Bigger Than the Facts

SEVENTY-FIVE STORIES

PORTRAIT OF AMERICA - Vol. III

G. Lowell Tollefson

ISBN-10: 0-9983498-0-1
ISBN-13: 978-0-9983498-0-0

LLT Press, P.O. Box 378, Eagle Nest, NM 87718

Contents

Village Search

We entered the village near dawn, at the first full light of day. It wasn't very big, just a small hamlet tucked into the brush jungle of the lowland country. It wasn't even near a road. But it was considered heavily fortified and under Viet Cong control. That's what made it important.

I was one of the first people in, riding on top of a tank with the first squad of the second platoon. As we rolled into the village from an open field on its south end, the Vietnamese were gathered together in a group at its center with huts on either side. The whole crowd backed up together as we came slowly toward them.

The tank stopped. Sgt. Derek ordered his men to dismount and sent a fire team along the rows of huts on either side. The second and third squads had deployed on the outer perimeter of the village, to the East and West, and were closing in together on the north end. This village had created a lot of problems and we were going to flush the Viet Cong out.

In a few minutes the two fire team leaders returned and one of them reported to Sgt. Derek that he had found a small cache of weapons in a hut. The villagers who were gathered before us continued standing there looking at us. We looked at them. How do you pick out a Viet Cong or a sympathizer, especially from a bunch of women, old men and children? There weren't any young men anywhere. There never were.

"Where are the VC?" I asked in Vietnamese. I had come along for that purpose. They all just looked at me.

"We won't harm you if you tell us where they went," I said. "Don't be afraid."

No one said anything. Sgt. Derek looked wearily along either row of huts. This clustered silence was the usual procedure. Whether they were afraid to answer or didn't want to was hard to tell.

"Get on the tank," he said.

"You going to burn it?" the tank commander asked, sticking his head and shoulders out of the hatch above the turret. The platoon leader, a young lieutenant who was now with one of the other two squads, had given Sgt. Derek the authority to make that decision.

"I don't know." He turned to the fire team leader who'd found the weapons cache. This guy was an Alaskan Indian whose left hand was badly scarred from an explosive charge left behind at an observation post bunker that had been overrun by sappers a week before he'd occupied it. His name was Mike, corporal Mike we usually called him.

"What do you think, Mike?"

"Marines have been fired on from this village. We've got every right. Especially since they won't talk."

In the front of the crowd I could see one woman whose face was thickly pockmarked. I had been studying her for several minutes thinking she had the worst case of acne I'd ever seen. Now it suddenly dawned on me that her face was full of tiny bits of shrapnel. She held a small child about a year old. It didn't look very healthy, though the breast she was feeding it certainly was ample.

Now we were all looking at them. Two very different groups of people trying to figure each other out.

"Let's go," Sgt. Derek said. All the men in the squad had returned from the search. A couple were carrying the few weapons they'd found in the cache: a Russian AK-47 automatic rifle and a couple of Chinese SKS rifles.

The tank screeched and groaned backwards out of the village with its ninety millimeter gun still pointing at the small crowd of Vietnamese.

Two days later another patrol was sent into the village to burn it.

Jennifer Neal

A young art student sat on a wooden bench at the University of Washington campus, sketching. Small, thin and blond, she presented a somewhat frail appearance in her white cotton blouse and shorts. She was in a wooded alcove of evergreen trees and was concentrating on an herb garden planted in a patch of sunlight just beyond her. Her right hand moved a slender black charcoal stick quickly, lightly over the sketch pad she held in her lap with her left hand. Crows carried on noisily overhead, cawing and flapping from branch to branch, obviously offended at her otherwise unobtrusive presence.

"Jennifer."

"Mark." She turned as a young man approached. "How did you find me?"

The young man sat down beside her. "It wasn't hard. You've been here before. You weren't trying to avoid me were you?"

They sat in silence for several minutes as Jennifer continued sketching.

Finally he said, "I've been thinking. You could move into my apartment now, and in the spring we could be married when I graduate."

Jennifer did not answer. They had been through this before.

"Well?"

"I can't, Mark. I just can't."

It was another three years before Jennifer got her degree, but Mark was so hurt, he had broken off their relationship after that morning in the alcove. Upon graduation from the University, Jennifer moved to New York and worked for an advertising firm. She hated commercial illustration, but it was a living. Eventually she returned out West, got a Master of Fine Arts degree and obtained a teaching position at the University of New Mexico, where she remained for some years.

She was now thirty-eight. She had had several lovers but never married. And she had never lived with anyone, having carefully restricted her relationships with men to preserve her freedom. She occupied a small flat in Northeast Albuquerque where she lived simply, frugally. Her second floor apartment, sparsely furnished and limited to a kitchen, bath, living-room and one bedroom, was full of paintings, some hanging, others stacked against the walls. She had had several showings, one modest retrospective in New York, and her work was represented in the best galleries in Santa Fe. But she still depended on teaching as a principal source of income.

Jennifer would often spend time, when not teaching classes, at a small cafe in the University district, where she occasionally sketched the passersby. She loved her art though it had been a demanding occupation through the years. Teaching was a necessary evil as far as she was concerned.

"Hello, Ms. Neal."

"Hello, John."

"Mind if I join you?"

"No. Go right ahead. Sit down." She looked across the small cafe table at the young man who had joined her. They were out on the sidewalk in the sun under an awning. Someone was laughing at the table behind her. A female voice. Jennifer continued looking at John, who was excusing himself to the person behind him for having to crowd his chair back against the other person's. He was one of her senior year students, and she thought how refreshingly young he was. He was pleasantly unaffected too by the rough manners of so many young men she had taught. Or so many other men she had known, for that matter.

John smiled. His teeth were clean and white, his smile unaffected. The sun was brilliant on the busy street beside him. "I was in Santa Fe the other day and saw some of your work," he said. "Why don't you ever bring it to class like the other professors?"

"I'm there to teach, not show off my own work."

"Oh. I don't think some of the students realize how good you are."

"Well, thank you, John."

"I mean it." He looked at her intensely.

She looked at him and smiled. Then, quite unexpectedly, her heart burst. It had been building up for some time. Twenty years of feeling welled up into her throat. She glanced out into the busy street, not wanting to look at this young student who seemed so unaccountably attractive to her.

"Thank you, John," she repeated softly. "I must be going. I..." She was confused. "I have a class to prepare for." She stood up.

"See you Thursday, Ms. Neal."

She did not go to class, but reported to the department that she was not feeling well and took the day off. On Thursday she felt she was a bit formal in her treatment of John. He seemed hurt, or perhaps she only imagined it. She was embarrassed. She had known men, and here a mere youth... She could not explain the sudden intensity of her feelings. Was it lust or the desire to simply recapture her own youth? Were all the years of careful self-preservation a mistake?

Over the ensuing weeks she regained her composure. Any woman would experience these matronly instincts toward such a gentle refinement. He was different. And even lust was natural in a woman for whom sex was occasional. Yet never had she been so acutely aware of her own desolate loneliness. She even asked herself if her art had been worth the years of sacrifice.

One day, feeling she had fully regained her sense of person and being quite certain again of the disinterested nature of her own motives, she asked John to come by her office after class. He did so, and they went out for coffee, returning to the cafe they'd been to before. The sun was hot, so they ordered cold soda instead of coffee. She noticed the strong chest behind the unbuttoned collar of John's shirt and forced the image from her mind.

"I thought we might discuss some of your work," she said. "There's... John," she said softly, looking down at her own hands. They were trembling. This was not right. This was not what she intended.

He touched her left hand.

G. Lowell Tollefson

On the street cars honked, stank of fuel in the heat, and roared thickly. People crowded past them on the sidewalk, and the sunshine all about them was like a halo of light.

Young Man

A young man stepped into a diner on a busy street in Seattle. He sat down at the counter.

"What'll it be, young man?" The waitress behind the counter was middle-aged. Her hair looked uncombed, falling down about her forehead and over her ears in muddy gray curls and long strands. She looked as if she had just gotten up or never went to bed.

"I'll have some of the pumpkin pie." He pointed to a glass case in the approximate middle of the counter. He was at the far left end.

The waitress grunted, pushed a curl behind her left ear, walked over, opened the case and took a plate from the second shelf. On the plate was a perfectly formed piece of pie, shiny, wet and slim. It looked as though it were molded in plastic. She laid the plate on the counter with a fork on it and gave it a shove. It slid over to the young man, half a counter length away, past several indifferent customers. "Anything else?"

"No thank you. Yes, please. Coffee."

The waitress, who had turned away at the words "no thank you," grimaced, came over, clattered a heavy cup and saucer onto the counter in front of the young man and poured boiling coffee into it. The saucer was chipped. "Cream and sugar are over there," she said. Just out of reach on the counter in a dish were packets of cream and sugar.

"No thanks."

"Is there anything else?"

"No thanks."

"Hey, Mack, what are you doing in here?" A man obviously down on his luck had come in and sat down at the opposite end of the counter. "You owe me for the last time. I told you never to come back." The waitress headed back down the counter toward him. The man hurriedly got up and went back outside. He could be seen passing in front of the big window as he went on down the street.

"Mildred ain't so bad," a man sitting on a stool next to Jim Latrec said. Jim Latrec was the young man. "She just hasn't had her morning coffee. Isn't that right, Mildred?" Mildred had left the counter and gone over to one of the small tables lining the opposite wall. A pretty young woman sat there with a cup of coffee, now empty, and a small dish which had apparently contained a breakfast roll. Mildred took a pencil from behind her ear, wrote rapidly on a check pad, tore off the check, pushed a string of hair behind her ear, and presented the check to the woman. The woman reached into her purse and paid the waitress.

Mildred took the money and went to the manual cash register at the far right end of the counter, next to a low swinging door that led behind the counter to the open cooking area. She rang the register open, put the money into the drawer and slammed it shut. Also behind Mildred, the register and the counter, with his back to them all, was a hairy, dark, thin little man with big ears who was busy at the grill. The young woman, who Jim noticed was wearing a nice, slim cut, beige, long coat that came to her knees and who had very pretty legs, got up and went out.

"They's lots of pretty ones like that," the man next to Jim said. "Been here long? You're new in town, aren't you?"

"Yes, I'm looking for work."

"That's what I thought. What kind of work you looking for, young man?"

"Something to do with writing. I've got an English degree..."

"Good luck with that!" The man, who was very heavy and balding, smiled. "I don't mean to discourage you. This just ain't a literary town. I got a son who wants to write. He drives a truck up in Redmond. We're into making airplanes here and ships. Heavy stuff."

"I'm going to try the papers."

"There's only one. It looks like there's two, but there's only one. They own each other."

"Oh."

"Good luck, young man. I wish you the best." The fat man laid some money on the counter, got down off his stool and went out. He bobbed along in front of the window as he went on down the street.

The sun was out somewhere, but the sky was gray with a high thin layer of clouds. This added to the general atmosphere of depression as Jim stepped onto the street. He walked along the row of small restaurants, office supply places and other small shops. He thought of the young woman with the pretty legs. The good things in life seemed very far from him. A bus pulled up to the curb, groaning and screeching its brakes as it stopped a little ahead of him. It was not the type that ran on electric wires, so common in this city, and it stank of diesel fuel. It lowered a lift, and a man in a wheelchair backed his wheelchair onto it. The bus driver got out and helped to position and strap the wheelchair onto the metal lift. Then he climbed back into the driver's seat, and the hydraulic system began to haul the disabled man and his chair up and into the bus.

Jim looked at all the dusty cars on the street, the people crowded about the bus stop waiting for the lift to finish its work. It all seemed so ugly, distasteful and unromantic.

Night Probe

The rain came down for days, slowing to a fine spray only occasionally. The nights were wet too, the bunkers and trenches full of water, so that the men on guard stayed on top of the bunkers. The probes came often, almost nightly, the enemy firing from the village across the river. The rounds went high because of the angle of trajectory over the hill, and you could hear the faint whisper of their passing.

A machine gun opened on the left, sending a stream of red tracers into the lower hillside. Nothing. Just the movement of shadows from the flares.

"I don't like it," one man said. "One of these times it's going to be the real thing again."

"The probes have been picking up," another man said. "It'll probably be soon."

"This is it!" the first man said. "Look." There was much movement in the village. The dogs were silent.

The Attack

The attack began with mortars. Somehow in the dark, troops had been ferried across the river in sampans. No one had seen it, not even the guards on the bridge, but now they were massed at the bottom of the hill. Hundreds of them. The bridge was under heavy fire, and mortars slammed into everything on the hill. Men were running to the perimeter.

A corporal yelled. "Get some ammo up here! We're running out."

The mortars were concentrating on the ammo dump in the center of the compound.

"Grab that box," said the ammo tech. The man with him did so, and they ran together toward the perimeter through the exploding mortars, a mat of tracers overhead. In the confusion of the fight, the man with the ammo box did not realize he'd been hit. A small piece of shrapnel had penetrated his lung. He had difficulty breathing.

Med-evac

In the morning, helicopters were taking out the wounded, the whack whack whack of their blades and dust filling the air. A corpsman was adjusting an IV bag which he had hung on a volleyball net the officers had erected the previous evening.

"Hey, doc," the marine attached to the IV shouted, "when are they going to take me?"

"You're up next," the corpsman answered.

"Good, I think this thing is hemorrhaging."

The corpsman knelt down to take a look. "Hey gunny," he shouted.

A gunnery sergeant who was organizing the med-evac came over. He took a look. "Okay," he said. He gestured to some men, who came to get the stretcher.

"I'm sorry," the wounded man said. "I thought I'd better tell you."

"Nothing to be sorry about," the corpsman said. "You'll be home in a few days. Your war is over."

The marine closed his eyes.

Elsa Mae

She had taught in the public schools in her day, when the schools were much better. Then she had lived in the predominately Greek but ethnically mixed, Astoria section of Queens, New York for a number of years, but she was not Greek. Neither was she Italian, Asian Indian, Middle Eastern or Hispanic. She belonged to that most nebulous and indefinable of ethnic groups in New York City. She was an American.

Elsa Mae was the name most people knew her by. Since retirement from teaching many years before, her last name seemed to have been lost in the mists of memory. It didn't matter.

"Morning Elsa."

"Good day, Elsa Mae. You think those pigeons will not survive if you do not feed them every morning?"

"Hush, Esteban. I feed them because it makes me happy. You go on about your business and catch your train."

"Oh, no, mother Mae. I do not have to work today. Today is Good Friday. I will go to mass."

"Well, God bless you, Esteban. And see that you do not sin, for one day at least!"

Elsa Mae pulled the last of the crumbs from her bread sack and spread them on the ground in front of the pigeons, who were always arriving and departing, flapping their wings noisily as the morning crowds streamed past them into the subway station. She contemplated their feeding with satisfaction for a moment, then walked over and threw the clear plastic bread sack into a waste bin along the sidewalk.

Two men sat on a bench beside the waste receptacle. One was a thin, stooped older man with a cane and a straw hat, the other much younger, in his early twenties. He was olive skinned, a second generation Italian, and wore blue jeans and a sleeveless shirt which showed him to be the muscular, working class person he was.

"Good day, Elsa," the older man said. "I am sorry about your friend there." He pointed to a mass of dark gray feathers that had been flattened into an irregular disk in the middle of the street by the passage of many cars.

"Oh, him, yes—Timothy. I have been warning him to stay out of the street. But not Timothy. No, it was always the peanut shuffle out in the traffic for him. Well, I guess even the Good Lord grows weary of defending the foolish."

Both the men laughed, and the younger one moved to one side as the old woman carefully deposited her short, stocky body on the bench beside them.

"It's a beautiful morning," the older man said.

"Yes, if you don't mind the smell." Elsa grinned slyly. You could not expect fine odors where so many cars, people, pigeons and fruit and vegetable stalls all came together. It is like too many opinions and ideas, which sometimes also rankle in the big city. The younger man laughed again. "Gregor here is in a very good humor," Elsa continued. "Everything seems to tickle his funny bone."

"It's you, Elsa Mae. You're making me laugh." Gregor was short for Gregorio.

"No, it is my belief that when most people laugh, they laugh only at themselves. Others are just an excuse." She grinned slyly again, glancing from Gregor to the older man on the other side of him.

The older man smiled, and he and Elsa looked at each other in silence for a moment. This slim, impeccably dressed older gentleman had obviously held his own in the world in an earlier time. In fact, there had once been a time when Clem, the older man in question, had vigorously courted Elsa. It was in the year after he'd lost his wife that he had discovered a deep affection for her, then newly retired from teaching and relocated in a nearby apartment high rise in the present neighborhood. But Elsa, a spinster all her life, had never indicated a willingness to go beyond the simple overtures of warm friendship. So in time, his ardor and his hope for a second close companion had sunk within him, where it smoldered, never quite going out.

"Well, I think I will leave you two lovebirds," Gregor said, getting up. "Some of us have to work." He turned and walked over to the stairs leading to the subway platform above.

Clem and Elsa averted their gaze and devoted themselves to observing some of the passersby. A young woman went by in a halter top and short shorts.

"Never in my day!" Elsa observed.

Clem watched the young woman climb the subway stairs. "Not in mine either," he said, shaking his head.

They both sat in silence for several minutes. Then Clem turned and looked at Elsa. He leaned over and gently touched her hand on the bench. It was not something he'd done in years. "You know, Elsa," he said, "I've been thinking. Maybe we were wrong."

"Wrong? Wrong in what way, Clem?" She had not taken her hand from beneath Clem's. It was an old friendship.

"I mean when we were very young. If we'd been freer, more natural then, perhaps later..."

"Perhaps later it would not have been so hard," Elsa said, quietly finishing his sentence. The rumbling of the train as it left the station scattered the pigeons.

Today and Forever

It was their anniversary. They had been married one year. There were differences. Sally was a socialite, loving parties, enjoying good restaurants, liking to have friends over for chips, wine and animated discussions on literary topics. John had a research fellowship in Pharmacology at the University. He seemed always to be preoccupied with his work, with the future as he saw or hoped to see it.

"Honey," he would argue, "if you want a nice home with good friends, we're going to have to pay for it. And a little prestige doesn't hurt either."

This was the general tenor of his conversation on the morning of their anniversary: the future was to be paid for by the sacrifices of the present.

"But, John, I don't just want a brilliant future. I want to live now, to savor every moment of the present. Like the sparrows here on the sidewalk beside our table. 'They neither sow nor reap nor gather into barns.'"

John looked at the sparrows on the pavement. They were doing the usual chirping, bickering, preening. A male hopped about after a female, who kept a certain distance. The male's chest seemed to be sticking out.

"We aren't sparrows," he said.

"Maybe we should be," Sally said. She tossed her head back, uncrossed and recrossed her legs. The sun shown down on her lap, on her red shorts and very white skin. She tossed her head again, the blond hair clearing her shoulder. She pushed back another strand. "Come on, honey. It's our anniversary."

"Oh, all right."

This meant that, though they'd made it as far as the University district that day, John did not make it as far as the University itself. Sally, an undergraduate, missed her classes as well.

In the afternoon, after some casual morning shopping for picnic supplies, they rented a boat and rowed out upon the nearby lake. They rowed far out to an unpopulated border of the lake, then rested their oars in the boat. The water was blue in the sunlight. The green all around them sang of bird song and springtime fruitfulness. The air was sweetly warm with only the slightest breeze.

"Isn't it lovely," Sally said, "I love the sound of water lapping slowly against the sides of the boat—the feel of the boat rocking. We're part of the gentle rhythm of it all, John. Blue sky, blue water, green trees, yellow sun."

"And no clouds."

"Yes there are."

"Where?"

"There's one over there by the mountains. See how slowly it moves. So white and billowy and peaceful. It's like us."

John laughed, bent over and kissed Sally's cheek. Her head was lying in his lap.

"John."

"Yes."

"Let's go ashore."

In the evening they went to a restaurant, a seafood place on the waterfront, rather expensive. They ordered wine. The baked salmon John ordered was light pink, partially uncooked, and he had to send it back. They ordered more wine. Then they strolled along the boardwalk under the warm lemon glow of electric lights made to look like gas lamps. They were holding hands, looking in the shop windows, mostly closed.

"I never made love like that before. Out in the open, I mean," Sally said.

"Me neither."

They both laughed. They never found it easy talking about a subject they'd learned together entirely by impulse and feel.

"Are you sorry?"

"For making love?"

"For not going in to the University today."

"No."

"Neither am I." Sally laid her head on John's shoulder. She felt a weight fall from her. For the last several months she had been struggling with John's preoccupation with his work. Research, research, research! She didn't care what great discoveries there were to be made. She wasn't as concerned with the future as John was. At least, not in the same way. Things would work out. They always did. As she saw it, life was a precious gift. It was to be lived at the finger tips, as well as in the mind. She supposed that was what made her and John so different. He was driven. She both admired and resented it.

"Honey."

"What?" John put his arm around her waist and pulled her close to him. His hand felt strong against her hip.

"I wouldn't care if we spent the rest of our lives in a little cottage reading good books. If only every day could be like today."

"It will be. We'll have the best of both worlds. I promise," John said. He kissed her hair. They walked along in the lamplight, surrounded by the big dark night which, along with the distant stars, had a pleasing chill of the cold bay water to it. The black tide water of the harbor could be heard softly slapping the log piles beneath them. They were happy together in each other's arms, felt pleasantly warm and secure. Sally was especially content, and John was calm and assured as he laid out the future for Sally and himself in his mind.

Daily Business

We could see them down on the road. Actually see them planting the mine about a quarter of a mile from us. Not far. It was Sunday afternoon. We were taking it easy sitting on the hooch steps. It didn't really matter that it was Sunday, only what day of the month it was. The day of the month determined the number of days you had left in Vietnam.

A jeep pulled up. The first sergeant from Mike company got out, then hauled out his prisoner. A patrol had picked him up for trying to peddle marijuana to some of the troops. The first sergeant grabbed the prisoner by the shirt. He had an ordinary shirt on, not a peasant's smock. The first sergeant yanked him out of the jeep, then, as he was stumbling forward, slammed him back against the side of the jeep. The prisoner's hands were tied behind him, so it was just a balancing act to see if he could find a way to stand on his legs.

"So you speak Vietnamese," the first sergeant said addressing himself to me.

"Yes."

"Well, tell this asshole if I catch him peddling junk to my men again, I'm going to cut off his balls. You hear that, asshole?" he said, turning back toward the prisoner and giving him another shove. "Goddamn VC!"

I figured the prisoner was in his late thirties, but it's hard to tell. These people are born old and die young. Meaning they're worldly wise. They always know what's going on and they seem to always look about the same age once they're grown. Until they get old anyway. They get old in their forties.

I've never been in the place where they put this guy. There's a hole in the middle of our helicopter landing zone, and they put him down there underground. The French built the cells down there as part of the fort on a hilltop overlooking a river that we used for Third Battalion headquarters. We had gotten orders from the Seventh Marine Regiment that he would be picked up by helicopter when one was available and taken to Division headquarters. They must have thought this guy was into more than selling marijuana.

Before we took him to put him down that hole, the other guys were taken care of. The ones planting the mine in the road, two of them. A volley of three shells was fired. They had variable timing devices on them and their effect could easily be seen from our hilltop position.

They exploded in black puffs one right after another directly above the heads of the two Viet Cong. Thousands of needles rained down on the two figures. Of course, you couldn't see that part from a quarter mile distance. A patrol was sent out to see what we got.

The first sergeant had two other guys with him, a corporal and a lance corporal. They got out of the jeep and were the ones who took the prisoner to his holding cell. The first sergeant and I walked along behind them, while the first sergeant explained to me his hopes of starting up a boy scout troop among the local village kids.

The corporal was stocky with hairy arms. He held the prisoner with his left hand on the prisoner's left wrist behind the prisoner's back where his hands were tied together. With his right hand he had a hold on the shirt collar which he used to shove the prisoner forward. The black lance corporal held the prisoner in the same way on the right side. Twice on the way to the helicopter landing zone the corporal kicked the prisoner in the back of the legs. The second time the prisoner fell to his knees. The lance corporal cuffed him on the side of the head with the back of his hand and jerked him back to his feet.

The first sergeant paid no attention. He wondered if I'd mind doing a little interpreting for him in starting up the boy scout troop. I tried not to sound enthusiastic because the idea seemed ridiculous to me.

When we all got to the hole the prisoner had a tired look on his face but didn't say anything or show any resistance. They put him down there in the dark

Voices

"Sarah always looks like she has consumption," John's mother had said. "You must do better than you have in providing for your family, son."

But the truth of the matter was that Sarah was strong, and John was doing the best he could. Now they had come to the bottom. They had fallen through the social net and landed in a homeless shelter with only a few hundred dollars left, which they were careful not to let anyone know they had.

"Honey, could you get me Aaron's bottle?"

John got off the lower bunk in the tiny, single room apartment. He pulled a cold bottle of prepared formula out of a travel bag and handed it to his wife. They had earlier tried heating the bottle on a radiator but it hadn't worked. Outside the thick wood frame sliding window of the stuffy, overheated room, it was raining ice on the corner of Ninth and Pine streets in Seattle.

"I'm going out again tomorrow. I'll try the taxi companies."

Sarah did not answer. She was young, not yet twenty years of age, and very thin. She removed Aaron from her small breast. He began immediately to scream. Sarah plunged the bottle into the child's mouth and he proceeded to suck furiously.

John looked at his wife. Having both hands occupied, she was unable to cover her breast. The exposed nipple, large and dark, made her seem especially vulnerable.

"We never should've dated in school. I should've left you alone," he said.

"Alone to do what?" Sarah looked up at him. She smiled. A toilet flushed. It was in the bathroom that they shared with the occupant of another room.

"If that jerk puts another damned apple down the toilet..."

Later that evening John lay on the upper bunk. Sarah was on the lower one. The child, in towards the wall beside her, was asleep.

"Oh, I hate these horrible things!" Sarah slapped at a small, very quick, light brown roach on the wall with a slipper, then at another and another. In fact, they were all over the walls and the rails of the bed.

"You can't kill them all," John said wearily.

"I can sure as heck try!"

Three days later they were on the road again, headed east from Seattle towards Denver. There was no work there either. Heading back, they were caught in a snow storm in Wyoming on Interstate 80. They pulled off at a rest stop, one that had no facilities but was just a strip of concrete off the freeway. The snow piled up around them. Inside the car John and Sarah sat close together in the front seat, huddled under a blanket. The baby was asleep, tucked between them for maximum warmth.

"Shouldn't we go on?" Sarah asked.

"We can't. There isn't enough gas to get to the next town."

"We have to try."

"No!"

They sat in silence for awhile. The snow continued to fall in a thick curtain of small flakes. Now and then a wind blew the white flakes in a sudden whirl toward them, and wherever it touched the glass of side window, rear window or windshield, it stuck, matted and further darkened the interior of the car. The cold of the dark, unlimited spaces of the night could be felt penetrating the blanket.

John turned on the engine heater but shut off the ignition upon realizing once again how low the gas was. He knew they might not get through the night but he didn't think he was frightened. In fact, he was calm, sitting for some time in silence, his mind beginning to wander.

"Did you hear that?" he said suddenly, throwing the blanket off.

"What?" Sarah roused from a half sleep.

"I just heard someone." John looked into the back seat, then got out of the car. Through the heavy snowfall he could see at a considerable distance the outline of an eighteen wheeler parked a good eighty yards behind them. Being outside in the freedom of the open air, however forbiddingly cold, broke the suffocating film of doubt that had encased him. He got back into the car.

"There's nobody out there."

Sarah looked at him.

"I heard someone say, calm and clear as day, 'What's the matter?' It came from the back seat, I thought."

John started the car. He realized he had been numbed by his own fear of going on in the storm with so little gas. He turned on the headlights and backed up.

"Stop!" Both he and Sarah heard it this time. They looked at each other in surprise and laughed. John, in his rush, had almost backed into a snow drift. He now eased the car out onto the road.

Shortly after they had started out again, the morning light came over them and the snow stopped falling. There was a white powder on the freeway and that made the road very slick. When an eighteen wheeler—perhaps the very one John had seen parked behind him at the rest stop—passed him at a high rate of speed, it sent his car into a spin. The car slid off the road and came to a stop against a snow bank. Its engine had shut off.

They sat for several minutes in stunned silence. The baby started crying. John started the engine and let out the clutch. The wheels gripped, and he eased the car back onto the road again. Unconsciously, Sarah was also easing her foot off an imaginary clutch on her side of the car as she undid her blouse for Aaron.

The Tyrant

She had said, "If you forget your red correcting pencils I will give you an F for the day," and no one in Mrs. Brown's high school senior English class would have ever thought to doubt her word. She was tough but you learned something, and a few of her students valued her for that. Today, as she erased the board and the scuffle of students leaving the room could be heard behind her, she knew one student would be waiting.

"Richard," she said, clamping her piece of chalk into the trough at the bottom of the blackboard and turning about abruptly, "you do want to pass this class, don't you?"

"It's Dick, ma'am."

"Yes, I know, Dick. Sit down."

Dick straddled a desk in the front row. He was a large fellow with dark hair that fell into his eyes. He brushed it back, the biceps standing out on his arm.

Patricia Brown looked at him for a moment. She wondered what in her young girlhood had ever attracted her to boys like this. Now in her late forties, she saw him simply as a red-necked youth bent on disrupting the class and interfering with her efforts to teach more promising students.

"Dick, I want you to start turning in your homework."

"What for, ma'am?" There was a slight grin at the corner of Dick's eyes. Patricia suppressed the anger rising in her.

"So you can pass this class. If you don't, you won't graduate this year. You understand that, don't you?"

Dick nodded, the smile leaving his face. A warm breeze and the smell of cut grass drifted through an open window.

"And no more cat calls from the back of the room. I'm putting you in the front row tomorrow. You're to exchange desks with Alison. She knows about it and I've already made the change on my chart."

There was silence, then "Anything else, ma'am?"

"No, that will be all."

Dick sauntered out of the room. The shiny new chassis has got a dent, Patricia thought, but he'll recover.

In the evening Patricia relaxed in her garden. She had been teaching for most of twenty-six years. She wondered if any eighteen year old had the capacity to understand Chaucer or Beowulf. The daffodils were lovely this year. The soil was rich and dark and smelled of humus. There was a scent of spring all about the garden, and there was also a secret Patricia never let anyone know. She was mortally afraid of her students. Afraid of—she wasn't sure what. Afraid of being embarrassed, compromised in some way, she supposed. But that had never happened. It never would. She smiled. Still, it bothered her. The smile faded. Even after all these years, she thought. Even after all these years she had to brace herself.

"Now, class," she said the following morning, "I want you to try something new," She walked between the rows of desks as she spoke. "Close your books. Imagine that you, yes you, are Petruchio, and you have brought home a shrewish wife." She looked about the room at the expectant faces. What impossible task would she require of them? Patricia returned to the front of the room. Sally, who wore a short skirt and sat in the center of the front row, next to Dick now, had her legs spread as usual. Patricia wondered if she did this in any of the classes taught by the men. She paused. Mike Bromfield coughed from the center of the room. "I want you in five hundred words to write me a defense of the action you, Petruchio, are going to take to bring this very difficult but desirable woman under control."

A moan went up all around. Patricia Brown went back to her desk and sat down. Pencils could be heard scraping on paper. Finally the bell rang. In a flurry of activity students gathered up their books and began to leave the room. The last few essay assignments were turned in.

Patricia did not have a class the next hour. In the silence of the room she went through the papers. Sally had written a surprisingly good essay. Or perhaps it was not surprising. Sally was an intelligent girl—in most things. Patricia came to Dick's paper. She crossed her legs and folded her arms together on the desk, the paper laying out flat before her. The essay began boldly, became confused, and ended abruptly two thirds of the way down the page. Then scrawled at the bottom of the page was the following plea.

I can't do this, Mrs. Brown. Why do you ask us to do things like this? What good is it?

Patricia felt a knot in her throat, a heavy anvil on her chest. She felt as if she might burst into tears. I try, she thought. I try so hard! She sat in silence for several minutes, in a cocoon of her own thoughts. A fresh scent of approaching summer, wafting through the open window, irritated her at first. Then it soothed her. There was one thing she knew she could never do. She would never slacken in her effort to educate these rough, young minds. Some of them, she thought, or at least hoped, some of them would carry the light of human reason into the next generation. It was the one clear thing in a clouded world.

The Cost of War

Several village women were keening hysterically with varying degrees of sincerity. Squatted about the corpse, they were friends and family members of the little girl. She had been killed by a mortar.

Two young marines walked over to have a look.

"It's always like this," one of them said.

"What?"

"All this keening. It's what they do." He slung his rifle over his shoulder and walked away.

The other marine stood for a moment before following his companion. Nearby, automatic rifle fire could be heard. Several grenades exploded.

"They're clearing the village on the other side of that tree line," someone said.

No one noticed the young Vietnamese sitting apart from the keening women. She could not have been twenty. Her face was expressionless, and she made no sound. She was the mother of the child.

The sun was hot. It was a very hot morning.

Michael

Joan Merril was a woman of conviction. She believed in the imminent appearance of the Lord. It was the business of everyone to make ready for his coming and hers especially to prepare them.

Joan's son, Michael, was of a different temperament. He was private, hated confrontation and was a little too sensitive, some said even effeminate. Home from his second year at college, he sat bolt upright on the living room sofa, preparing himself. It was Sunday morning. His mother came into the room.

"Son, the others will not be able to make it for service this morning, so we will have time to ourselves." The service Joan referred to was a regular gathering of six or eight people in a private home, often hers. "Praise the Lord, he is coming! Open your Bible, son."

"I already have."

"Have you been reading it?"

"No."

This was the morning Joan received the shock of her life. Her son confessed to her that he was gay. Michael, though scheduled to remain a week, left the next morning and returned to the University.

Upon graduation, Michael moved from the Midwest, where he'd grown up and had been attending school, to the city of New York. A film arts major, he took a job as a clerk in a book store and moved in with another young man on the upper west side of Manhattan. Within a few months he and his friend disagreed and he moved to an apartment near Greenwich Village occupied by three women.

These young women, all of whom worked in the book store on Fifth Avenue, were close friends of his. They knew Michael very well, were aspiring actresses, and had made numerous attempts under his direction to produce a good street film which might then propel them to more serious film or theatrical careers. One young woman in particular, Janet, became a very close friend to Michael. Had they not known Michael to be gay, the others might have suspected a budding romance.

One evening around ten thirty or eleven, when only Michael and Janet were home, they fell into a discussion concerning Michael's strained relationship with his mother.

"She's a strong woman," he said. "You should meet her sometime."

"I'd like to."

"I don't think so." Michael smiled. He looked wistfully from the chair where he was sitting toward Janet who was sitting with her legs folded under her, dressed in a light cotton gown, on the sofa across the room. The day's temperature and humidity had both reached well into the nineties by early afternoon and had not dropped significantly since. The breeze coming through an open window in the room was heavy and warm. Janet was small featured, rather pretty in an unremarkable way, and quieter, more reflective somehow than the other two women with whom they lived. Michael felt she was the sister he'd never been fortunate enough to have. Conceiving him out of wedlock in a less disciplined period of her life, his mother had never married.

"What do you mean?"

"I mean she's kind of overbearing. She's a big woman with prematurely white hair and she's, well, forceful."

"Forceful?"

"Yes. I mean she comes on strong. She's a big breasted woman, and sometimes you feel as if she's going to walk up and knock you over with them."

Janet laughed. She was not herself a big breasted woman. Michael laughed too.

"I think I'd still like to meet her," Janet said.

That Christmas Michael took Janet home with him. His mother was, of course, delighted for reasons Michael had in no way led her on to believe.

"This is Janet," Michael said matter-of-factly. "We spend a lot of time together in New York."

"That's wonderful!"

"We're not lovers, mother."

Christmas Eve service was simple and short. It was conducted in the home with no Christmas tree present. Several couples of varying ages attended. There was prayer and the first demonstration of tongues and prophesy Janet had ever seen.

She felt uncomfortable but wanted very much to be there. She wanted to be with Michael anywhere because, in spite of what she knew about his sexual orientation, she was certain she was in love with him. She knew she would at any time give him anything he wanted. She wished he would press her for something more than friendship. She had even prayed God would work a miracle, open a way. She had fallen desperately in love with this intense, sensitive, creative man with whom she shared a close emotional bond but physically careful, circumspect relationship.

They flew back to New York together. In the plane Janet turned to Michael, who was sitting beside her, and said, "She's not so tough."

"Who?"

"Your mother."

"Oh her. That's what you think!"

They both laughed.

"I'm serious, Michael. She just doesn't understand, that's all."

"I know. She thinks you and I should get married, that, in spite of what I've told her, we must already be sleeping together since we live in the same apartment."

Janet was unable to respond. In the silence, Michael looked at her, saw tears in her eyes, and bent over close to her face. He kissed her lightly on the cheek then fell back into his seat.

"You're the best friend I'll ever have," he said from the depths of the seat, "the closest person to me."

As they sat there side by side, a mere pinpoint in the blue American sky over the northern Pennsylvania wooded mountains, he thought: But I would only hurt you.

Who Are You?

Jennifer Cisneros did not remember from her childhood the language of her father's family. She could understand certain phrases and expressions which had been frequently used by her paternal grandparents but that was all. Her grandparents were gone now, her father was not close to any other member of his family, and her mother was an ethnic Vietnamese who had thought it a good thing to give her daughter an Anglo-Saxon first name.

Now an Amerasian with an Hispanic last name, living in the Rio Grande River valley in central New Mexico, is a strange thing. But it is even stranger when the Hispanic father of such a person prefers to speak only English and gives his daughter the ambition and privilege of going to an exclusive eastern school for her higher education.

Her history professor there said, "Cisneros. That's Mexican, isn't it?"

"Spanish."

"Yes, that's what I mean."

A fellow student in an economics course she took, who knew her mother was Vietnamese and that she was conversant in the Vietnamese language, once asked, "How'd you ever get a name like Cisneros?"

She married a young lawyer. He was tall, thin and blond, and his name was Amundsen, like the explorer. Jennifer had coarse, shiny, coal black, shoulder length, straight hair, high cheek bones, round eyes, small stature, a full mouth, dark complexion and a good figure. She did indeed look like a new world Hispanic, and she was attractive. But she was confusing to meet because her name was Jennifer Cisneros Amundsen and she was, after all, Vietnamese, or so she often told people.

This only began the confusion, for she got a degree in creative writing. That meant she was destined to teach. "I'm a writer who teaches," she would say, or "I'm a teacher who writes."

"It must be dreadfully difficult," a colleague of her husband had once commented at a party.

"Teaching?"

"No, writing." In the background was the tinkle of glasses and much noise of conversation. It felt very impersonal.

"Oh, I find writing much easier than teaching. It's what I really want to be doing."

The colleague, a smartly dressed, blond, female lawyer, looked blankly with cold blue eyes at Jennifer. This complex state of affairs was clearly out of her league. She didn't understand. Why would anyone want to do anything as impecunious as writing? Few people ever made money in that field!

"It isn't that I don't enjoy the things we have," Jennifer told her husband one morning as they sat in their large, expensive kitchen full of the latest appliances and rushed through a breakfast of toast and coffee. "I just think there is more to life than a nice car, an expensive house in the suburbs, and parties attended by people who act like conversational robots and emotional zombies."

"But what would you prefer, Jenny? To bum around the country or starve in some exotic slum somewhere? Poets and novelists aren't worth much in this country, and most of them are pretty strange, you have to admit. A weird bunch from what I've seen."

"No, it's just..."

"What?" Her husband poured himself another cup of coffee. The gold cuff link on his immaculate white shirt twinkled chilly in the morning light filtering through the delicate white lace curtains partially covering the kitchen window.

"It's just that all this keeping up with the Joneses seems pointless. I mean the car, the house, the fancy clothes, the parties and dinners, where's it all getting us? It seems like we just go around in circles. And nobody understands me anyway."

"Poor Jenny, nobody understands her. You could try to make a little more sense to people, you know. You seem to enjoy confusing my friends about your background and your work."

"What about my friends?"

"What friends? I haven't seen you make any."

"That's what I mean. I'm not happy here, Leonard."

"You want to just pick up and move? I've got a good job with a prestigious east coast law firm here. You want me to give that up?"

"No."

"I understand you're not happy, honey. But you have to try harder. Figure out who you are." Leonard tossed the hot coffee into his mouth and got up from the kitchenette table. Jennifer wondered that it didn't scald him. He was always in such a hurry.

"I know who I am," she said as he left the room.

Several times Leonard had suggested having children. This seemed to be a solution to him. Jennifer steadfastly refused. She didn't want to become just a suburban housewife. At least teaching kept her in contact with the world of imagination and possibility. She was afraid of losing that.

The sex in their life had been good at first, when they had fallen in love and married. But now Leonard seemed so demanding at times. The tenderness, that special waiting and warmth, seemed to have gone out of their relationship. She felt used, thrust at and pawed like a rubber doll. Leonard was always in a hurry and preoccupied, it seemed, even in lovemaking.

One day Jennifer simply packed up and left. She went back to the Rio Grande valley. It was the most frightening period of her life. She had no job, no idea of what she would do. She stayed with her parents for several months then accepted employment as an English language teacher in Japan. Leonard rushed out to persuade her not to go. He asked her to return to him.

"I can't live the old life, Leonard."

"Why not?"

"I...I don't know. Something's missing."

"I'll be more considerate, Jenny."

"I know you would."

"We can work it out."

Jennifer tossed her dense black hair behind her shoulder. She put her face into her hands. "There isn't anything to work out, Leonard. I'm not who you think I am."

"Well then, who are you?"

"I don't know."

Jennifer went to Japan.

A Complete Joke

She was nine years old. The bullet went into her left cheek and came out her neck on the same side. It must not have hit anything solid like teeth or bone because the damage wasn't that bad, though it wasn't pretty to look at.

It was her sister's fault. She was carrying a rifle when we spotted the two of them crossing a rice field. We ordered them to stop but they didn't. So we fired, two or three guys in the patrol, and that brought them down. Killed the older and wounded the younger one. The rifle was an AK-47. Pretty sophisticated for a mere peasant.

Our corpsman patched up the little girl and we radioed for a chopper. It took fifteen minutes for the helicopter to get there. She'd probably have bled to death if the corpsman hadn't put compresses on her face and neck. Nothing major had been severed, but the wounds were bleeding quite a bit, especially the one in her neck.

After the chopper came we continued our patrol. Our platoon encampment was in a swampy area, partly stuck back in some trees beside a rice field. It was a miserable place. We had sandbags strung out in the wet places for stepping stones. What a mud hole!

The lieutenant wasn't with us when the thing happened but he took a special interest in the case. He kept wondering how she was doing, so one day about two weeks later we went in to see. She was at the civilian hospital in Da Nang. The lieutenant had some other business at First Marine Division Headquarters and that was our excuse. He took me along.

What a stench bucket of a place that hospital was. It was a complete joke. They didn't seem to have anything in the way of supplies. The morgue was in a separate building. It was a bare room with its door hanging ajar and containing a couple of bodies and a lot of flies.

When we entered the hospital a doctor met us in a small room at the end of a long hall. There were a few bottles of this and that and a few medical tools I didn't know the use of. For the most part the room was just empty and dirty.

When we entered the hall, the lieutenant, a short, young, kind of peach fuzz looking guy, stopped and stared. All along both walls were people sitting in silence. I mean absolute silence. They were all women just sitting there on the floor, some holding children. Several of the white cotton blouses were blood stained and, as we walked along, the three of us, I saw that one of the women was dead. Another, several really, had very small children in their arms. And one of these was holding a child that was also dead. I can't explain death, but it has a kind of presence. It's as if a personality had suddenly left the room. You always recognize it.

Anyway, in this hall the silence was enough. Not even the children made any sound.

"This morning the VC come in. They mortar the village. We don't know yet what was their reason. Maybe the people won't give them the taxes. Maybe they are too friendly to the Americans."

The lieutenant listened to the doctor and nodded. He also kept looking up and down the rows of people lining either side of the hall. We walked quietly between them.

Upstairs there was a room full of South Vietnamese Army soldiers. I just glanced through the door as we passed and saw that the beds were so close together you couldn't see the floor. There were a lot of people in there, and they were noisy.

This was a two story building, and since we were on the second floor it was as far as we could go. The hall was bare with a few windows lining it on one side, the recovery rooms on the other. The windows were dust streaked and only let the light in intermittently.

At the far end of the hall was a tiny room. In the room was a straw mat. No window. It was more like a closet than a room. Kneeling on the mat was the girl we had shot. Her wounds looked almost healed and there were no bandages on them.

The lieutenant knelt down and asked her in English who she was—what her name was.

The doctor translated for him.

"What village are you from?" And so forth. That's how we found out the woman we'd killed was her sister. As she told us, she cried quietly.

Afterwards, on the way back in the jeep, I kept looking over at the lieutenant. He sat on the passenger side looking out over the fields, his M-16 rifle slung across both arms pointing out towards the fields on the right. The normal procedure is to have the safety switch off for immediate use. But he left the rifle locked on safety. He left it that way all the way back to our little home in the swamp.

Independence

She wore glasses, her hair was a messy mud brown and her breast swell rose to the level of two fried eggs. She was eighteen.

"Janene," her mother had frequently pointed out that summer of her high school graduation, "when you go to the University this fall, you must comb your hair and look after your appearance a little more." Mrs. Jones had even offered to have her daughter fitted for contact lenses, but Janene was indifferent. She went away a disappointment to her mother.

Janene spent four years at the State University, didn't date much, maintained a casual appearance, to say the least, and left after those four years with a degree in wildlife biology. She had specialized in raptors. Why, her mother could not possibly imagine.

It helps to understand that Melodie Jones was not at all like her daughter. She had given birth to Janene out of wedlock at the age of sixteen, and in her middle to late thirties she could have rivaled any college cheer leader in physical attractiveness. This after giving birth to four children and being married since the age of eighteen to the same man, who, she once told a close friend, and not without relish, pumped her day and night like an oil well.

Janene got a job with the Idaho State Fish and Game Department. Stationed in Boise as the junior biologist, she received the dubious honor of spending weeks in the field doing population surveys of hawks and eagles. She was, after all, a liberated woman, according to several of the older men with whom she worked. They did not understand her interest in a man's profession. But she didn't mind. She did much of this work to the northeast of Boise where the terrain was hot, dry, rocky, forested, rugged and beautiful. She was alone, but the poet in her soul sang in the presence of God.

Camped in the forest on the dry, pungent needle floor near a river where she also parked her departmental all-terrain vehicle, she loved to spend the evening by the wood smell of her fire observing the silver percolating sweep of the water over white and gray stones. In places the water was clear and heavy as glass. In others the current rushed by over foaming rapids, spewing upward in a white drifting spray. Its mist, floating over the banks and into the forest, smelled clean. And when the sun dropped suddenly into night, a chill wind came up and roared through the evergreen trees, swaying their tops back and forth, revealing the clear points of distant stars overhead and an occasional ghost of a small cloud in the moonlight.

In her bedroll Janene carried a little silver flask filled with cream sherry. The sweet nut flavor of the sherry warmed her by the fire.

"In the name of God," her mother once told her on one of her visits home to the San Francisco suburb where she'd grown up, "a woman doesn't do these things."

Janene, sitting in a chair in the living room, wearing shorts, smiled self-consciously, looking down at her crusty knees. They were wind dried and sun burnt. Her step-father, a welder of stocky build with a butch haircut, and a man of few words, was sitting in the room with them reading a newspaper. Janene and her mother never seemed to understand one another. But she and her step-father were close. It was he who had encouraged her to read when very young, though her eyes were weak, who had spent time with her outdoors, teaching her to fish the rivers of northern California, and it was he who had pushed her to get a higher education, to pursue her interests without concern for what others thought.

"Mother, I'm happy with my life."

"Oh!" Melodie had recently learned of the silver flask, and that was the last straw in shattering any appreciation she might have had of her daughter's ways. "Look at you! Can't you at least comb your hair back, tuck your shirt in, wear a blouse once in a while, for Lord's sake!"

"Mother, I'm outdoors a lot."

"Leave the girl alone. Can't you see she's happy the way she is?" Janene's step-father said, glancing up from his newspaper. Opinion stated, he turned back to the article he was reading.

For a moment Melodie sat speechless. Anger surged through her and subsided. Really, what was the use? She went into the kitchen to make popcorn. Her two youngest children were in bed. Her teenage son had not returned home from a date.

Janene came into the kitchen. She got the hot popcorn out of the microwave. Her mother was getting dishes from the cupboard. With her back to her daughter, Melodie asked, "Do you think you'll ever marry?"

"I don't know, mom."

"You do like men, don't you?"

"Yes."

"Have you dated?"

"A few times in college."

"But not since?"

"No."

Her mother sighed. "I don't understand you, Janene. Honestly, of all my children, I understand you the least."

"Don't try to understand me, mother. Just let me be who I am."

Her mother looked at her, appearing to travel far away in thought for several minutes. Then she came over and put her arm around Janene's shoulders. "Okay, daughter," she said. "What have I got to lose?" They both stood there for a moment in silence.

Janene never married.

Newlywed

"I think," she said, "that people who drink too much should be flogged."

He did not answer, but rolled over onto his face, putting his pillow over his head.

"Matt, listen to me! You made a fool out of yourself last night, and you embarrassed me."

"Sarah, I didn't mean to." He sat up bleary-eyed, hair sticking out at odd angles.

Sarah, who was dressed only in a bra and panties, went over and pulled up the second floor studio apartment blinds. Brilliant light flooded into the window. "Get up," she said.

"Ow! You didn't have to do that." Matt rolled back under the pillow.

At breakfast they had black coffee, bacon and eggs. The bacon was burnt, the eggs fried hard, and the coffee manly.

"What're we going to do this bright Saturday morning, honey?" Matt asked, swallowing his first egg in a lump.

"You mean, what're you going to do today."

"Oh, come on, Sarah. Are you still mad about last night?"

"Well, I should be." She smiled. "Matt, the Watsons think you're some kind of animal. Worse. They think we're trash."

"I guess we are by their standards."

"Didn't you know that was good crystal?"

"I didn't think. Besides, I didn't really throw it off the balcony. I dropped it. Accidentally."

"That's not what they think."

Sarah and Matt had been married for only two weeks. Already there were numerous adjustments. Sarah was not always as modest as Matt thought she should be. And she was a bit of a flirt. On the other hand,

Matt bit his nails, couldn't hold his drink and was generally awkward among strangers.

Saturday afternoon they went book shopping on Bainbridge Island. They returned by ferry boat to Seattle across Puget Sound at dusk and took a bus through the gray, dreary neighborhoods east of Lake Union up to the University District.

There they came across a brown bearded man in his thirties dressed in olive green army fatigues, sitting on a low wall fronting the post office on University Avenue. Next to him, mounted on the same wall, was a small cardboard sign reading, "Questions answered. Fifty cents."

"The meaning of the universe," this street philosopher repeated in response to Sarah's request. He paused and stroked his beard. He looked slyly at his two interlocutors. They were coolly dressed in shorts, tank top or T-shirt, holding hands. It was a warm, pleasant summer evening. There were stars already showing in a darkening sky that was rarely so clear in the Pacific Northwest.

"The meaning of the universe is simple." He looked up at the night sky. The yellow of the street lights faded into blue black starry darkness above the two story buildings. The air was sweet. "It is," he said quietly, looking down and motioning them closer. "It is that all things are one." He leaned back and smiled.

"Is that all?" Matt asked.

"Fifty cents. All questions answered," the man on the wall called out to other passersby. He seemed to have instantly forgotten about them.

They walked on and passed the inset door of a small shop selling souvenir bric-a-brac for high prices. In front of the door, under the covered entranceway lined with glass window displays, a tall Caribbean black man dressed in a bright red and orange shirt and stringy blue jeans cut off at the knees, with long hair braided into corn rows, was standing on his head. He said nothing, but discreetly placed in a corner of the shop entrance on the pavement between him and the sidewalk was a cup into which passing people were occasionally putting money in bills and coins. Rastifari music played from a transistor radio set next to the cup.

"Have you seen the blind woman?" Sarah asked.

"Yes. She's usually down there in front of the bank with her little girl in the afternoons during the week," Matt said. "Sings really badly and plays the banjo even worse. The little girl just stands quietly beside her and waits. I gave her ten dollars once."

"Why'd you do that, Matt?"

"I don't know. Must've been drinking."

"Probably."

They both laughed. They went into a small Japanese restaurant and ate squid and rice. The juice the squid had had cooked out of it was very good on the rice. But the squid itself was like rubber. They drank a little plum wine.

At home in the tiny studio apartment they sat down on the fold-out bed in the semi-dark. The blinds were down but canted open, so that city light filled the otherwise unlit room with soft shadows. A TV was blaring something from across the hall.

"Matt," Sarah asked, "Do you want to have kids?" The wine they had had with their dinner was working, and she felt a little light-headed.

"Kids?"

"Yes. You know. Little human replicas of their parents that spit at one end and squirt colored fluids out the other."

"Oh, one of those. I don't know. Do you?"

"I think I would like to when we can afford it."

"Well, me too then." Matt had Sarah's tank top off and unsnapped her bra. He began kissing her shoulders and breasts.

Sarah pushed Matt back. "I'm serious."

"Okay, hon. Let's do it then." He began kissing her again. Sarah fell back into a swirl of her own chestnut brown hair on the bed. She closed her eyes. Matt pulled her short-short jeans and panties off, observing the dark, curly mass of hair almost breathlessly, and discarding his own clothes as fast as he could. Their union was warm and sweet. Sarah bit Matt on the shoulder and moaned. Matt groaned, thrusting involuntarily now.

In the morning Sarah pulled the blind up again and let the bright sunlight in on her semi-naked body. Matt, who was reading a book in bed, was unconsciously chewing his nails. In the kitchen a pan of muffins, which was burning in the oven, began to fill the room with smoke.

Summary Justice

In the dark morning hours, three Viet Cong entered a village. They went into a hut. There was shouting.

"You didn't pay your taxes. Twice you refuse."

"I need money for my family."

The guerrillas dragged an older man into the street. He lost a clog in the struggle. One of the guerrillas had an American pistol. The old man stumbled under the grip of two men. The one with the pistol waited on the dirt road. The old man began to plead.

"I must help my children and their children. The crops are meager with this war. I could not spare any money, or they would go hungry."

The guerrillas did not speak. They were all business. There were no villagers in the street, but they were listening. The man with the pistol raised it to the old man's temple and fired.

A dog was barking the whole time.

The Burgeoning Poet

On the morning when the well-known magazine editor, Mr. Gornam, came by the house to have breakfast with her father, a college professor, she tried to remain upstairs. But her father wouldn't let her. He called her down to meet his friend.

"Susan, I want you to meet Jeff Gornam. He has expressed an interest in seeing some of your poems."

"Pleased to meet you, Mr. Gornam."

"The pleasure's all mine, Susan."

Susan knew her father had pressured his friend to look at her work, and she felt embarrassed. Mr. Gornam was a small man with heavy rimmed glasses. His manner seemed casual and at the same time distant, notably patient.

"I would be interested in seeing some of your work, Miss Dawson," he said. He peered at her with small blue eyes through his glasses and smiled with his mouth.

Susan went into the living room. In the corner was a large, antique, roll-top desk, which had been in the family for several generations and was kept unnicked, unscratched and spotlessly clean and polished. The room was shadowy, being lit only by what light could pass through the heavy living room drapes, which were still drawn. With a rattle Susan pulled back the flexible, slotted desk top and retrieved a packet from one of the pigeon hole compartments inside. It was a sheaf of small sheets of paper, rolled and bound together with a red ribbon, the same kind of ribbon she was using to tie her coal black hair into a ponytail that morning.

She paused. She had never shown her work to anyone outside her family. It seemed to her very intense and personal. Showing it to a stranger was like publicly removing her clothes. She took a deep breath, pulled down the top and marched into the kitchen. There she unrolled the packet on the counter, took several sheets from it and, smiling nervously at her mother who was getting eggs out of the refrigerator, took them into the dining room.

"I don't think modern poetry has much at all in common with Donne or any of the others of his school in the seventeenth century," her father was saying. "In my opinion Mr. Eliot and his associates simply used the Metaphysical Poets as an excuse for attacking the Romantics. It seems to me most moderns substitute a kind of technical complexity for the multifaceted states of consciousness evinced by those earlier poets."

"I don't think I follow you, Tom."

"Dad. Excuse me, Mr. Gornam." Susan handed her poems to her father.

"Well, take a look at these, Jeff. I think Susan's work will illustrate my meaning very well. They were certainly a surprise to me when I first read them."

The room felt stuffy with the smell of omelet coming from the kitchen. Susan was beginning to get a little light-headed and sick. Pressing her hand to her stomach, she pulled a heavy, dark reddish-brown mahogany chair out from the large dining room table and sat down. Mr. Gornam read intently, his piercing blue eyes moving back and forth in jerks over the pages he now had spread before him on the white linen lace tablecloth. He read each poem several times.

"Well, these are...good," he said, looking up. "They're certainly different." He smiled.

There was a pause.

"Yes, different," Tom Dawson said, coming round to his thought once again. "That's what I wanted you to see." He hesitated. It was clear his friend didn't see at all and didn't fully appreciate the poems. "What I mean is that among a good many contemporary poets whose work I'm familiar with, there's been a kind of slackening or loosening of tension in the verse as the fashion for technical complexity has worn off. That's why I wanted you to look at Susan's work. She..."

"It's free verse, Tom. That's the way it's supposed to be written. More relaxed now, I'd say. Like the human voice."

"It doesn't have to be. Verse isn't speech. It's evocation."

Susan's mother came in with the omelet on a large silver platter. Over food, the conversation turned to inane topics. After breakfast, Mrs. Dawson, being fully aware of her daughter's awkward situation, sent her into the kitchen with the empty platter. She followed with other dishes.

"I'm sorry, honey," she said in a hushed voice. "Your dad's right. Your poems really are very good. But this Mr. Dornam—Gornam—Doorknob—whatever his name is. Well, he's a professional editor, you know. You know what that means."

"Go with the flow."

"That's right. And old beady eyes out there..."

They both tittered with whispering laughter. Susan's mother snickered with the vindictive pleasure of her remark.

"He looks like a grasshopper," Susan added. They both laughed out loud.

"What on earth's going on in here?" Susan's father asked, coming into the kitchen. "Listen, Jeff and I have got to be going now. I'll talk to you later, daughter." he said, putting an arm around her shoulder and hugging her. "I'm not through with this guy yet," he whispered. The living room door softly closed as they went out.

Susan gathered up her poems, bound them to the others in the kitchen with the red ribbon and took them back to the roll-top desk in the living room. Then she went softly upstairs to her bedroom and shut the door. She threw herself crossways onto her bed, onto the familiar white bedspread with its raised pink floral design. A curtain blew back from the window, introducing a suburban smell of mown lawns, and the fresh breeze brushed her tears. A robin began to sing. Exhausted, she fell asleep in the familiar and comfortable surroundings of her room.

The Lord's Anointed

Spiritual life had always been important to her. Even as a child she had found strength in the quiet places of her own heart.

"Mary Lou. Mary Lou, where are you?"

"I'm in here, Ma. Down in the old chicken house."

Mrs. Bethsen crossed the back yard, fat gray-barred Plymouth Rock and reddish-brown Rhode Island Red hens scattering before her. "Why, I declare, Mary Louise. Why you would want to go and hide in this filthy old chicken pen the way you do..."

"I just need to be alone sometimes, Mama."

"You having one of them visions again, honey? I told your pa he ought to have torn this thing down when he built the new one. 'The child will catch ill playing down in that filthy old pen,' I says. 'Oh, let the girl alone. It can't hurt,' he says. Well, I'm still so worried you're going to get some kind of sickness in here."

"I'm okay, Ma."

Mary Lou grew up in spite of her strange ways and left home at sixteen. She went up north and had a child. For years she made her living waitressing in Chicago. She was divorced, working in a truck stop. Then she married again. Edward was a good man. He drove the big rigs for awhile and then went out west and got into construction work.

Edward never understood Mary Lou, but he respected her. And he raised Purdy, her boy, as though he were his own. Purdy grew up and did even better than Edward in the construction field. He made a good deal of money.

What Edward didn't understand about Mary Lou was her religion. He respected it, but its intensity and the way it drew her off from him were disturbing. He would sometimes awake in the middle of the night and there she would be, up on her knees in the middle of the bed, deep in prayer, rocking back and forth, moaning or singing, laughing or weeping with her eyes closed and maybe with her lips trembling if she was crying.

Once, observing her in this state, speaking in tongues and then prophesying in song in her loose fitting nightgown, he had suddenly acquired an intense physical need for her but was afraid to touch her. So he lay in the dark waiting, heart racing and gasping for air in the heat of his desire. But after praying, Mary Lou crawled under the blankets and went to sleep.

Edward was miserable. He couldn't sleep. Finally he reached over and touched her on the hip. She awoke immediately and crawled over onto him, sitting down on his chest and pulling her nightgown off over her head as she did. They did things that night he had never dreamed she would do. It was strange how religion affected her.

In her fifties, her son grown and she and Edward comfortably settled in a small house on Driscoll Boulevard on the northern outskirts of Spokane, Washington, Mary Lou began to have her deepest revelations. She saw that God not only lived in her but in all men, that we were all part of one Christ body. Jesus had already returned in the flesh in us, once and for all. She gathered a small group around her and taught them this simple truth. They met every Sunday in her home.

One afternoon Mary Lou was arrested for shoplifting. She had done nothing but eat a handful of grapes in a supermarket, having grown tired and hungry from a long day's casual shopping. The day was hot and she had stepped into the grocery store for a few minutes to cool off in its air conditioning. But a disgruntled stocker had considered her free-handedness theft, since she hadn't paid for the grapes.

"Ma'am," the arresting officer, who was hardly more than a boy, said to her, "Mr. Carter, the store manager here, says he's willing to drop the charge if you'll consent to pay for what you've taken." The officer seemed anxious, not willing to arrest the woman on such a trivial charge.

Mary Lou looked at the young police officer. "Don't you know, son, that all these things belong to the Lord?" she said quietly.

"Yes, I understand but..."

"Then how can you accuse me of stealing? The Lord lives in me. He lives in you as well. All the earth is a gift of his spirit."

"I..."

"You don't understand, but you will some day, I know, because the Lord has given it to me to tell you that he would have you turn your heart to him. He will bless you as you come to know him, and he will free you from the burden which is troubling you now." The young officer looked at her with curious surprise. Mary Lou fixed a disturbingly penetrating gaze on him for a moment. Then she reached into the large bag which she carried for a purse. "He loves you, son," she said. The policeman blushed.

The store manager, a balding, perpetually concerned looking man in his early thirties, with knit brows in a pale, fleshy face, was standing there with her and the officer just outside the electrically operated doors of the supermarket entrance. People were going in and coming out with shopping carts, looking at them with mild interest because of the presence of the police officer. As Mary Lou rummaged for her wallet in her purse, the store manager bent over a little closer to her, as though wondering if there might not be a few other store items concealed in that large, brown, patterned purse that looked more like a carpet bag.

Mary Lou pulled out a five dollar bill and handed it to the manager.

"Well this is too much," he began.

"And what price would you put on the Lord's produce?"

"Well, we generally charge..."

Mary Lou walked away toward her car. Neither the manager nor the policeman chose to follow her.

Bullhocky

The last time I saw our combat correspondent he was gaunt looking with sunken eyes. He'd spent a few months in the A Shau Valley and had seen too much. A correspondent can get out of a firefight just about any time because he has the same priority as wounded on helicopters, but Corporal Stoddard didn't do that. He used his privilege to go from one hot spot to another.

But that's not the Stoddard I remember. He was easy going, the kind of guy who laid back, took it easy, and wrote news stories about heroic battles we'd been in that none of us ever heard of. Like the time the sapper was found dead, stretched over our perimeter wire in the morning. We took casualties that night, but that one body on the wire was as far as the enemy got. Not according to Stoddard. According to him the North Vietnamese Army broke through our wire and spread themselves all over the compound. By the time we beat them back, there were only a few of us left standing. We read some of his garbage in the Stars and Stripes. Most of it didn't get through because the editors weren't that stupid. But now and then we got a good laugh.

"These gooks aren't human," he told me one night. We were lying on the perimeter answering fire from a Viet Cong probing action coming from a village across the river.

"Yes they are," I said. "They've got feelings."

"Not like you and me. They've been here thousands of years. Have you ever seen a wheelbarrow?"

"No."

"Well keep shooting. You're not going to hit anything human."

One day Stoddard got a letter. His girlfriend was having a wonderful time with someone else.

Three days later we were on hole watch together. It rained all night. We sat on top of the bunker in our ponchos because the inside of the bunker was a pond. I remember sitting there, my rifle sticking up under the poncho and my boots sticking out. The water poured off me, making gullies out of the folds in the plastic. It was cold and all I could see of Stoddard in the dark in his poncho was his face and his wet blond hair stuck to his forehead.

"Crap," he said, and he sat there for an hour without saying anything else.

He didn't have to be there. As a correspondent he wasn't supposed to be pulling perimeter duty. There was a third guy with us but he was asleep. I was imagining what Hawaii would be like if I ever got there on R and R. After a long while the downpour slowed to near a cold sprinkle. It never stopped, just slowed down.

"Ever been to Hawaii?"

"Yes."

"What's it like?"

"Nice."

"What's nice?"

"Doesn't have any gooks. Doesn't have any bitches either. Not anymore, anyway."

"I thought you had to be married to get Hawaii for R and R."

"I'm a correspondent." He smiled.

Stoddard the genius. For a while we sat there in silence. Finally I said, "It's Mckenzie's watch."

"Let him sleep," Stoddard said. "I'm not tired."

Stoddard left us at the end of the rainy season and went to the A Shau Valley. The first time I saw him again he was really gung ho. The Marine Corps wanted to send him home and he was fighting it.

"They claim I was wounded three times," he said, laying out his blanket roll on the hooch floor, folding it, then mounting it on his haversack. He was getting ready to go back and was preparing his pack. Three purple hearts for three wounds and you're automatically sent home. "I was only wounded twice."

He explained that he'd been in a firefight after previously receiving a wound in another one. In this one he got shot in the hand and caught shrapnel in the back from a Chinese Communist grenade. They weren't serious wounds and he insisted they were only worth one purple heart since he got them together.

The Marine Corps must have accepted his argument because they didn't send him home. He went back to the A Shau Valley. It was the beginning of 1968 after the Tet Offensive and there was a lot of activity there: Khe Sanh and the battles of hills 861 and 881. He was in the middle of it.

As I said, the very last time I saw him, a few months later, he looked like he'd had enough. And it was only a week after he left again to go on an operation south of Phu Bai that I heard he was in a village with a patrol and tried to enter a hut. A forty-five caliber automatic pistol was facing the door, rigged to a wire. He was killed.

I remember a conversation we had some time that night on the bunker in the rain shortly after he got the letter from his girlfriend. We'd been hearing about all the anti-war sentiment and protests, so we were discussing our reasons for fighting for our country.

"I'm not fighting for my country," he said. "I'm fighting for the Marine Corps."

Points of View

She was young, neither plain nor strikingly pretty, and had a vigorous temperament. But she was not well educated. On the day they were married, she explained to her husband the simple truths of her religious faith, which she felt he ought to share. After that there were problems.

"Thelma, I don't agree."

"You do believe in God, don't you?"

"Yes, but I don't think it's so easy to know who he is or what he is. Maybe..."

"There can't be any maybes with the Lord, Dick. He's in authority over all."

"I was saying, maybe he doesn't want us to know everything about him. Maybe there's some mystery involved. Where would life be without any mystery? We need to be wrong sometimes, so we can have the deeper pleasure of knowing when we're right."

"That's crazy, Dick."

"Crazy?"

"Blasphemous."

"Oh."

"He has already sent his prophets to tell us his will. And Jesus let us see him as he is."

They were sitting on the living room sofa, having one of their many interminable discussions on the subject. They'd been married now for about six months. There was no TV, and several hundred second-hand books lined the room on improvised and somewhat rickety board and cinder block bookshelves. They were Dick's books.

It was blistering hot and muggy in Philadelphia. Their second floor apartment was stuffy. It was located in a row house on Brown Street in North Philadelphia, not far from downtown and a few blocks east of the

Philadelphia Art Museum. They were in their underwear. Dick put his hand on Thelma's thigh. Thelma was a densely freckled redhead, very slender with small, girlish breasts and narrow hips.

"Not now, Dick."

"Yes." He began to kiss her on her stomach, putting his tongue into her belly button.

"Oh, what are you doing?" She pushed him away. "This is serious."

Dick sat up uncomfortably, feeling awkward with an erection. He was tall and lanky and wore glasses that darkly framed his brown eyes.

"I'm just trying to get your mind off religion."

"It isn't religion."

"It ain't religion. Well, if it ain't religion, what is it?"

"It isn't religion. Are you trying to make fun of the fact that I've never been to college? Just because you have, doesn't mean you know everything, Mr. book-and-pen-and-broken-down-typewriter, or that you have all the answers."

"I didn't say I did."

"Well, that's what you meant."

"No I didn't, Thelma. Honest."

Thelma sat silently for several minutes. She was obviously angry. Dick watched her but said nothing.

"I'm getting dressed," she said.

"It's too hot."

"I'm getting dressed anyway. And I'm going down to the park." She got up. They both got up, went into the bedroom and dressed.

Outside, the neighborhood gang was gathered at the corner of the block of reddish-brown brick row houses they lived in. The teenaged ruffians had joyously and loudly broken some bottles on the cobblestone street and two of them were now engaged in a slap fight. They were hanging around in their usual place in front of a boarded up store. It was generally from this vantage point that they watched the neighborhood to keep out anyone who didn't belong in it.

As usual, the couple and the gang acted as if they hadn't seen each other. The gang was at the corner of Twenty-fifth and Brown. Dick and

Thelma walked away from them and turned the corner at Brown and Twenty-sixth streets, heading west toward the Schuylkill River, Fairmount Park stretched along both its banks, and the Philadelphia Museum of Art. It was dusk. The one or two empty lots they passed were forming dark recesses in the growing shadows, and there was an odor of sulfur pollution in the air.

In the park by the museum, it turned dark. Stars shown clearly in a deep sky. They stood looking at the river, at the stars and moonlight reflected in broken rivulets and circles of moving water.

"It's beautiful!" Thelma said. She put her head on Dick's shoulder. He put his arm around her waist.

"There's been a lot of violence in this park," Dick said somberly. "Remember that young couple that was down here a few weeks ago? Three guys raped the girl and drowned her boyfriend in the fountain in front of this museum. And then there was that newborn baby they found buried in the middle of the park near here. Never did figure out whose it was." He looked at Thelma. He was determined, in his own right, to educate her about the realities of this world. She was looking up at the stars in the sky.

"Thelma."

"Yes."

"Did you hear me? I mean about the rapes and the infanticide."

"The what?" She looked down.

"Baby killing."

"Oh. Yes, I remember. It's so sad!"

"I'll say it is! Just a little perverted too."

"What that poor mother must be going through."

"Poor mother? What about the kid?"

"I'm sure he's with the Lord."

Dick looked at Thelma in amazement. He wanted to ask her, a little contemptuously, how she knew the child was with the Lord. But the sincerity of her tone and the sweetness of her expression kept him silent. The problem was that he loved her for the very thing that drove him nuts.

Intimations

They were twins and had grown up on a small dairy farm in the bucolic, green hill country of Southeastern Pennsylvania. But in their teens the bank had foreclosed on unpaid loans and the family had been forced to relocate to a small house in a nearby drab and crowded industrial town, where their father found intermittent work at various grinding mechanical occupations.

At eighteen John and Teresa, named for the two sixteenth century Spanish mystics their mother admired, sought their fortunes elsewhere. Teresa, through a series of loans and grants, eventually obtained a bachelor of arts degree in American History, as well as a teaching certificate. She went to work in a high school in the town of Paoli just west of Philadelphia. But that was later on.

Upon graduation from high school, John joined the Marines. Shortly afterward, while still a freshman at college, Teresa felt a sharp pain in the shin bone of her left leg. It came upon her suddenly one night and would not let her sleep. In the morning she phoned her parents to learn what she already knew. John had been injured in a training accident. He had broken his leg.

This close affinity does not normally occur between fraternal twins, as it is said to do between identical twins. But John and Teresa had always been very close. They had rarely fought with one another in childhood and were always good friends, even confiding their tenderest emotional misadventures to one another during their teens.

After boot camp, hospital convalescence and infantry training, John got himself into language school. The Marine Corps sent him to Washington, D. C. for a year to learn Vietnamese. That was a very pleasant year. He spent a number of weekends staying with his sister and her roommate in the small apartment they shared near the university they both attended as freshmen. Patricia, the roommate, and John fell in love. They were married only a few weeks before John went to the West Coast to await orders to Vietnam. Patricia remained in school and in the apartment with Teresa.

One evening as they were sitting quietly in the tiny living room of their one bedroom apartment, Patricia said, "I envy you, Terese."

"Why's that?"

"I don't know. The way you and John are. The way you can feel things about each other. I love John and I'm sure he loves me, but we don't get those feelings about each other."

"We were close when we were kids. When mom and dad lost the farm... Well, it made it easier to have each other. We didn't have any other brothers or sisters." Teresa put down the novel she was reading. It was a paperback Martin Chuzzlewit. She should have been studying for a history exam.

"But how do you do it? How do you know these things?"

Teresa thought for a moment, sitting in her stuffed naugahyde armchair with one bare slender leg folded under her. "I don't know. I really don't. It's just always been that way." She smiled and looked at her friend. "Mom used to always say that she believed we had the spirits of the original saints we were named after living in us. I think she wanted to believe that."

"Do you believe it?" Patricia was eating crackers and had dropped crumbs onto her nightgown on her lap. She was picking them off one by one.

"Sometimes. Saint John of the Cross and Saint Teresa of Avila were close. And they were both mystics, which may have something to do with the intuitions we get."

"Why? Just because they were mystics, Terese, doesn't mean..."

"I know. I don't understand it. Anyway, what difference does it make? It's just the way things are."

"I guess. ...Terese."

"Yeah."

"I'm pregnant."

"You're kidding!"

"No. You've got a potent brother."

They both laughed and embraced in tears.

John wrote regularly and Patricia answered as often, hardly able to wait for the day when his tour in Vietnam would be over. During her sophomore summer break, well along in her pregnancy, Patricia went to Hawaii to be with her husband during a week of R & R. It was a wonderful week, full of warm, but not too hot, pleasant weather and "clean beds, white sheets and clean streets," as John kept remarking. Emerald blue water, quiet isolation, and the many hued greens of Kauai Island.

Sex might have been a problem at this advanced stage in Patricia's pregnancy, but in their hungry, joyful, kissing, touching, caressing nakedness nothing was a problem. The last evening back on Oahu Island was spent in the lavish dining room of an expensive hotel. The wine was good and a warm rain blew fresh and clear against the floor to ceiling glass window that faced out onto the beach and night darkened ocean. They later strolled on the beach on the wet sand in the damp air after the rain. The foaming sound and salt smell of ocean waves washing up the beach under a quickly cleared, starry sky somehow felt clean.

Patricia had the baby in the early fall and stayed out of school. She remained in the apartment with Teresa, since she didn't know where John would be stationed when he returned from Vietnam in a few months.

A month before John was to return, Teresa collapsed while attending one of her classes. She was taken to a hospital where nothing could be found wrong with her. Patricia was at her bedside when she awoke in the morning. Patricia had been crying. Her eyes were dark, her cheeks red.

Teresa put her hand on Patricia's and asked sadly, "You've heard?"

"No. No one's been to see me. But I know." She laid her head on the side of the bed next to where she was sitting and wept bitterly. Teresa pulled herself close to Patricia, kissed her on the forehead and tried to comfort her in her arms.

Shortly, word of John's death by a land mine came from the military.

Overrun

At a small firebase, they had been overrun during the night. They had taken casualties but had held their position. In the morning, the choppers came and took out their wounded and dead. The firebase was nothing but a clearing in brush jungle on a hill. The remaining members of the platoon ate their C-rations in silence.

Several of the wounded ended up in an aid station. It was further south, down country. One of these men lay on a cot. He and the other seriously wounded would be transferred to a hospital ship. The surgeons had only been able to stabilize his wound.

As he lay there, he thought about the night's fighting. He remembered the shouts, the explosions lighting the dark, and the screams. Everyone had fought like a devil, and no one had thought he would make it. He wondered how many had, feeling sick about it.

The Bear and the Wildcat

She was like a wildcat. He was a bear. When they married, the institution of matrimony became a Roman arena.

"I'll look at whomever I want."

"Look, yes...but"

"And flirt a little too, if I feel like it."

"No. You married me," he said.

"I didn't give you my soul. Just the use of my body now and then."

"Now and then?"

"Well, I mean when we both feel like it."

"I always feel like it."

She was a fine looking young woman. And he was strong and virile but seemed to have lost command of himself from the day he first met her. He loved her passionately. There was no doubt about that. She had a kiss like fire. Her lips actually burned. At least this was his view, his experience of the matter.

What Paul couldn't see was that Sally was just as much in love with him. That's why her kisses were so warm, why her love-making left him as exhausted as the embers of a burnt over forest. Even their fighting was a kind of love-making. They kindled each other like dry twigs under an intense heat. And there was never a day without a lightning strike somewhere in their hearts.

The problem arose from his insecurity and what Sally considered to be Paul's suffocating possessiveness.

"I don't want to feel like I've got chains on me," she once told him. "I'm not an ox cart. I don't want to spend my life clunking along behind my big bull." Sally was sitting naked on the mussed sheets of their bed, her legs folded under her. Paul was lying on his back, his hands under his head. He was admiring his wife's breasts, the shape of her body, for

Sally had a narrow waist and strong, smooth thighs. There were several damp spots on the sheets from spilled semen. The morning sun was bright behind the curtains. Its warmth filled the room, and already they were arguing again.

"I'm not asking you to."

"Then why are you always jealous?"

"Because you're always flirting and dressing like a tart."

"Like a tart!" Sally became red in the face. "I do not! I do not!" She turned her back to Paul, putting her hands over her eyes, and began to cry.

"I'm sorry, honey." Paul sat up and touched her shoulder gently. She jerked it away from him.

"I give up," Paul said to himself. But of course he didn't. He put on a robe, left the room for a few minutes, then came back, and they finally made up.

One evening, as was often the case, they went over to Sally's parents' home for dinner. Sally's father was an accountant with a law firm that handled tax problems for corporations and the rich. Balding, he wore glasses. He was quiet in manner, and Sally always felt he seemed cool, or at least unaffectionate, toward her mother. Sally's mother had become heavy-set over the years and tended to fuss over guests, including her daughter and son-in-law. Sally was an only child.

They had mashed potatoes, fried chicken, gravy and green beans on a big, blond wood, dining room table without a cloth. Steam rose from the white potatoes in the big stoneware bowl on the table. The bowl was chalk white with a blue farm motif of cows and sheep etched onto its outer surface. The platter of chicken was ample, the pieces crisp and golden brown. So was the gravy, though a little peppery in flavor, Paul always thought. The green beans, Paul also thought once again, since they frequently had this meal at their in-laws', were one of those necessary ornaments, like the fake, green turf out on the front porch that didn't do anything to improve its appearance.

The Gates' lived modestly in a big rambling frame house, though they were by no means without money. They lived in Franconia, a Virginia suburb of Washington, D.C.

"Mom," Sally asked her mother during the otherwise quiet meal. Her father was eating and wiping his mouth with his napkin, making serious business of his supper. Her mother asked intermittently about the food, receiving the accustomed compliments. "Did you ever flirt much when you and Dad were first married?"

Paul looked at Sally in surprise. She must be feeling a little contrite over our last fight, he thought.

Sally's father looked up from his plate, as though glancing up from his newspaper. He peered over his glasses with steady gray eyes. "As a matter of fact, yes she did," he said. "And I was very jealous. But we managed to survive somehow."

Mrs. Gates was flushed with embarrassment. "Your father was quite the Don Juan in those days. I had to make sure he understood he had something worth keeping," she said, smiling.

"So what happened?" Sally asked. She didn't mean for her question to sound quite the way it did. "I mean, you're so calm and domestic now."

Mrs. Gates laughed. "I guess we got used to each other." She got up and went into the kitchen. "What'll it be?" she called cheerfully from the kitchen. The question was always the same and the choice always the same: vanilla or chocolate ice cream.

On the way home in the car, Paul said to his wife, "You think we'll ever be like them?"

"I hope not."

"What do you mean?"

"Dad's so indifferent now. At least he seems that way toward Mom."

"I don't think I could ever be like that with you," Paul said. He put his arm around Sally's shoulder and pulled her over to him. She laid her head on his right arm.

It was raining and the nearly deserted suburban streets were wet and glistening under the street lights. They turned a corner, Paul working the steering wheel with his left hand. On making the corner, his car veered a little into the oncoming lane. A car approaching them honked.

"All right, all right," he said. "I'm just trying to love my wife." The young man in the other car was good looking. Sally gave him a coy smile. The young man stared back at the couple as he passed them, wondering what could be the matter with them.

The Play

As a child she had been domineering, tomboyish, her dark hair cut short, straight and in bangs. And she was always organizing her brothers, sisters and playmates into theatrical performances for her parents and neighbors to watch. She generally took the lead part. And when they applauded, she beamed.

In high school she participated in school plays: Twelfth Night, Macbeth, Julius Caesar, and a few, more frivolous, popular works. She loved it all but had a taste for serious drama. For this reason she never aspired to movie stardom, nor coifed herself to a soft prettiness. She was striking: lean, tough, athletic, yet somehow feminine in appearance. And she was a true artist.

"I'm a chameleon," she told her associates in a small theatrical company which they had formed together in a large mid-western city. They performed in city parks on weekends and holidays and made their living by other means. What she was trying to explain in this instance was that she could capture the spirit of Telva, the house servant in Alejandro Casona's play, The Lady of the Dawn. Telva was by turns wise, impertinent, humorous and sardonic.

"I want you as the Pilgrim," Martin, the director, said. "You have that kind of tall, willowy beauty. We won't have to make you over. Besides, it takes a lot of skill to be Lady Death and convince an audience that you mean it when you say you don't enjoy your work."

"If I was Lady Death, I would enjoy my work." Danette raised her hands like talons. "I wouldn't disguise myself as a pilgrim. I would come boldly looking for victims with blood dripping from my teeth, smoke pouring out my ears, and hair rolling in tufts over the tops of my socks."

"Yuck!" Joanne said.

"Well?"

"Well, this role is more sophisticated than that," Martin said.

That night in their small apartment, Danette said to Martin, "I really do want to play Telva."

"We have someone for Telva. And she's built for the job, a middle-aged house servant. We need you as the Pilgrim. You'd make a good Lady Death."

"Thanks."

"I mean it, Danette. There's mystery in the way you move, so deliberate and catlike, and in your dark eyes and your precise gestures. You're too deep for Telva."

"You're not going to flatter me out of it. Telva's smart."

"Smart, but not deep."

"All right, I'll do the Pilgrim."

An extraordinary thing happened. The play, like others they'd done, had been put on over one weekend in a city park, in the muggy heat of a summer afternoon on green grass under tall trees. And it had been reviewed in the Sunday supplement of the city's largest daily newspaper. A lengthy and positive appraisal had been made of Danette's performance.

Years passed. The company prospered, became self-sustaining, had its own theater. Rather small, they built a stage closely surrounded by the audience on three sides. The seats mounted upwards like bleachers, creating a close-in, intimate quality. The players concentrated exclusively on classical performances, often doing the Greeks, but also Moliere, Racine, Goldsmith, O'Neill, Calderon and so forth. They did comedy, tragedy and epic, from modern to ancient. The only criterion was the quality of performance the play could occasion.

One evening a young man began to shout obscenities from what was usually the well-behaved audience. It was during a performance of Euripides' Medea.

"Bitch! You can't do that. Women don't kill their own children."

Danette was in the midst of the dialogue that took place between Medea and Jason, her husband, after she had just killed their children. Danette went on with the role of Medea, stating her lines clearly, slowly, with a controlled anger and that strange mixture of grief and vindictive exultation which she could perform so well. Her slim, dark, sinewy looks and arched eyebrows expressed pride, cunning and unpredictable determination.

"No one kills their own children!" The young man was standing up. He was in about the fifth row of seats, was obviously very drunk, and had difficulty maintaining his balance. Danette could certainly hear him and could see him beyond the lights, but she continued with her lines. Her heart began to race and she feared she would falter, forget her lines.

Two men got up on either side of the drunken one and pulled him down. Two others came and removed him from the theater.

Danette continued on as Medea. Jason pleaded to no avail for the bodies of his children. The chorus bemoaned the unpredictability of fate.

There was no curtain for this theater-in-the-round. The players simply quietly left the stage at the end of the play.

Then there was silence as the heavy emotional weight of the play sank into the audience in the darkened room. A shout could be heard from the outside reception area—probably the young man. Outside, cars passed and honked, their headlights flashing in the semi-dark under streetlights. Far above the city, in a clear night sky, were quiet stars.

Night Attack

They shot him because there was an order out to the surrounding villages not to swim in the river. We didn't want anyone trying to cross the river near our firebase because we'd just been through a North Vietnamese Army night assault. It was an NVA regiment designated R144. If we hadn't used the gunships, they'd have probably overrun us. So we wounded a seventeen year old from the village whom we later judged to be innocent.

We brought him up onto the hill to patch up the bullet wound in his shoulder. One of our bridge guards had shot him while he, as he put it, "was just going for a morning swim."

That's the way it was. You put out the word and they did stupid things anyway. They might as well go strolling in a mine field. But that was a privilege they always reserved for us.

The night attack came at two in the morning. That's usually when things like that would happen. It gave them time to get themselves and their gear up close enough to do something and time enough to clear out before dawn.

They slipped into the village across the river and set up their mortars. Then they started the barrage, walking the mortars in bright flashes over our compound and trying to hit the ammunition dump that they knew was in the middle of it. The mortars made a crumping sound like big hand grenades. As we woke up, dove into the mud puddles inside the low-walled sandbag bunkers beside our hooches, pulled on our pants and boots, and then headed with rifles and helmets (some with flak jackets) toward the perimeter, they crossed the bridge.

There was a bunker on their end of the wooden bridge and they hit that with a rocket propelled grenade, killing all but one of the guards.

The other one, who was on watch in about the middle of the bridge, they cut down with automatic fire as they went across.

By this time we were all pretty much in the trenches along the perimeter firing back. That didn't stop them. You could see them coming, intermittently. They were backlit by some flames on the smoldering wooden struts of the bunker. You'd see a shadowy figure or two in the dark and knew there were a lot more of them pouring over the bridge.

We sent a reaction platoon out to meet them. They lost a guy before they ever got to the bottom of the hill. Our eighty-one millimeter mortar crew finally got some flares up. The flares hung like balls of fire swinging from parachutes in the black sky.

We could now see the North Vietnamese soldiers hurriedly massing at the bottom of our hill. Some of them had on those helmets that looked like World War One helmets. When they started coming up the hill, they came in a line, shooting steadily, and we were getting heavy fire from the village across the river as well. It was hard to do anything but keep your head down. There was a smell of damp earth, brass and gunpowder with orders being shouted. I heard someone call for a corpsman way down the line on my right. Some of the NVA soldiers were using tracer bullets, so even if you were deaf and couldn't hear the rounds thudding into the sandbags in front of you, you could see how close the ones were that went over your head. You just waited for what seemed like a lull and jumped up, holding your rifle over your head firing a burst, and got down again.

Mike Barnes was right next to me.

"Did you see them, Corporal?" he asked. "They're coming thick as tent caterpillars."

A little ways down the line to our left, a Marine threw a grenade but it fell short and exploded without effect.

"It's hard to make anything out," I said. "The damned swinging flares are making shadows move everywhere. I can't tell if there're a million or a few hundred of them."

"I hope it's only a few hundred. God, I hope it's only..."

Then the choppers went up. The three helicopters lifted off our landing zone and circled around until they were directly over the massed NVA. One of them turned on its spotlight and the other two canted over to one side and went around and around it firing their M-60 machine guns out their side doors into the NVA line of assault. The tracer bullets came down out of those gunships in two pencil thin red lines. When they hit anything solid on the ground, they ricocheted away softly into the night like fireflies.

The assault was broken up and that made it easier to return fire, though we were still catching it from the village across the river.

Private First Class Barnes stood up, getting his head above the line of sandbags. He carefully squeezed a round off at one of the muzzle flashes we could see across the river. At the same time, with my rifle set on automatic, I emptied a magazine into the troops now broken up and running down the side of our hill near the bottom. As I pulled out another magazine of twenty rounds and shoved it into my M-16 rifle, I heard the most sickening sound, a kind of wet slap. Barnes fell down in the trench at my feet. His face was turned toward the ground but I could see the piece missing from the back of his skull, on the left side near his neck. The collar on his flak jacket was already soaked in what looked in the dark like black blood.

I was back in the States before I discovered I'd been wounded too. It was a pin head sized piece of shrapnel in the muscle on my chest just below the skin, which I must've gotten while running across the compound toward the perimeter during the mortar barrage. I never even felt it, and it was the only contribution I ever made to that war.

Family Matters

He had married into a dark, mysterious family and did not understand them. They, for the most part, kept him outside their innermost bond of emotion. There were always secrets.

"Myrna, what's the matter with your dad?" he asked one day. It was a Saturday morning, shortly after breakfast, and Myrna was feeding their newborn child from the breast.

"I told you, Dan. He was injured in the war."

"Lots of people were wounded. He looks alright now. But he's always brooding. At least, it seems that way."

Myrna pulled the child free from her breast. It immediately began screaming, angry at the sudden loss of the teat. The wet nipple stood out large, dark and firm on Myrna's swollen breast.

"I don't think he's done," Dan said.

"I know, but he's soaked. I need to change his diaper. Could you get me one, honey?"

Dan found the carton box and pulled out the paper diaper. It had elastic sides for a firmer fit. He brought it over.

Myrna had the baby on the living room couch, the old diaper already unfastened.

"Whoa! Smells of ammonia."

"Yes, it is pretty strong. I waited too long." Myrna held the baby's feet up, pulled out the deep yellow, urine soaked diaper, laid it dry side down on the ugly, pea green living room carpet of their one bedroom apartment and put the clean, white, dry diaper under the baby. She did this in what seemed to Dan like a single motion.

"I mean your dad was in some kind of a terrible situation, wasn't he?"

"Yes. He was a platoon leader. All of his men were killed in an ambush."

"He was the only survivor?"

"Yes."

"Wow! But that doesn't explain the rest of them."

"Rest of whom?"

"Your brothers. And your mother. They're all weird."

"You just don't know them well enough." Myrna picked the baby up, shifted her open blouse to the other breast, and attached him to it. She was so rich in milk, Dan had had to take some of it from her at times. It tasted thin compared to cow's milk.

"How could I?" Dan said. "When you're together, you guys always close ranks on me, it seems."

"We do not."

Dan was silent for a moment. Myrna was now in the rocking chair with her head back, eyes closed. The baby sucked furiously, making slurping sounds.

"He's a regular little pig," Dan said.

Myrna smiled.

"What I mean is you guys always seem to be saying things no one else understands."

Myrna rocked quietly.

"Martin's gay, isn't he?"

Myrna started to an upright position with the rocking chair. She looked directly at Dan but didn't say anything.

Dan looked into her dark eyes, so intense, so veiled with layers of emotion he felt he couldn't reach. He wanted everything to be simple and open between them. The living room was dark except for one lamp at the end of the couch where Dan was sitting. They hadn't opened the heavy, brown, floor length drapes yet.

"I can tell," Dan said simply. "The way he talks, the way..."

Myrna leaned back in the rocker again.

"Is that the big secret?" he asked.

"Part of it."

"What else?"

"Nothing."

"Come on, Myrna. I'm your husband, the father of your child, who is their nephew and grandchild. I'm family too."

The baby was almost asleep. Myrna got up and gently laid him in a small crib they kept in a corner of the living room. She covered the child, who remained asleep, or partially so, now sucking its thumb, and went back to the rocker. It was a big rocker and there was a large bookcase behind it.

Myrna looked at Dan. There were tears in her eyes.

"So what else?" Dan asked.

"There really isn't anything else, Dan. It's hard to explain."

"Well, try. Please."

"When we were young, Mom and Dad used to beat us. Pretty severely sometimes. Martin has some scars on his back to prove it. When he was about eleven he smarted off to Mom, and Dad took a belt to him. He hit him with the metal buckle end of it a couple of times."

"Ow!"

"Yeah. My parents can be very strict. We weren't allowed much freedom. My mother came across my older brother, Bob, masturbating when he was about fifteen. I was home at the time. I thought she was going to have a seizure."

"Did she tell your dad?"

"I don't think so."

"So why do you guys stick so close together? Your family life sounds horrible. It sounds—I don't know—repressed."

"It was."

"So why do you stick together now?"

"We're family."

"What about Martin's homosexuality?"

"We don't talk about it."

If I came out of a family like that, Dan thought, I'd be gay too. Who'd want to start another family like that? He wondered why his wife wasn't sexually inhibited herself.

He never asked Myrna any more questions about her family.

The Budding Theologian

She did not think she believed in the doctrines of her church, which was Episcopalian, though she loved the service, its beautiful ritual, particularly the celebration and receiving of the Eucharist. She had been precocious in early childhood and now, in her early teens, read philosophy, often arguing with her father, a professor of philosophy at the University of New Mexico.

"To say that God is three persons doesn't mean anything," she stated emphatically one morning at the breakfast table.

Her father looked up at her with that glint in his eye that was always present when his daughter challenged an idea.

"Oh, children, must we ruin our vacation on the first day, before we even get started?" Mrs. Eliott was addressing both her husband and her only child. "It's getting late, Dick."

"I know, Margaret, I know." He stuffed a piece of toast into his mouth and held his fork at the ready with a bite of egg on it, should the way for its consumption be cleared. This demonstrated his hurry.

"Well, if all three persons of God are said to be one substance, what is a substance, anyway, Dad? It's easy to put a label on nothing."

"Well, I'm going to get something done," Mrs. Eliott said. She got up from the table and went into the kitchen, muttering half amused, half vexed comments about her husband and daughter.

"The point, little miss enlarged brain pan, is that God can be understood as acting and presenting himself to us in three ways." Mr. Eliott had eaten the egg on his fork and was speaking almost in a whisper, so as not to disturb his wife. He had resumed a normal pace of eating, now that she was out of sight. "Come on, Marge, we need to hurry," he said aloud to his daughter, who shared her mother's name. He spoke loud enough for his wife to hear.

"But, Dad, it's important. Why can't we just say God is a spirit and leave it at that? He was in Jesus and present to him at the same time."

"That involves some rather contradictory presuppositions. If God's spirit were wholly present in one place, and it wouldn't be God if it wasn't, how could it be simultaneously present somewhere else?" Mr. Eliott smiled. He felt he had his daughter in a corner, at least for the moment.

"So how does the Trinity solve that problem?"

Mr. Eliott looked at his daughter. He didn't have an answer. "The Doctrine of the Trinity solves certain historical problems," he answered lamely.

The drive north from Albuquerque toward the San Juan Mountains in Southern Colorado was beautiful. New Mexico always gave the feeling that light itself was a physical presence. Approaching Santa Fe on Interstate 25, for instance, the soft pastels of dry, sandy wash and desert flora began to give way to a more intense green of piñon and juniper covered hills. To the northwest were flat, red mesas. The sky rolled overhead with its iceberglike white cumulus clouds and blindingly blue open spaces. Often in the late hours of the day, the clouds would thicken, darken, becoming gray, and increase in number, particularly on the horizon, where they would veil the direct sun, which would then fill them with red, salmon and maroon sheets of liquid color. Breaking through them, heavy shafts of light would fall on the hills bright and dark, looking like pillars holding up the sky.

Marge was thinking of those evening skies when she said, "Dad, do you think the human mind is a prism, breaking up the light of God into different colors?"

"Well, I suppose you could look at it that way," he said, watching the road.

"Then how do you account for the dark places, the shadowy places, like the broken sunlight on the hills in the evening along here?"

"I thought we were talking about prisms."

"We are. Well, I think the dark places are the light that reflects back on God and that we don't see."

"Point taken," her father said laughing. "Maybe we don't know everything and should leave definitions to the things we do know."

North of Santa Fe, Marge fell asleep. She was in the back seat. Her mother also dozed in the right front seat. That left Dick Eliott to his own thoughts. He had imparted his love of speculative thought to his daughter, and their endless debates gave him much pleasure. The girl's religious views often disturbed her mother, who felt such questions were better left to prayer and tradition, but Dick didn't mind if he had a budding theologian in the family. After all, he had always encouraged her wonderful questioning mind and frankly was a little in awe of it at times.

Dick looked at his daughter in the rear view mirror. Leaning her head against the right rear window, she was wearing a loose, cotton, sleeveless blouse. He looked at her soft rounded left shoulder and long, slender arm, where they lay in sleep against her side and hip. Her blouse was white and tied in a knot above the waist. Beneath the knot were her midriff, bellybutton and denim shorts. Marge had long slender legs and straight blond hair, which fell in disarray over her left shoulder as she slept. Some strands fell over the front of her blouse, over the almost unnoticeable protrusions of her young breasts. She seemed so vulnerable to him when he contemplated her at such times. Such an active mind to be contained in a fourteen year old girl's body! What would become of it? Though he felt a special closeness to her because she was a girl, he sometimes wished, for her sake, that she wasn't.

An Old Woman's Memory

The nine year old girl didn't know why her older sister was carrying a rifle. But she knew enough to be afraid because her sister was telling her where to step and what to avoid as they crossed a rice field along one of its dikes.

Suddenly several shots were fired, the bullets snapping through the trees behind them. There were shouts from an American patrol several fields away. The girls were being ordered to halt. Instead, the older girl grabbed her sister's hand and ran through the paddy water toward the trees.

Bullets hit the water around them, and the older girl fell face down into it and did not move. Simultaneously, a bullet passed through the younger girl's neck and cheek, and she also fell.

The last thing the younger girl remembered that day was flying through the air in a helicopter. She never saw her sister again.

Eccentric

He was a socialist in principle but lacked any kind of sentimental fondness toward the working classes. Not an atheist either, he would turn to prayer when in dire straits. Yet his spiritual views were indefinable, either to himself or to others. Masculine in physical makeup, abrupt in character, his sensibility was nevertheless of a feminine delicacy. He was easily moved to tears, though he never shed them. In short, he was considered an eccentric by those who knew him, who were of thicker skins and thinner souls.

This man lived alone in a dingy, two room, fifth floor apartment, with peeling wallpaper and one crumbling wooden window sash, on the upper west side of Manhattan. He worked in a bookstore on Fifth Avenue, which was, though a good hike, within walking distance of his apartment. Tom Banks was his name. His friends and acquaintances called him the "banker" in fun, because he was anything but that in deportment, attitude or character. This was plain enough for anyone to see.

A typical scene: It is the middle of winter and Tom's day off, a week day. There has been a heavy snow and freeze, and there is salt everywhere on the streets, far too much for anyone's good, in Tom's opinion. Salt, too much salt, rots out the bodies of cars. Why don't they ever think of that when they put down so much of it? Must we go to the limits of dromedarian surefootedness every time a little snow falls? People aren't camels. They aren't trying to cross the Sahara on shifting sands. They just need to get to work.

Oh, what does it matter? Tom has set up an easel on the south end of Central Park. Painting is his hobby. But in freezing weather? Well, he is an eccentric.

It is between seven and eight in the morning. People are going to work. They are streaming out of the subway tunnel on Fifty-ninth street, just around the corner from Fifth Avenue. A black stretch limousine pulls up to one of the multistory apartment buildings facing Central Park. A well dressed middle-aged woman steps quickly out of the building and into the limousine. The limousine whisks her away, turning south on Fifth Avenue. As it goes through the light and turns the corner, it reveals a man in a long, dingy, wool, military green overcoat, feet and head wrapped in rags against the previous night's bitter cold. He is awkwardly stooped over, leaning to one side, right arm reaching into the metal and concrete garbage receptacle on the corner. A few things, such as paper wrappers and cans, have fallen from it to the ground.

None of this is of interest to Tom. He is on the east side of a pond in the park. A man is feeding bread to some pigeons a few feet away from him. The pond is more than half frozen over. A powdering of white snow covers the ice. Ducks, mostly mallards, are swimming in the black, unfrozen water in the northwest corner of the pond. Beyond them are trees, dark, looming, massed together, also covered with a powdering of white. Some ducks take off, leaving a silver trail of water droplets behind them; others splash down, skidding to a landing in the water, quacking loudly, fluttering their wings and wagging their tails. The ones that take off circle the pond, sailing in a wide arc to the south as they bank against the solid, unbroken masonry wall of tall buildings on Fifty-ninth street.

The birds obviously think the buildings are cliffs. It is a good thing that no peregrine falcon has moved over from the Palisades, rock cliffs on the nearby Hudson river, to take up residence on these man-made cliffs. Plenty of ducks and pigeons here to tide a falcon or two through the winter.

Tom, in an oversized, thickly padded jacket, is bent over his canvas. Wearing knit gloves with holes cut in the ends of the fingers for dexterity, he carries tubes of oil paint in the specially sewn inner lining of his jacket to keep them warm against his body. He has taken several out to smear gobs of paint on a palette. Quickly working the paint together into the color combinations he desires—an ash-white, several grays, gray-blue and black—he works feverishly to capture the effect of the ducks wheeling like dive bombers against their man-made cliffs.

It is bitter cold. Only the pigeons, which the man nearby is feeding, could be oblivious to it. They are pecking away at the pieces of bread thrown on the pavement of the walkway that runs along the east side of the pond. Like dogs when they are busy eating, nothing else can be worthy of consideration to them. Not the cold nor the people walking past on their way to work.

The man feeding the pigeons, an Italian who works in a nearby restaurant, empties his bread sack and walks away. Snow begins to fall. Small, dry flakes. A wind picks up, gusts past Tom's easel and blows on down the walkway into the dark trees beyond. Tom is left holding his easel with one hand, still trying to paint quickly with the other.

"That man must be crazy!"

Tom looks up from his canvas. A young couple is strolling past him. The man appears to be prosperous, wearing a fine cashmere overcoat. The woman looks somehow too fresh and noticeably pretty. A secretary perhaps. No doubt trying to rise above her station. The young woman seems to shrink into her escort's shoulder as Tom looks up at her. Snow is gathering on Tom's uncovered head, his heavy beard, the broad shoulders of his powerful frame. He turns back to his canvas, then suddenly gets up, folds the easel, and trudges off towards his apartment, easel under one arm, palette in the other hand.

The snow is falling thicker. The wind bites. With head lowered, his face turned part way out of the wind, Tom pushes himself half-blindly through the thinning crowd up the west side of the park. He is muttering, and the people, who can afford it now that more of them are already at work, are giving him a little room. You never know about some people in New York, what they might suddenly do, especially those who talk to themselves.

What these people don't know about Tom is that he is angry with himself. There is a burning acid in his throat. He feels both bitter and defiant. Whose business was it anyway? It is in this manner that he has always felt himself to be so much alone.

Grief

He had been their only child. When the leukemia had been diagnosed, they had sworn to fight it. They prayed and sought medical answers. But the end was not long in coming, for the disease progressed rapidly.

Four pallbearers were chosen from among their friends, members of their church. The casket was lowered by these four men into the ground. The attending group of mourners, numbering between twenty and thirty family members and friends, stood silent about the open pit. Above them, a blue sky with few clouds.

Pastor Davis opened his Bible, held the pages down in a light breeze, and read, "Blessed are they that mourn: for they shall be comforted."

It was summer and the warm breeze blew across the cemetery. Margaret wept openly, quietly while her husband, Anthony, stood silent and dry-eyed with his arm around her waist.

When the service was over, many of those in attendance offered their condolences. It was all in a blur. Then the funeral party broke up, got into their cars and drove away. Margaret and Anthony went home.

Margaret entered the house, which seemed dark, musty and cold on such a warm day, and began cleaning, straightening things. Tears filled her eyes and were on her cheeks. Anthony went out and sat down on the rattan and wicker lounge on the back patio. Robins were very active on the lawn and among the flower gardens and trees. The air was sweet with the smell of roses. Anthony sat there for a long time.

Finally Margaret came out and sat beside him. She put her hand on her husband's, which were clenched together in his lap.

"We had precious little time to prepare for this," she said.

"I know."

"It doesn't make it any easier. But we have to go on."

They sat together for several moments in silence. Anthony found the robins irritating. Their joyful song, activity and chatter contrasted with his emptiness.

"I can't believe he's gone," he said.

"I can't either."

"Do you remember that rickety fort he built last summer here in the back yard?"

"Yes. What a mess!"

"He used up all the lumber I'd saved for the utility shed."

"We didn't need it."

"No. But he should at least have asked."

"So why didn't you stop him?"

Anthony smiled. "Because I did the same thing when I was his age."

"Really, Tony. You never told me that."

"I meant to. I just never got around to it. I didn't see you stopping him."

"That was your job."

"My job? Why my job?"

"Well, it was your lumber."

"The shed was for both of us."

"Well, you can build it now."

"I don't want to build it."

They both lapsed into silence. After a while, Margaret got up and went in to fix dinner. They ate dinner on the patio. The house seemed too stuffy by late afternoon and evening. They ate without speaking, but afterwards Margaret said, "It makes me so sad."

"What does, Marge?"

"This house."

"You've always loved this house."

"I wanted it for our son." Margaret began crying bitterly. Anthony took her into his arms, sitting beside her on the wicker and rattan lounge, a glass topped, rattan coffee table in front of them. On the coffee table were their dishes of food.

"It'll be alright, Marge. We have to believe the Lord has him now."

"Has him! Where was the Lord when we prayed for help? Why couldn't he do something? And if he couldn't or wouldn't do anything, why did he ever give us John in the first place?"

"I don't know, Marge. I don't know." Anthony rocked Margaret in his arms. She wept bitterly against his chest, the deep sobs shaking her shoulders, her entire body.

After a while the sobbing subsided. "I'm sorry, Tony," Margaret said.

"That's alright, honey. I understand."

"Do you? He was your son too." She looked up at him. "I'm sorry," she said. "I didn't mean that. I know how deeply you loved him. What'll we do, Tony? What'll we ever do?" She began crying again, her shoulders shaking gently. She was exhausted. After awhile she almost fell asleep in her husband's arms.

Two days later, on a Sunday afternoon, Pastor Davis came by. He was a young man, a fellow who one might have assumed would not have much experience in such matters.

"I thought I'd drop by, since I was headed this direction," he said smiling when Margaret answered the door. In the living room he sat down with a face full of the energy of youth. "Where's Anthony?" he asked.

"He went out for some bread and milk and a few other things."

"Oh. How's he taking it?" he asked confidentially.

"All right, I guess. I seem to be the weak one. Though I know he hurts deeply."

Pastor Davis sat quietly for a moment, looking with sad eyes at Margaret, who avoided his gaze, fingering the pages of a magazine on the heavy, somewhat ornate, solid oak coffee table in front of her. Finally he said, "There's no weakness in love, Margaret." Then he added something surprising, something Margaret hadn't known. "You know Alice and I lost a child several years ago. Yes, it was a case of SIDS. Just before we were called to this church family." He paused. Margaret looked at him. "You know," he continued, "I almost left the church then."

Human Error

When I arrived for the first time at the firebase on hill 55 and was still new in Vietnam, I saw my first USO show. It wasn't much. The Marines there had built a small wooden platform and the performers, several men and women who were comedians and singers, four people in all, were using it as a stage. They had arrived by helicopter and were working through their act when I got there. But they were so nervous their performance wasn't very good.

They weren't doing well because there was a firefight in progress somewhere off the south side of the hill. You couldn't see much because of the thick brush jungle near the bottom of the hill. But the gunfire was steady and automatic and there were occasional shouts. While this was going on there were Marines sitting all over the tops of tanks and amphibious vehicles parked in a ring that went completely around the stage. They were wearing flak jackets and helmets, had M-16 rifles, grenade launchers and M-60 machine guns and were covered with belts of ammunition which were slung over their chests and shoulders. But they weren't interested in the firefight, the racket and commotion. That was a problem for the unlucky squad that wasn't on top of the hill watching the show with them. The shooting finally ended, and I think when the choppers took out our guests they were more than happy to go.

I was brand new and trained as an interpreter, so right away they had a use for me. A dirt road ran straight through our compound. It was a major transportation route. An old woman had come to one of our checkpoints and wanted to pass on through. I went down to interpret and saw that she was carrying a split bamboo pole loaded with straw baskets. Heavy too. She was bent over and wrinkled but had that endurance and strength Vietnamese peasants always seemed to have. She said she wanted to go to market in a nearby village down the road. I told the sentry I'd take her through. Since I was a non-commissioned officer and he was a lower rank, he figured I knew what I was doing and let her go.

Well, I didn't. I had no idea about these people. We walked along, the old woman trudging very slowly under her load. Believe me, that pole was heavy! I tried it. I don't know what those baskets were loaded with but they weighed a ton and the pole's sharp edges cut into my shoulder. As we walked, she kept looking all around. Just curious, I thought. But a week later we were hit at night with a sapper attack. We fought them off but they managed to plant a plastic explosive charge on every listening or observation post bunker we had on the west side of the hill, as well as on our bridge down below. They knew where everything was, thanks to that old woman. They even broke through our perimeter wire at one place and killed six Marines, wounding twelve. We never knew what their casualties were, but at least they didn't have time to set off any of the plastic explosives they'd planted.

The worst part was knowing what I'd done. But I never told anybody. Not for a long time anyway. Finally one night I opened up. The lieutenant and I were walking the perimeter line at dusk, distributing ammunition and helping to set up claymore mines for the night perimeter guard.

As we walked from one bunker to another, I said, "I killed those guys."

"What are you talking about, sergeant?" The lieutenant was a very tall, thin faced looking guy, whose brown eyes would get big when he was excited or confused. It made you laugh sometimes.

"Those seven Marines, sir." Another one had died after the wounded were taken out by helicopter for med-evac.

"You mean, sergeant, you were running around on the outside of the perimeter shooting at them.

"No, that's not what I meant, sir." Why was I bothering?

"I don't understand you, sergeant."

"It's nothing, sir."

"What do you mean nothing?"

"I was just talking."

"Those guys over there need ammo. And you'd better show them how to set up their claymore. They leave it like that, they're going to blow their own faces off."

"Aye Aye, sir."

After my tour of duty was over and I was back in the States, having learned a little more, it still bothered me sometimes. Like that nervous USO troop I saw, I was still trying to make sense out of what was going on. Both here in America and over in Vietnam. I thought of the lieutenant sometimes. He had been transferred to another assignment several months into my tour over there. They often did that with officers. Well, I had heard later that he'd led a patrol into an ambush that should've been obvious to him and had lost some of his men. It was a stupid thing that he did, and any one of those guys he was leading could have warned him. But he was the lieutenant and I guess they figured he knew what he was doing.

Luisa Aragon

Luisa Aragon had arrived in New York one year ago, and six months later it was discovered she was pregnant. She lived in a small apartment with her sister and brother-in-law in the Washington Heights section of Harlem.

"What will you do today," her brother-in-law said to her one morning at the kitchen table, cupping his mug of boiling coffee in both hands. The heating in the apartment did not work right.

"I have an interview."

"Another one? Mother of God, Luisa, do you not understand that a woman who sticks out so far in the belly as you do cannot find work in this city?"

"I must find a way to feed myself and the child who will soon be with us. We cannot always burden you and Angela, Ramon."

"I told you not to concern yourself at this time."

"I must."

At seven twenty Luisa walked to the subway station. The streets were grimy and the stairway leading down into the subway tunnel stank of urine as always. She thought of the beautiful green hills of Puerto Rico. The tropical green there, with its bright hint of yellow, even in the intensest green, always had the fresh look of new shoots.

George Carlson had a job with an investment firm in Manhattan. He was twenty-two, single and had had the job for one week. He lived in the Jackson Heights section of Queens. He took the train in to Manhattan, crossing under the East River from the Queensborough station. It amused him to frighten himself with thoughts of what would happen if the river were to suddenly break into the long, poorly lit tunnel while he was in it. He was headed downtown to the financial district today and made a switch in Midtown to the train coming out of Harlem and the South Bronx. He was lucky enough to get a seat.

The train roared and stopped, roared and stopped, lights flashing in the tunnel. People standing in the aisles were jammed tight, someone's knees shoved between his. In the Downtown area the train began to clear. The knees got off. The aisle was partially empty. You could breathe.

Suddenly a door slammed open on the forward end of the car. The train was screeching and jerking around a bend. Unbelievably, a small thin unshaven man with a white-tipped stick entered the car. In one hand, along with the stick, he held an empty coffee can. In the other an ice cream cone.

"Help for the disabled. Won't you help?" The blind man strolled confidently through the car, apparently familiar enough with the surroundings not to need the stick. A few people dropped money into the can. As he passed through the car, the blind man took several stabs at eating his ice cream. Due in part to the rough, uneven movement of the train, he missed his mouth with every attempt, but this did not seem to perturb him. The ice cream stuck to his face and ran along his chin. Then, as the train was violently jerking around another bend in the tracks, he passed calmly from the other end of the car, stepping out onto the twisting iron couplings between it and the next one.

"Only in New York!" a heavy-set woman said, sitting across from George. She was middle-aged, hairy legged and dressed like a domestic. She spoke English with an accent.

Probably headed for Brooklyn, George thought, glancing at her with curiosity but without answering. He was watching closely for his stop now. He didn't want to end up in Brooklyn too. He could see the light begin to increase in the tunnel as they approached another station platform. The train was screeching as it slowed. Suddenly it stopped with a jerk.

They sat there. Finally, a sound of sirens could be heard on the street above. It must've taken forty minutes for the train to start moving again. George was worried about being late.

The following morning Angela Hernandez sat alone in her kitchen. She was in an old cotton housecoat which should have been replaced long ago. It had a faded rose pastel floral pattern which, though clean, could no longer be made to look so.

"Luisa, Luisa, oh my Luisita," she whispered. She was embracing her shoulders with both arms, her face down, her elbows on the table. There were no lights on, not even in the kitchen. A hot cup of coffee sat steaming in front of her. In the living room on a chair was the morning paper, which Ramon had bought and left when he went to work.

Of course, they already knew. When they had become worried the previous evening, Ramon had called the police. The police had not until then been able to determine Luisa's next of kin from identification found on her body.

Her unborn child was also lost under the wheels of the train.

Mores

Janet Somersby, a brunette with a small attractive figure, pushed the drawer in on her gray metal desk at the Naval Testing Center on Overland Road in Boise, Idaho. She got up and walked down the long narrow hall of the first floor of the building where she worked. Wearing a short skirt that was hemmed several inches above her knees, she felt self-conscious as she passed the row of military recruiting offices. She could see the men inside lift their heads and set down whatever they were doing to watch her go by. It was embarrassing, but she would not have wanted to have missed this ritual which occurred several times each day.

Janet lived in a small house in old Boise, a quiet residential neighborhood of both run down and well kept up older homes located just behind the Idaho State Capital building. It was a green neighborhood of tall dark trees, hedges and the sight and scent of many flowers. She shared the house with another young woman who was an English professor at Boise State University.

"Hi Meg," she said as she came in the screen door. The rusty metal spring on the door creaked and slammed the door in the chipped paint wood frame behind her.

"You're early," Megan said. She walked out of the kitchen, then came into it again. Megan was a tall, large boned woman with long reddish blond curly hair that fell uncombed in tangled ringlets over square shoulders. Janet had entered by a side door into the kitchen, which was at the front of the house.

"I took an hour off."

"Why?"

"I just felt like it."

"Want some coffee?"

"Sure."

Meg poured a hot cup at the kitchen table. It was a yellow formica table. She spilled some of the coffee on it and wiped it up with a dish towel, setting the glass coffee pot back into the coffee maker. The relatively bare room, made impersonal and cold by the harsh afternoon light coming from large wooden frame windows, was softened by the rich brown aroma of the coffee.

"Meg."

"Yeah." Meg threw the dish towel on the counter. Though it was only late afternoon, she was already undressed and in a housecoat. On the days when she did not have a class, she often spent her afternoons in this way, leisurely correcting papers. Then she would go out again in the evening, leaving Janet alone until well after she went to bed.

"Meg, who was that you brought home last night?"

"A friend."

"Anyone I know?"

"No. Just a friend."

"Just a friend. I could hear you guys. You kept me awake until four o'clock."

Meg laughed. "Were we that loud?"

"Yes."

Meg looked at Janet. She tossed her hair over her shoulder and adjusted the cloth belt on her housecoat. "Well, you should try it sometime."

The next day, walking down the hall at her place of work, Janet thought to herself, Why do I do this? But she knew that in spite of the unrelieved tension it built in her, she could not sacrifice the enjoyment of having men look at her. Nor would she do anything about it. She couldn't accept casual sex.

In time Janet began to date one of the men where she worked, a Marine recruiter. He treated her with the greatest consideration and restraint, in spite of what she'd always thought about Marines. Within a few months they were married, and she moved out of the house where she'd been living with Meg. Shortly after that a man she hadn't met took up permanent residence with her old roommate.

One afternoon Janet again took off work early and paid a visit to her friend. Meg's boyfriend wasn't home and Meg seemed tired and dispirited. She puttered around the kitchen while Janet sat at the formica table with her cup of coffee.

Meg came over to the table and leaned forward with both hands on the table top. "I'm being rifted."

"What do you mean?"

"They've denied me tenure, Jan. After this semester I'm out of a job."

"I don't understand. I thought you were confident. You weren't even concerned about it."

"I wasn't. But that old biddy, Dr. Ogleby, did me in."

"Why?"

"I don't know. Something about my writing not being good. Not good enough for an English professor. I don't meet 'professional standards.' And I haven't been publishing."

"What'll you do now?"

"I don't know. Jack and I are about through. I applied at Hewlett Packard as a technical writer but I haven't heard anything." She sat down at the table, put her head down on her arms, then got up again. The kitchen door had been left open and the afternoon sun came warmly through the screen door. Meg went over to the sink.

"You could teach somewhere else."

"No. I've only got a Masters degree. Boise State's getting bigger and more important. That's one of the reasons I'm being rifted. They want PhDs. Besides, who's going to give me recommendations when I'm being denied tenure." Meg began to cry, leaning on the edge of the sink.

Janet got up and took her in her arms. She felt terrible for Meg.

That night, as her husband lay exhausted and quiet beside her after lovemaking, Janet thought, Poor Meg!

She didn't know Dr. Ogleby had strongly disapproved of Meg's involvement with several of her own students through the years. A number of the faculty had known about it. Janet thought only about the contrast between her own present happiness and Meg's misfortune.

But is there really any difference between us? she thought. We both really want the same thing. We want to be loved, to be held, to be made love to, to feel good.

She fell asleep beside her husband's naked body with the pleasant odor of lovemaking in her nostrils.

Priorities

The head mechanic came out and looked at the history professor. The professor was wearing dark blue tennis shoes which were decidedly not of an athletic variety.

"We have taken a peek under the hood, sir, and I believe you may have a serious problem."

The professor looked tired. His shoulders were rounded. He had been through this before. He had shelled out money he didn't have. Brushing a gray-white wispy strand of hair back from his forehead, he said, "What's the problem?"

"You've blown a gasket. There may be some pitting inside the cylinder sleeve causing a loss of compression. We'll have to remove the head to have a look." The mechanic was a large fellow with dull, tiny blue eyes and big gnarled hands like hunks of coal.

"When can you do this?"

"Maybe this afternoon, perhaps early tomorrow. We're stacked up tight."

The professor abandoned his car to this surgeon with rough hands. It was a large, older, middle priced car. He had had it a long time and it had once looked very good and run smoothly, but his professor's salary at a small, western, liberal arts college had never substantially increased. On the other hand, his family had. He had a couple daughters and a son, all away from home now, two of them at the State university.

Alone the next day in his cubbyhole of an office on the upper floor of the college administration building, Professor Daniels was reading a book. He had papers to correct, but he was reading a book. College professors do this sometimes because they are generally scholars as well as teachers. It is also nice to relax and think instead of talk and critique. So many people talk and critique but never think.

It was an unfortunate characteristic of the roof of the administration building that it overhung and obscured much of the light that might have come in through his tiny window. A result of pompous academic architecture, the professor thought, but he had never openly expressed his opinion about it or about any other unimportant matter—not in thirty years. There were better things to worry about.

At exactly five minutes past two in the afternoon a student tapped lightly on the door of his office.

"Come in," he said and set the book down.

A young woman of nineteen or twenty stepped through the door, holding the door knob with her left hand as she carefully pushed it open, presenting a slender wrist. She held a load of books to her chest with the other arm. She was quite slender, in fact, with long dark hair and even darker, deep set, expressive eyes that offset a pale, delicately bridged nose.

"Good afternoon, Dr. Daniels."

The professor crinkled his face up in a smile. It was a warm smile that covered him from ear to ear and centered in his eyes. He got part way up out of his chair and moved another chair out beside his desk. "Have a seat, have a seat. How are you doing today, Vicki? What can I do for you?"

Vicki sat down. "I don't think I'm going to make it, Dr. Daniels." She started to cry right away. "I'm sorry," she said and wiped the tears with the back of her arm. "I didn't mean to do this."

"Oh, that's fine, dear," he said. He was up and bustling around the tiny room. "I've been here thirty years and seen plenty of upset students. Plenty of them." He pushed out the dusty glass pane of the narrow window. It was winter and a cold gust of air came in. "No, no, that won't do!" he said and pulled it shut again. He pulled off his reading glasses, set them on the desk, then picked them up and put them into his shirt pocket. "Yes," he said, "that will never do."

Vicki had recovered control of herself and smiled at the professor. He sat down.

"I think I won't have enough money to cover next semester," she said calmly.

"You know I put you in for the Mortimer Harrison Scholarship Award, don't you?" Professor Daniels asked. He was Vicki's academic advisor.

"Yes, but..."

"You must be patient. You know we are authorized to give this award each year to a promising student. I've spoken to a number of my colleagues. All of your professors think highly of you." Vicki was looking down dejectedly at the pile of books on her knees. Professor Daniels looked kindly at the top of her head. Her hair was neatly parted in the middle, and there was a small, brown, tortoise shell beret holding it back out of her face on either side.

She's such a lovely young woman, the professor thought. And so perceptive too. A fine student.

"My dad lost his job."

"Oh, I'm sorry to hear that!"

"I think I may have to..."

"No, I will not hear of it!" The professor jumped up and went angrily to his window. Or so he seemed. He looked out over the sodden dead brown grass of the winter campus. Students were going back and forth between classes. A bell rang. The last of them disappeared into a building. The professor was standing with his hands clasped behind his back.

"Miss Harper," he said sternly, without looking away from the window. That was Vicki's last name. "I would like to have a word with your parents. Can you arrange that? I believe you are from this area, aren't you?"

"Yes, sir."

"Good. Then you needn't worry, dear." He turned around and looked at her, a gentle smile lighting his face again. "I'm sure we can come up with something that will keep you in school."

Vicki left Dr. Daniels' office without the slightest notion of how her problem would be resolved. But she placed full confidence and trust in her advisor.

That evening Dr. Daniels returned to the garage to retrieve his old car.

Gung Ho

Sam Houston really was his name. I don't think he was any relation to the first president of the Republic of Texas but you couldn't help making the association. He was a big guy with dark, curly hair. Kind of quiet, unless he was drunk.

We didn't drink often then because beer usually wasn't available at our firebase. But they brought some in for us on Christmas Day so we could celebrate the twenty-four hour truce. Might as well relax while the Viet Cong had time to gather in their ammunition and rice.

Sam was a forward observer. So when he wasn't out in the field with an infantry company calling in artillery missions, he did other things. Once they had him doing the daily burning of latrine receptacles. He loved that and did a lot of grumbling. Would even be sullen in the evening in the hooch with us. But normally he did more dignified chores when he was with us at the battalion command post. For some reason, the Colonel wouldn't allow him inside the Command Operation Center to do counter-mortar fire and things like that which would have been his normal mission. Though a good F.O., he was considered too wild. So he went out early most mornings with the mine sweep team to clear Liberty Road. The VC mined this dirt road almost every night without fail, and it was the mine sweep team's job to clear it of mines before the day's military traffic started passing over it.

Here's what he told me one morning. We were casual friends and he wanted to talk, having just returned to the compound with the sweep team. It was about eight or nine A.M. and I was still lying on my cot, since I had the lazy job of a Vietnamese Interpreter.

"Morning, Don," he said cheerfully.

"Forget something?" I asked. I had noticed the magazine, as usual, still loaded into his forty-five automatic pistol. He was also carrying an M-16 rifle.

"Oh yeah." He unloaded the pistol. "We lost our lieutenant today."

"The new guy?" I knew the lieutenant wasn't well liked. He was considered dangerous and naive by the men who had to go out on these patrols with him. They provided security for the men who actually did the mine search.

"Yeah." He crouched down beside my cot, speaking quietly. "We were ambushed. The crazy, gung ho bastard took off after them over a rice field with his forty-five. Got shot through the head."

"Anybody else hurt?"

"No." Sam had the weirdest grin on his face.

On Christmas Day in the middle of the day a little U.S. Army one engine spotter plane flew over our hilltop position and dropped a box of books into our compound. I was surprised because I had always heard the Army was of the opinion that Marines couldn't read. On the same day one of our own trucks brought in a load of Red Cross care packages from First Marine Division Headquarters in Da Nang. They were full of odds and ends like gum, candy and a better quality toilet paper. That truck also brought the beer, enough for each of us to have two cans.

Not everyone drank. I didn't. And Sam got the extra beers. He got good and drunk.

In a way you couldn't blame him. For months the constant gunfire all around and the artillery and bombs in the mountains never stopped. Suddenly it was dead silent. It was unnerving.

Several of us were sitting in our hooch enjoying a big can of spam for which we'd traded some Marine Corps combat knives to the Air Force in Da Nang. Christmas dinner, a few letters from home, and a card game. In comes Sam, waving his loaded pistol.

"Screw this Marine Corps! Screw you bastards! Screw Vietnam and all those damn VC getting their stuff together so they can come out and kill us tomorrow!"

"Take it easy, Sam."

"Put that gun away."

"Crazy fool. Don't you know you can't carry a loaded weapon in the compound."

He went over and collapsed on a cot, sobbing. Somebody quietly took the pistol out of his hand and unloaded it. A warm breeze flapped the canvas sides of the hooch. The naked light bulb flickered on its wire. We went back to our card game while Sam slept off the beer.

Later that night when we were all sacked out, except for the guard, the mortar crew decided to help out in the celebration. They set off a tear gas grenade behind our hooch.

The stuff was thick when it entered the hooch in the pitch black night. And when we woke up with burning noses, lungs, throats and eyes, we knew what it was. One guy fell vomiting on the ground as we ran along in our underwear toward the perimeter of the compound and fresh air, mucus pouring out of our noses. Two of us grabbed him up by the arms and kept on going through the dense fog of tear gas that followed us in a cloud.

Later when we came back to the hooch, we found Sam still dead asleep.

"Can you believe that?"

"Must be his mosquito net protected him."

It was worth a good laugh.

The next morning I told Sam about the tear gas and then asked him what had gotten into him with the beer and waving the gun around.

"I kept thinking about that lieutenant," he said.

It had been more than two months and I'd forgotten him. But it was only then that I realized what had happened to that lieutenant might not have been the result of an ambush.

Springtime

She was thin, a little too thin perhaps, and for this reason did not consider herself attractive. Standing in the shower, dripping wet with the water turned off, she pulled back the yellow and green patterned shower curtain and got a towel off the rack. The towel was white with a blue trim. As she bent over, drying one brown leg then the other, she observed the slender bones in her feet and the protrusion of her knees. They're too knobby, she thought.

Timothy Knowls, a tall, good looking, black, medical student at Georgetown University, was Helena's new date. He took her to a nice restaurant in Washington called the Brickskeller. It was in a basement, softly lighted, and the red brick walls were atmospheric. Helena had braided her hair in corn rows and wore a light green, summer dress. After dinner they drove over and went for a walk in Rock Creek Park near Georgetown, something they really shouldn't have done after dark. Then Tim took Helena back to her third floor apartment. He was very polite and did not even attempt to kiss her good night.

Sitting in her living room in her night shift, turning the pages of a women's magazine, Helena wished he had. She wondered what those warm lips and strong arms were like. She shook her head to throw the thought out of it. She'd had a conservative, Christian, middle class upbringing in the Midwest—her father was a welding supervisor at a large auto assembly plant in Detroit and an usher at the New Congregation Baptist Church—and she did not think she should be thinking such things. A warm, sweet feeling made her breathe unevenly. She opened a window to let in the cool night air and street sounds. Someone, a man's voice, shouted outside, then a woman shrilly, but there was no response after that. It must have been from one of the other apartments.

The following weekend when Tim brought her home, he did kiss her and they fell to some very passionate caressing on the living room sofa. Suddenly Helena pushed him off her and sat up, straightening herself. She was breathing heavily.

"I'm sorry," Tim said.

Helena's bra, though still fastened, was off one of her breasts. She quickly repositioned it. "I'm not that kind of girl," she said.

"I know."

"You know!" Helena got up indignant, standing over a very contrite looking young man. "If you know that, then what are you doing?"

"You're beautiful."

"No I'm not."

Tim looked at Helena. It was absolutely incomprehensible to him that she could mean what she'd just said about herself. She had high cheek bones and a soft golden glow to her skin. Her manners, if a little abrupt, were neither thick nor heavy. In short, he found her appearance and demeanor quite stunning. "I'm sorry," he repeated.

Helena sat down next to him. "I'm sorry too," she said quietly, smiling. "I didn't mean to blame it all on you. You frightened me."

Tim looked at her with surprise. Before he could think he said, "You're a virgin?"

"Yes."

"Wow."

"What do you mean 'Wow'?"

"Nothing, Helena. It's just..."

"Virgins are rare these days."

"Well, most women your age..."

"I'm not most women."

"I know. That's why I'm falling in love with you." Tim felt the heat rising into his face. He didn't seem to be in control of his tongue. Helena looked at him. "What I mean is..."

"I'm not ready for being in love," Helena responded curtly and moved a few inches away from him.

Both Tim and Helena were embarrassed. They sat in silence for several minutes. Then Tim succeeded in lightening the conversation. By the time he left, they had achieved the softer tones of friendly laughter and Tim departed with the promise of a date for dinner at Helena's apartment the following Saturday.

For a long while after Tim had gone, Helena sat in the living room and chastised herself for her behavior. I was mean to him, she thought. He didn't do anything I didn't want him to do. Etcetera.

At five fifteen on Saturday Tim was due to arrive in less than one hour. Having just bathed, Helena was still naked, posing in front of the wall mirror in her bedroom. She looked at her slender hips, the large dark brown nipples and areola of her, in her opinion, small breasts. What does he see in me? she wondered in delight. Then she quickly dressed.

Helena had been a Biology major in college in the Midwest. But she had accepted an airline hostess job and had not completed her senior year. The airline job lasted for six months. It was not for her. After that she'd gotten a clerical job with the U.S. Department of Justice in Washington, D.C.

Every window of Helena's apartment was open when she went into the kitchen. Birds were singing gloriously outside. She checked the pot roast in the oven. The very smell of it was a rich brown, and it was swimming in the makings of a fine gravy, rich and creamy, Southern style, as her grandmother had always made it. The roast was nearly done. The spring air of the outdoors felt warm and pleasant. Helena's heart leapt at the thought of Tim's arrival and seemed to be perpetually beating at a rate a little faster than normal. She felt tense and nervous, more than she had before with him. Tim was certainly handsome. And well educated. Would he repeat his declaration of love?

Oh, I mustn't think of that, Helena thought. She took the biscuits out of the oven, then set the table with a clean white cloth. Tim was bringing the wine. A chianti, he'd said. Sounded good. But dangerous, Helena thought. She didn't care. Yes I do. He's so handsome. And gentle. His touch... I must be careful. Oh, it's a wonderful evening!

The doorbell rang as she was checking the pot roast again. Helena closed the oven with a bang and went to the front door of her apartment. She pressed the button that released the lock on the downstairs entrance, so Tim could come upstairs the four flights to her apartment door.

Maturing Vision

Throughout his life he had taught art in various schools around the country. He had shown his own work a number of times and had had a retrospective exhibition at the age of fifty. Then he had come to be almost entirely overlooked, mentioned only occasionally in a magazine article or two but never discussed among important critics.

It seems he had been a close follower of the abstract expressionist school of painters, which fortunate practice had kept him in vogue for a number of years, as it was the style of the times, especially if you knew the right people. Advancing through the decades into a quieter, more restrained, geometrical formalism reminiscent of Mondrian and the later Kandinsky—and thus still within the abstract mode—he had kept himself visible within the national art community well into middle age. As the critics saw it, this formal cooling in style in later life brought about an inevitable solidification of the wild and vigorous lava flow that had been characteristic of his energetic youth. He was complete in their eyes, a fine fulfillment in himself of the direction he had established, and he was soon forgotten.

Tom Forman was now seventy, pensioned and alone. Hardly anyone had spoken of him in years.

"Who is it? Yeah, yeah, just a minute, I'm coming. Get off the damned doorbell, will ya. I said I'm coming!"

The door of the second floor apartment on Sixth and Seneca in Seattle opened to the length of its security chain.

"Mr. Forman?"

"Yes."

"I'm Steven Velasquez with Art Forum."

"Never heard of you."

"Mind if I come in?"

"What for?"

"Well..uh..to interview you, sir."

Tom Forman unlatched the chain and opened the door. The hall light, shafting suddenly into the apartment, revealed a wizened little old man in worn-out clothes, slender, small of frame, a bit stooped with his age. Nevertheless, at seventy he still had a full head of silver hair which hung over his forehead and which he now brushed out of his face. A sweet, acrid smell emanated from the dark interior of the efficiency apartment.

"May I come in, sir?" Steven Velasquez smiled, youthful and nervous.

"Enter at your own risk, boy."

"You know, Mr. Forman," Steven said, entering through the door into the musty interior, "I consider it a great privilege to have this opportunity to..." Steven stopped just inside the door. As his eyes adjusted to the dark (There were no lights on in the apartment. There was only the dim light of day filtering through filthy curtains.) he saw that the floor was littered with paper, old clothing, old paint brushes, even, it appeared, such things as dried orange and banana peels. "Oh."

"I said to enter at your own risk. Didn't you hear me?" The old man, still standing by the door and bent over just a little, round shouldered, looked keenly at his interlocutor. "I don't get visitors often," he said more gently, apologetically.

"Yes sir." Steven regained his composure. "Mind if I sit down?" He made his way over to a dark green couch, which was really in good condition, he observed, once he had pushed away a sufficient amount of debris in the form of dirty overalls and oily paint rags, so as to be able to sit down. There were a few other pieces of furniture in the room, including an easel. "Are you still painting?" he asked. The smell of paint, turpentine, unwashed clothing and something, well, indefinable made breathing a somewhat laborious and delicate operation.

"I paint for my own pleasure now," the old man said in a gravelly voice. He was standing in front of the young man, looking him directly in the eyes. He seemed wary of the intruder. "You here for any good reason?"

"Yes, sir. I told you I was doing an article..."

"You didn't say anything about an article."

"An interview. Look, sir, perhaps I should come back."

"State your case."

Steven looked at the wary old man. What the hell, he thought. "I'm here to see what you are doing now," he said matter-of-factly. He tensed for the response, for there was no evidence of work in progress in the room. The acrid odor of dirt and whatever else, which he still hadn't determined, seemed overwhelming. He felt anger, embarrassment, a desire to get outside into the fresh air. Why had he ever come to see this old fool? Obviously the real Tom Forman was dead. Replaced by this...this ghost of decay.

The old man stood in silence before him, studying him for several interminable moments. Then he abruptly went into the kitchen, came back into the room, and turned on the light. The sudden light from an uncovered bulb in the middle of the ceiling was almost blinding. Under Tom Forman's arm was a large canvas. It still had about it a faintly fresh odor of oils. Tom pulled the easel over to where he stood in front of the couch. He set the canvas on it. "I paint in there," he said pointing to the kitchen. "Light's better through the small east window."

Steven sat in silence. The painting was not like anything he'd seen. Gone was any hint of abstraction, yet the word realism would not properly describe it. It had a dreamlike, intensely evocative power. A movement that was more spirit than natural. It was clearly a painting of faded white and yellow houseboats on gray Lake Union. But the shadows, the light that welled hauntingly upward out of the seemingly murky, slate green water, the substanceless hulk of the houseboats themselves. It was as if everything dissolved into something which was neither there nor absent. It was as if Tom Forman had learned to see what we all see but from the other side of the curtain of his physical existence.

The Philosophy Club

In the Corner Book Store on Central Avenue in Albuquerque, New Mexico, beyond the pedestrian hustle and the noise of traffic, a singular event is taking place. It is the bimonthly meeting of a small group which has come to call itself The Friends of Philosophy. This evening, a Tuesday, five people are present: a young couple, a middle-aged couple and Patricia Jensen, the store owner, who is a woman in her fifties. The present tenor of conversation, were it overheard, would probably be considered abstruse, perhaps ostentatious, by American standards. But our participants are oblivious to any form of imagined public censure.

"There is nothing in George Berkeley to convince me that the floor I am sitting on isn't real," the young woman says. She is a slender woman of medium height and straight shoulder length black hair. She has a narrow nose and thin lips, which give her a determined look.

"Nobody said it wasn't." The middle-aged man looks at the woman, whose name is Karen. The five of them are gathered in a far corner of the book store behind a set of bookshelves crudely constructed with one by six inch white pine boards. The two couples are sitting on the floor, the men positioned cross-legged, the women with their legs swept back along one side of them. Patricia sits on a folded out metal chair which she has pulled away from a nearby desk. There are no other customers in the store.

"Berkeley's idealism denies the reality of material substance. Only spirit, or mind, is held to be real." Karen directs her remarks to the middle-aged man. There is a feeling of tension in the way she holds herself.

"Words, mere words," he continues. He is also slender of build and has a long, graying pony tail. "What is substance anyway? And what is spirit? The point is that we only know things in our own minds and, if that is so, we can't assert their independent existence."

"What about the existence of another person?" Patricia asks. The two look up at her. She continues, directing her remarks to Barry, the man with the pony tail. She is obviously enjoying her role as both interlocutor and mediator. "It would seem a rather lonely existence to me if you didn't quite believe either Karen or her husband or your wife were real." There is a twinkle in her eyes and a general titter of laughter follows her remark. She has spoken in a soft voice and in the kindly, sincere manner with which she always speaks. Patricia's age and experience show clearly in the deep lines about her eyes and on either side of her small nose. She also has a slightly rounded stomach which shows clearly beneath her tight jeans, but she is otherwise well preserved for her age. Sandy haired and hazel blue eyed, there is a general smoky softness about her whole character and appearance.

"That's the trouble with this kind of philosophical idealism," contributes the husband of the young woman. "Karen and I were talking about it on the way down here tonight, and I think that what she's really getting at is this: if you don't believe in the physical reality of things which we see and touch, then even people become insubstantial. Nothing matters because the only reality is your inner self."

"That's not it," says the man with the pony tail.

"Oh, come on, Barry. Like Pat says, what the hell is there if people aren't real?"

"Calm down, honey," Karen scolds in a hoarse whisper no one can miss.

"I didn't say that," Patricia adds. She smiles sweetly. "All I said was, or at least all I meant to imply, was that an assertion of the insubstantiality of material things brings up the problem of any individual existence outside that of the particular consciousness in question."

"Well that's what Mark's saying."

"What Mark seems to be asserting is that Berkeley is taking an extreme position that denies reality to everything but one inclusive consciousness," Patricia continues. She smiles again, and the sweetness of that smile, which is in her eyes, seems to soften, at least a little, everyone it touches.

The wife of the middle-aged man says nothing. Her role tonight seems to be that of observer.

There is a pause while everyone turns over his own thoughts. Patricia Jensen then continues, warming to her subject, "Look, I don't want to turn this discussion into an argument." She pauses. The friendly unaggressive expression of her eyes finally seems to be calming Mark. Barry is lost in his own thoughts, as if he is gathering force for a counter attack.

Karen sits looking at the floor. Her husband has sprung to her defense and she feels it is her argument that is on the line. At any rate, the absurdity of any view other than her own prevailing in this matter seems clear enough to her. She says nothing at all now because that is her way. She can't see the point of belaboring the obvious. Her strength has always lain in the reserve of her nature, sometimes in the power of silence. Besides, she loves her husband in her own careful way and she appreciates his defense of her thesis, but his emotional outburst has embarrassed her. It looks like weakness, weakness for everyone to see, which puts her argument at a disadvantage.

Patricia goes on. "The problem with philosophical idealism of the type Berkeley espouses is that it becomes subjective or pluralistic. I mean," she says almost inaudibly as she triumphantly and modestly approaches her point, "that you are left isolated within the limitations of your own awareness. That means you have to take another person's reality on faith, positing it as separate and valid like your own without any direct assurance that that is the case."

"Isn't that what we do?" Barry asks.

"When I make love to Karen, I don't make love to a ghost," Mark adds.

"Okay, Mark!" Karen snaps sharply.

Patricia Jensen blushes.

"All I'm saying," Mark continues.

"Just be quiet," Karen says.

"What Mark is saying is true," Patricia continues. "We do believe in the reality of one another. And of most other things as well."

"But if we asserted the absolute integrity of material things," Barry adds, running his hand along the side of his head and pulling his pony tail out over his shirt collar as he weighs his words. "I mean if we went to the other extreme of making consciousness depend on physical reality, then consciousness would become just as unreal. None of us would really exist. At least not as agents of free will. We'd just be processes, bubbles rising and popping in the big kettle of the universe, and consciousness and freedom would be illusions."

"Precisely," Patricia says. She is smiling happily. "We get in trouble at either extreme, and finding a convincing halfway point has been the eternal problem of philosophy."

Barry's wife speaks up for the first time. "The only reality," she says dully, "is that we are what we are and we do what we do."

"And where does that lead?" Barry and Karen ask together.

"To next week's discussion," Patricia answers. She uncrosses her legs, gets up, brushes off her tight jeans, and puts the chair back behind the desk. She knows that at her age she is still a good looking woman. She is single and proud of her mind, of her philosophical education, which is why she started this discussion group.

The two couples browse about the store for a few minutes and then leave without purchasing anything.

Patricia Jensen has never been married.

Tet

The first night of the 1968 Tet Offensive took out one of our Combined Action Platoons. The Marine contingent was made up of nine men. All we knew was that in the morning they were gone. No bodies. Nothing. As far as I know no one ever knew what became of them. The Viet Cong took their ammunition; their new, expensive night vision scope; the machine gun (they had a fifty caliber); even their C rations.

The Popular Forces soldiers that were with them also disappeared, though one of them later turned up in a nearby village. When we questioned him, he claimed the VC had thought he was dead and left him. But if that was the case, why were there no other bodies?

One thing we did learn from him, if his word can be trusted, is how they did it. They didn't attack the position and assault its wooden tower and sandbag bunkers. They just showed up after a previous action an hour or so earlier, suddenly appearing in the middle of the night in such numbers they overwhelmed the Marines and PFs.

How'd they get so close without being detected? I don't know. I know the Combined Action Platoon was short handed. They always are.

The battalion command post didn't set quietly on its hilltop either. We were hit at the same time that the CAP unit was in that earlier firefight. The CAP unit was about a half mile away. I remember looking over in their direction once while helping to resupply ammunition to our own perimeter. It was easy to see that far from our hilltop, especially when the night was lit up with grenades and mortars. There were mortars coming in on us too and tracer bullets flying overhead but I still had time to notice the flashing lights of the explosions over there. As I was running toward the perimeter with a couple cases of M-16 rounds, I saw a long streak of tracers arc straight up into the night sky, followed by a shorter burst of fire. I wondered then who had gotten it. I knew those guys personally.

But as I said, I never found out. In their case, the night assault was just a diversion, a probing attack. It helped the Viet Cong figure out their defenses and numbers. An hour later in the dead quiet the VC just walked in and captured them.

Next morning we were busy with our own wounded and the choppers were coming in and taking them out. We had wounded from one of the line companies as well as from our own fire base. They were all on the helicopter landing zone. There was a volley ball net stretched across part of the LZ and plasma bottles were hanging on the net. Their clear fluid was carried down in plastic tubes to men who were lying close to the net.

"Arthur!" I said. He was one of my best friends but was over on the other side of the compound during the night with the heavy weapons platoon. I didn't know he'd been wounded. "What happened?"

"Took a couple rounds," he said. "One in the hip, one in the gut. Nothing serious."

Nothing serious? He was one of the guys with a plasma bottle attached to him. But that was Arthur. Glasses thick as coke bottles, a hooked beak for a nose, thick lips, pale blond kinky hair, and perpetual good humor. If he'd been dead he'd have had a comment on the funeral arrangements.

"Want to know what I think?" he said. I'd just handed him a lit cigarette and a chopper was taking off, blasting us with hot wind and choking dust from the prop wash.

"What?" I yelled, stooping over within two feet of him. The noise was deafening. He was smiling.

"I think they played their best hand last night."

"Who?"

"The gooks."

"Why?"

"Because it was organized. Too organized. You heard about CAP Charlie Two."

"Yeah."

"Must've taken a lot of planning putting that one together. Hitting us and them, then pulling back and walking in on them like that."

"I guess so."

"You guess so. Come on, man, when have you seen anything like that before? I've heard rumors..."

"Yes, I know. When S-3 called in our spot reports and casualties this morning, the Regiment told them Division Headquarters had said it happened all over Vietnam last night."

"Damn right. But we're after them now the sun's up. And we got a lot of air and fire power. They can't disperse as fast as they got together. We'll get them."

"I hope so."

He laughed and stumped his cigarette out on the ground. Two Marines came over and picked up the stretcher Arthur was lying on, one of them unfastening the plasma bottle from the net and laying it next to him. "So long, buddy!" he said. "See you back in La La Land." Just before they put him on the helicopter he propped himself up and looked back at me.

I must've been looking mournful.

"Cheer up," he shouted. "The war's over."

County Seat

The basement of the old Jefferson County Courthouse on the Olympic Peninsula in western Washington State. It is ten p.m. A dispatcher sits in a small room adjacent to the booking room of the county jail. The jail itself extends beyond the other end of the booking room. The dispatcher is speaking over the radio.

"County, twenty-six. County to twenty-six." There is a pause of silence as he listens for a response. Radio static can be heard when he presses the transmitter key to speak again. "County to twenty-six."

"County, this is twenty-six."

"What is the condition of your prisoner?"

"Can't you hear him?" Growling sounds in the background. "He's bloodied his face on the metal window guard. He's slamming his face into the window guard."

The dispatcher rolls his chair back from the wooden counter where he has been speaking into the radio transmitter. The room is tiny, perhaps eight feet by ten feet. There are rolled maps in a carton box. There is a bank of 911 phone lines. A computer monitor sits on the right side of the counter, and left of the counter on a small table is a printer. The room is full of smoke, although the dispatcher does not smoke. There is a sweet odor of tar, nicotine and sweat.

"Better get a cell ready for this one," the dispatcher remarks, looking up at a dark, curly haired man in his late thirties. "He's a mean one."

"I've seen worse." The jailor is standing behind the dispatcher. He is a man of medium height. He butts his cigarette out in an ashtray on the counter next to the phone banks. A few sparks fly off in the direction of the dispatcher.

"No 911 calls?" the jailor asks.

"No. Not yet. Except for this one. Pretty quiet overall for a Saturday night." The dispatcher brushes the ashes from his arm and shoulder.

There is an extra straight backed chair in the room. The jailor turns it around and sits on it, propping his elbows on the back of the chair. He seems unconcerned about the incoming prisoner. The dispatcher, a thin, nervous, balding man of about the same age, is visibly concerned.

"They're going to be here in a few minutes, Leroy," he says.

"Got any back-up coming?"

"A couple of patrol cars from the County. And I think twenty-seven is already outside waiting." Twenty-six and twenty-seven are city police units for the town of Port Townsend.

"Good. You open the door for them when they get here. I'll book him into the jail. We can put him into the holding tank until he cools off." The holding tank is a bare, concrete room with nothing in it. No windows. Just a secure door. "What, is he drunk?"

"No," the dispatcher answers. "Worse. He's on PCPs."

"Oh, one of those. Were you here the night they brought that Caitlan girl in? Drunk. Drunker than a hog in a fermenting mash bin. And mean! Squealing like she'd just been stuck, when they first came in with her."

"What'd she do?"

"Turned her car over out on old Highway One. Wasn't hurt. Just madder'n hell. You should've seen her."

"County, this is twenty-six."

The dispatcher swivels his seat back around toward the counter. He has a paper log sheet before him, upon which he records all radio transmissions.

Jefferson County is underpopulated, poor and remote, and the county jail is about thirty years behind the times. Inside the jail itself, the cells are composed of large, iron barred cages painted white. They were taken off a nineteenth century ship when the little county seat of Port Townsend was once a busy port. There are bare light bulbs hanging down from electric wires inside the cells. The wires are suspended from uncovered, irregularly cut holes in the ceiling.

"Twenty-six, this is county," the dispatcher responds.

"I'm outside and I'm bringing him in, county. Tell Leroy we've got a tough one."

The dispatcher gets up and goes to the side door of the basement. The door is located in a narrow hallway between the dispatch room and the jail booking room. The jailor follows him, continuing his story.

"Maude was on dispatch that night." Maude is a big, husky, older, white haired woman everyone gives plenty of room to. "Well, they bring this little slip of a girl in and she's madder'n hell because they arrested her for drunk driving. She can't be more than twenty. Her hands are bound in front of her and she stands there in front of the booking desk..."

The dispatcher opens the door. There is a sound of scuffling outside and a blast of cold night air. It is early winter. There is frost on the ground. Four squad cars, two white and two green, are parked in a group, one with its lights flashing, which can be seen through a thin veil of vapor rising from the hot car motors. Two deputy sheriffs and two city policemen are pulling the prisoner out of the back seat of the car that has its lights flashing. He is growling and struggling with his hands bound behind him. They shove him to the ground and bind his feet.

"She was all of a sudden as quiet as a mouse," Leroy continues. "I knew something had to give. I could see the anger in her face. I wanted to get her fingerprinted first, before putting her in a cell, but suddenly she lets out a scream and starts running around the room, cussing, kicking holes in the wooden door and in the walls. Nobody knew what to do for a few minutes. We were all too surprised. Then Maude comes burling in from dispatch and gets hold of this one by the hair and mops the floor with her. Ha ha. I'm not kidding. Down she goes, and Maude mops the floor with her!"

The deputies and police outside are moving toward the side door now. Leroy goes into the jail booking room. The dispatcher flattens himself against a wall by the door. Four officers sweep through the door carrying one husky teenager sideways like a suitcase. They lay him on the floor of the booking room. The prisoner is thoroughly bound up. His hands, arms, legs and feet are tied, and he can hardly move. Nevertheless, he is thrashing about on the concrete floor, growling and squealing. He is saying things, but none of it is intelligible. His face, hair, shoulders, and shirt front are matted with blood, some of it still fresh, most of it dry. A thin mucus is running out of his nose, drool from his mouth.

"Ugh. What happened?" Leroy asks.

"He walked into Henry's Garage," the city officer responsible for bringing him in answers, "took an ax off the wall and went to work, destroying everything in sight. Henry was open late to get some extra work done. Anyway, he and a couple of his mechanics piled onto this guy and managed to subdue him, and then that's when one of them called dispatch."

The dispatcher smiles to acknowledge his role. He is standing well clear of the frenzied prisoner. "Who is he?" he asks.

"Name's Billy Martin. Only sixteen. He's from Hippie Hollow," the same officer answers. "He's been raised on drugs. Been around them since before he was born."

"That PCP is nasty stuff," one of the deputy sheriffs observes.

"Angel dust," another repeats, tapping the long, black handle of his flashlight, which can be used as a nightstick.

The prisoner is still thrashing, growling, squealing and muttering nonsensical gibberish on the floor.

Young Married

"I'm pregnant," she said, sitting up on her knees, a soft breeze from the bedroom window cooling her body under her arms, along her stomach and between her legs.

He looked at her in dismay. "But I thought you were using..." He was sitting in the middle of the bed beside her.

"I was. I don't know what happened." They had just made love. She had waited until such a moment to tell him. It seemed best to approach him with it at a time of both emotional and physical release.

He fell back onto his pillow naked and stretched out his long legs. "It's too soon," he said.

Thelma, sitting up, looked at her husband under the glare of the bedroom ceiling light. He was slender, though not without muscular definition. Working outdoors, he had gotten a good tan on his face and arms. But his body was pale. His sexual organ lay moist and at rest in the dark curly hair between his thighs. Thelma so enjoyed being held in his arms, and feeling the hard manliness within her! She bent over and laid her head on his chest, her brown hair covering its whiteness. It was not a hairy chest. She could hear his heart beating, slow and strong after this period of exertion. "I love you," she said.

He didn't answer.

"You do still love me, don't you, Ken?"

"Yes."

"But you're mad at me."

"No I'm not. I'm just...surprised. Well, what am I supposed to think? I wasn't expecting it. Why did you wait till now to tell me?"

"I wanted to tell you after I'd made you happy."

"You always make me happy," he said laughing. He rolled her over and pinned her down with his arms, lying on top of her. She squealed happily. He took one of her breasts in his mouth, then gently bit the soft nipple.

"Ow!" she shrieked. She reached down and took his testicles in her hand. "You do that again!" she threatened.

"What?" he said. Her soft touch aroused him, reawakening the liquid warmth that spread within his pelvis and reached up into his chest. "Thelma." He pressed his mouth against hers. He was almost shaking with need. Thelma opened her legs, letting the warmth of his possession of her fill her consciousness. Involuntarily she thrust her hips upward, surrendering every fiber of her physical being to him. The sound of her moaning was sweet and brought Ken to a climax. He felt the terrible intensity, the concentration of his mind into a pinpoint of conscious fire, and a profound sense of his possession of her in her vulnerable nakedness. He wanted to hang on. He couldn't. As Thelma relaxed in the sweetness of her own release opening like a flower within her, she felt him convulse and groan, throbbing inside of her.

They lay for several minutes in exhaustion. He felt cleansed, emptied of his need. She felt full, complete, as if her being were a fluid.

"Thelma." He rolled to one side and onto his back to relieve her of his weight. "I'm glad you're pregnant," he said beside her.

"You are?"

"Well, I think I am. To tell you the truth, I'm afraid. We don't have much." The ceiling light overhead glared into his eyes and shone from the white bed linen. He put his arm over his eyes to shield them.

She rolled over and put a finger on his lips, her white buttocks and round shoulders now glowing in the light. "I know that," she said. "It doesn't matter. We'll manage."

"You know you could always..."

"Could what?" She raised herself suddenly onto her arms. Her long, brown hair fell onto his face and her breasts hung downward in tender youthfulness toward his chest.

He reached up and cupped her breasts in his hands. Even when the fire was put out in him, he loved the shape of her, the womanliness of her. It made him feel as if he were all earthly manhood absorbed in all earthly womanhood. "Nothing," he said.

"You want me to have an abortion."

"I didn't say that."

"That's what you were thinking."

"I wasn't thinking anything, Thelma."

"Then why did you say it?"

"I didn't say it."

"You were going to." She rolled over onto her back beside him, staring at the ceiling, her breasts flattening out on her chest. Though shapely, they were not large. Her pubic hair lay rich and tangled like a wild forest in a ravine. They remained silent for awhile.

"Thelma."

"Yes."

"It's alright. I love you. I swear I wasn't trying to suggest anything."

"It sounded that way to me."

"Well, it wasn't."

"Come on, Ken. I heard you."

"You heard me mention a possibility. That's all. I wasn't going to make you do it."

"You couldn't make me do that."

"I know," he said softly. "That's why I married you."

She laughed. "Because you can't make me do things?"

"No. I can make you do plenty." He ran his left hand along her soft belly, between her thighs, touching her clitoris with a finger. They both laughed.

"Don't" she gasped. "I'm still sensitive."

He removed his hand. He kissed her cheek. There were tears. "I'm sorry if I hurt you," he said.

"I'm not unhappy," she whispered. "I want to stay like this forever."

"So do I."

They both fell asleep. The bedroom light burned all night over their relaxed and naked bodies. The curtain over the window fluttered inward toward the bed.

Men at Play

Two gentlemen of Queens, New York, were engaged in a severe combat. They were seated at a small concrete table near the street end of an asphalt park which contained, among other things, a few trees and a basketball court that was separated from the rest of the park by a six foot chain link fence. The kids on the basketball court were putting up a considerable racket. The two gentlemen, ignoring them, were, with furrowed brows, drawn-in cheeks and pursed lips, each studying the most efficient means of annihilating his opponent.

"Check!" said the thin man, moving his white horse into position against the black king. He leaned back from the table and relaxed his tightened jaws. He even went so far as to interlock the fingers of his two hands, turn them inside out, stretch out his arms (over the very scene of battle) and crack his knuckles.

"Cut that out," said the other. "This ain't over yet." He smiled but did not otherwise move a muscle.

The thin man felt a sudden, if but slight, tinge of apprehension. What could Jake—his more generously fleshly endowed opponent—have in mind? "Pshaw!" He let out a breath of air. It was nothing. Jake always did this. He never conceded defeat until the guillotine blade fell right down upon his neck. Charley looked about, glancing up at the large limb of a sycamore extended overhead. All about him on the ground lay its spiny round fruit, some brown, some green. Above, on a smaller branch extending from the heavy limb, was a blue jay. It was putting up a considerable din of noise. "Worser'n a crow," he said.

"What?" Jake looked up. "Stop distractin' me," he said frowning with irritation. Then, smiling, moving his heavy jowls about to loosen them or slide his false teeth back into place—Charley wasn't sure which—Jake picked up Charley's knight and replaced it with one of his own. "Didn't

see that, did you?" he said smacking his lips. "I told you it wasn't over."
He leaned over and spit with satisfaction onto the pavement beside him.

Charley appeared not to notice the move, though, of course, he had
been struck through to the heart by the callous manner in which his
friend had removed his horse. Serves me right, he thought. I should've
seen it. But he continued looking up at the jay. "Appears those robins've
got him cornered," he observed. "He must be near their nest."

"You saw I took your knight?" Jake asked.

"Yeah, I saw it." Charley looked down at Jake and then the
chessboard, the squares of which were a permanent feature of the table
itself. "Scoundrel," he muttered.

Jake laughed. "Wouldn't be a bad sport now, would we? It's your
move."

"I know it."

"Well."

"I'm thinkin'."

"Ha!"

"What do you mean, ha?"

"Nothin'."

"Check."

"What?"

"Check mate, my friend. You see this here bishop. Didn't notice him
before, did you? And that pawn. You can't move your king no ways out
of the way. Gone into the pan sizzling. And not coming out till he's
eaten."

"Damn!" Jake shook his head, his loose jowls seeming to flap.
"Damn," he repeated. He was holding a corner of the concrete slab of the
table top in each hand. "You snake."

"Thems that stays low in the grass gets the bird."

"Damn." Jake got up and shook himself all over. He walked over to
the chain link fence that ringed the basketball court, leaning on it with
both hands clutching the wire. The hot New York sun fell onto the back
of his bull neck. Sweat ran down along his forearms from his upraised
hands to his elbows and beyond. He was a hairy, powerful man who

looked as though he could tear the fence down if he chose to join the boys at their game. They were running about on the court, shouting occasional jibes and obscenities at one another. It looked more like a free-for-all than an organized game.

In a few minutes Jake turned and came back to the little table. Charley was waiting. He had already set the chess pieces up for a new game. In a gesture of magnanimity, for he always preferred to use the same pieces, he had switched colors.

This generosity available to the large heart of the victor did not escape Jake's observation. But he made no acknowledgement of it. He sat down and moved a pawn forward two spaces.

Charley was alarmed. Such a simple move! He had expected something dynamic, as was the general habit of his friend upon opening a game.

"That's it?" he asked.

Jake nodded.

"That's it, huh. Well, we'll have to make the best of it." It was impossible to discern any game plan on the part of his opponent.

"Pretty rough game going on over there," Jake observed.

"Over where?"

"Over on the court." He pointed to the kids playing basketball.

"Well, those hooligans are always over there trying to chew on somebody's Adam's apple."

"You weren't ever a hooligan yourself, Charley?"

"No sir. I weren't. Well. Even if I was." Being a man of dynamic character, he moved a horse out onto the field of battle.

The blue jay, which had never ceased its rasping complaints, had moved to the main limb directly overhead. At this moment, wearied by the insistent robins, it took off and flew away, leaving a deposit of its disdain in the middle of the chessboard.

Both men sat silent for a moment, stunned.

Finally Charley commented, "Here in New York City they never curb their dogs."

"We will maneuver around the sacred spot," Jake said, bringing out one of his horse, "and continue the game."

And so they did.

Bigger Than the Facts

The first time I saw her was not a pretty memory. She was the bride-to-be taking part in a traditional Vietnamese wedding procession. It was a beautiful day and you could smell the green rice wafting in from the fields. She was dressed up in a white ao dai, the classic long slit dress with matching long silk pants, which always looks good on the women, especially when they're young. And she was.

We were guarding a bridge just outside the village. It was a temporary pontoon bridge which had only recently replaced a permanent steel one that had been blown up by the Viet Cong. There was a lot of bad feeling at the time because some of the guys believed that sympathizers in the village had been responsible for what the VC had done. There were five of us on the bridge and the same number of Marines had been killed there before.

So when the procession tried to cross, we refused to let them. That started an argument. The groom got excited—it was his party—and that only made things worse. Cpl. Thomas, who was in charge of the rest of us, was a big guy with dark bushy eyebrows, a square face that gave the appearance of an iron jaw, and a beard shadow that was plainly visible after he shaved.

"That's it, buddy," he said. He grabbed the groom by the shirt and pulled him up to his face. "You're not going across, and if I get any more crap from you, you're going in the river."

That's when the little priest in his black cowl stepped up. "Take your hand off him," he said.

Cpl. Thomas released him. "Look, Father," he said. "Nobody's coming across. You understand? Khong duoc lai day."

The priest said something to the groom and they all turned around and went back to the village.

Well, the story was bigger than the facts. I'm not saying we should have behaved the way we did. But that damned priest laid it on thick to the District Chief. Then the District Chief went to the colonel in command of our battalion, since he was responsible for security in Dai Loc District, which was part of the battalion's Tactical Area of Responsibility.

The Colonel had two of us in front of him, the Corporal and me, since I was second in charge of the bridge detail. The canvas sides of the hooch were rolled up so that warm air and sunlight flooded in. The Colonel looked very neat and clean.

"Corporal, what is this I hear of you and your men beating up several members of this man's wedding party?" The groom was present in the hooch, which was the Colonel's office and which we were standing in side by side, rigidly at attention just inside the door.

"Sir, that man is not telling the truth."

"There were others present, and there is a priest who was also a witness."

"Sir, I don't like to call a priest a liar."

"Corporal, I don't give a damn what you like or what you think you did out there. Your job is to provide security. Now that bridge is on a major transportation route. People have to cross it. Your duty is to screen them, not beat up unarmed civilians."

"Yes, sir."

"Do you understand me, Lance Corporal?"

"Yes, sir."

"I'll court martial both of you, the whole damned lot of you, if I hear of anything like this again. Now get out of my sight and perform your mission like Marines."

"Aye Aye, sir." We did an about face and left.

Walking back to the bridge, Cpl. Thomas seemed to be mulling it over. Finally he said, "That little sack of..."

"Hey, man, we weren't exactly civil, you know."

"One Marine is worth twenty of them. You saw what they did to those guys. What makes you think they weren't just checking us out for their guerrilla buddies?"

"Maybe," I said. "I don't know."

Several weeks later and much to everybody's surprise, the VC mortared the village.

"Hell of a way to treat old friends," the Corporal remarked.

There were quite a few casualties. The Colonel sent an interpreter and a corpsman down to the bridge to give first aid to some of the wounded. A young woman approached, and I saw that she was the bride from the wedding party. She didn't look as young and pretty. Her face was drawn, her white cotton blouse was smudged with dirt and had some blood stains on it, though she wasn't wounded, and she burst into tears when she got to us.

The interpreter translated.

"The VC came and took my husband away. I don't know where they have taken him. They said he didn't pay the tax, but he always..." She stopped and looked at us with fright, especially at Corporal Thomas. He listened to the interpreter without saying anything.

The interpreter told her to go to the battalion command post. He accompanied her. From there she was sent to the District Chief. Eventually, through the grapevine of village informers, the local Vietnamese officials were able to find her husband's body. It was buried in a mass grave a couple kilometers from the village. The heads of all the corpses were missing and the bodies were bloated, stinking and starting to come apart. But she recognized her husband's somehow. The heads turned up later in another nearby pit.

A Peculiar State of Mind

Thelma Duran's cat was of a peculiar state of mind. It generally held in distinct disdain all friends and acquaintances of its owner, but would act differently on unexpected occasions. It was resolute in the convoluted workings of its own secretive mind, haughty, at turns importunate or unapproachable. It had even been known, upon occasion, to slip up undetected and deliver a nip on the hand or foot of an unsuspecting visitor, especially if said hand or foot were tapping its fingers or toes or moving in some other rhythmic pattern. This performance had only been surpassed by a raccoon Thelma once possessed, for she was fond of animals. The beast had clambered up the back of an armchair and tied into a tangle of knots the hair of a young female Jehovah's Witness. The Jehovah's Witness never returned to Thelma's residence after that incident, and the raccoon caught distemper a few months later and passed away. But the distemper of Sam, Thelma's cat, a male seal point Siamese, whether haughty and disdainful or too friendly, was of a different variety altogether. It was more of an electrical nature, the mind of the animal shorting out in surprising ways. Or sometimes, one suspected, simply failing to activate.

Thelma also had a twelve year old son, George. He was her only child. Thelma was divorced. She and her son lived together in an apartment complex on Mercer Island in the middle of Lake Washington east of Seattle. This was when Mercer Island was a green, quiet, underpopulated, woodsy place. George, who was rather small and thin and wore very thick lensed glasses, spent much of his time wandering alone along the heavily wooded, winding roads and grassy open meadows of the island. He was a great lover of nature and a dreamy young fellow.

George had one other noteworthy trait. He loved to tease the cat. Oh, he was merciless! When he was ten and the cat a mere kitten, he introduced Sam to the game of shuffleboard. This took place in the long hallway outside his apartment entrance door. The hall had a wood slat floor, slick, highly polished, rich and glowing. George would simply hurl the cat along the floor. The cat would slide on the fawn-colored fur of its side to the other end of the hall. But just before knocking against the end wall, it would suddenly gain its feet. Thus, fur standing on end, all bristles, claws and wide blue eyes—with very large pupils—it would hit the wall. Then it would come prancing back down the hallway toward George, ears laid back, spine arched, body turned sideways and bent half moon so that fore and rear feet approached on the same line of advance. It hissed loudly but would allow George, so much bigger than itself, another go at the game. There are those, familiar with the family, who insist this may have been the chief cause of the cat's unpredictable perversity.

Thelma had a neighbor, a young man who lived alone across the hall from her. Not bad looking in her opinion, he was nevertheless a bit shy, and it was some time before they were on terms of exchanging occasional greetings. But close proximity among humans is a breeder of both joys and woes. One evening this young man was to be found sitting on the living room sofa of Thelma's apartment. George was away visiting an aunt for the weekend. A small wine glass sat on the coffee table in front of the young man, whose name was Bill. Another one nearby marked the place where Thelma had been sitting. A now half empty decanter was positioned between the two glasses. Bill's last name is unremembered and apparently of no consequence, as he has since left the State of Washington.

Thelma, who loved country and western music, was placing one such selection on her stereo record player. She was a brunette of attractive, but not exceptional, proportions. In her middle thirties, she was tall, and she was slender like her son. She was dressed casually as befit the friendly occasion and her desire to create an impression on her neighbor. She wore a simple white cotton blouse, unbuttoned to the brassiere, and a very short blue denim skirt, which was rather striking against her untanned legs.

Bill tried to clear his mind, but his mind was in the skirt, in the blouse, in fact everywhere but safely tucked, as he himself believed it should have been, in the vest pocket of moral resolve. A heat arose in his lower abdomen. He did not know that the same heat was invading Thelma at that very moment. But he was resolved to induce it.

Bill picked up his wine glass as Thelma straightened from placing the record on the record player, adjusting her skirt. The glass contained a red claret. He finished it off.

"Can I offer you more, Bill?" Thelma came over and sat down on the couch. She picked up the large, clear glass carafe of dark wine and filled Bill's glass, refilling her own as well.

"Sure. Thanks," Bill said thickly, his glass already filled. The thickness of his voice embarrassed him. But then it was always thick. He was no conversationalist.

Thelma looked at Bill, who was not more than a two foot distance from her on the couch. He was handsome, built somewhat like herself, but of male proportions, of course. She desperately needed a man. She knew it was wrong. But than what did Mother know about living single after being married? she thought.

It was somewhat later. The decanter was empty, only a delicious, irretrievable red stain remaining at its bottom. The lugubrious she-loved-me-and-left-me-for-some-other-fool music had stopped. Neither one cared. The couple, both naked, had fallen asleep, arms about one another. Brassiere, panties, skirt, blouse, trousers, shirt, a man's underwear, shoes, even socks—all were heaped upon the floor.

Thelma awoke first. Though lying side by side on the narrow width of the sofa, Bill's weight was on top of her. She felt she could hardly breathe. She also felt that sense of remorse that comes with the withdrawal of wine from the moral inhibitors of the brain and the subsidence of passion. Why had she done it? It felt good to be held, to be locked in a man's sexual embrace. But now it was over and she felt nothing. She was empty. She wished George were home and this heavy, slumbering, dead weight of a near stranger were gone.

Thelma tried to sit up, pulling herself from the weight of Bill's body. It was then she noticed Sam. The imperturbable, unpredictable Siamese was fast asleep, curled between Bill's hairy legs near his groin.

Thelma fell into uncontrollable laughter. Bill awoke. Moving his legs surprised the cat. Sam hissed and sprang from the couch, leaving deep claw marks on the back of Bill's legs. Bill let out a shriek.

Thelma, laughing and apologizing at the same time, ran naked to the bathroom medicine cabinet, returning quickly with a wet wash rag, a medicine box and a robe covering herself. She found Bill sitting upright with his pants already on, pulling on his shirt.

"Damned cat!" he said. "What the hell happened?"

"He was sleeping between your legs."

"People who have cats should declaw them," he said.

But Sam was never declawed. Nor could he be found for several hours, even after Bill left. Bill never returned. And Thelma eventually remarried, which was more to her mother's conscience and her own peace of mind, to be sure.

Coronado's Gold

Isabel Abeita and Joseph Carver were married in an old Spanish adobe church in rural New Mexico where Isabel had grown up. The church was painted white, had heavy, beautiful wooden doors and a simple cross at the top. It was a remnant of a time when Isabel's family had had possession of thousands of acres of land in the lower Rio Grande Valley and on the surrounding mesas. Now Isabel's father owned a welding shop and cultivated hay on a few acres. They were comfortable, for their needs were few; but they were not rich.

Joseph Carver, tall, blond and very Anglo, was a bit of a shock to the family. But Joseph, whose parents had moved from their Mennonite farm in southern Pennsylvania to the Rio Grande Valley when he was a small boy, was a quiet, circumspect, well-mannered young man, who knew more than a little Spanish. He was not Roman Catholic. This, of course, had been a major obstacle.

Joseph and Isabel lived in Albuquerque, where Joseph finished school while Isabel supported him. He then entered law practice. They had a prosperous, middle class lifestyle, producing two children. Their children, a son and daughter, both received a higher education and went away to live in other parts of the country.

Joseph and Isabel grew older. Isabel's parents died and the small farm passed to one of her brothers, the welding shop to another. Joseph retired from law practice. They traveled a little.

By this time, well into retirement, Joseph and Isabel are doing very well and possess a fine home in the far Northeast Heights, a semi-rural section of Albuquerque built in the foothills of the Sandia Mountains. Their home is perched on top of one of these hills and has a veranda, or long porch, extending three quarters of the way around it.

It is winter, late November. A vigorous snowstorm has blanketed the city during the night. In the bright sunlight of the following day, Isabel and Joseph have come outside with a broom and shovel and cleared the veranda. Joseph has not bothered with the walk or driveway. He has some reason to be careful of his heart. And, besides, they aren't expecting visitors.

At the evening fall of the sun into the West, they are seated on their porch wrapped in heavy parkas, blankets, gloves and mufflers. The temperature is near seven degrees. The cold air bites them on the nose and cheeks but they frequently do this on late fall or winter evenings, not to mention other, milder seasons. The many hues that can be broken out of the red setting sun by cumulus clouds gathering on the horizon are beautiful to witness across the snow covered mesas. Such a simple, stark setting as the present one almost always brings up reminiscences from Isabel, for many stories have been passed down through her family from Spanish colonial days. She loves to tell them all. Joseph has a few of his own about Mennonite and Amish life in Pennsylvania, little of which he remembers himself and much of which he's learned from his parents. His parents are still alive, but he and Isabel rarely see them.

"There was a time," Isabel begins, her eyes looking out into the distance over the city and across the mesas beyond. Some of the city lights are already twinkling on. "There was a time, when Coronado first ventured into this territory and stayed near an Indian pueblo with his soldiers not so far north of here at what is now the town of Bernalillo... The demands he made for food and forage were very hard on those Indians."

"I know," Joseph says.

"Yes. You've heard it before. You've heard about it until it's coming out your ears."

"No, Isabel, it's just that..."

"Hush. Be quiet. Never mind." Isabel laughs softly in her mountain of wraps. Her brown eyes glisten with energy above her age worn cheeks. "I'm going to tell you something I haven't told you before."

"I'm listening."

"Good. Coronado had brought a young Tlaxcalan Indian girl from the valley of Mexico with his army. This girl, not more than sixteen, was very beautiful and knew several Indian tongues, as well as fluent Spanish. She had a gift for languages, and Don Armando Abeita y Palacio, who was one of Coronado's lieutenants and who was the one actually responsible for bringing the girl..."

"Abeita? No, you didn't tell me this."

"That's true. It's a story for the quiet time of life when the soul looks with interest toward the setting sun."

"I'm not looking forward to dying, Isabel, if that's what you mean. We've still got a lot of living to do, you and I."

"No, Joe, I don't mean that. I mean when one takes the time, when he finally has the time, to observe the sun slipping over the edge of the earth at nightfall and wonders, in all that mysterious sea of fire and light, where it goes."

Joe looks out over the whitened and increasingly shadowy mesas. The sun is out of sight now and only a thin layer of red separates the graying horizon from black descending night. The ground squirrels have long since quit their high pitched barking from rocky outcrops, but a few birds can still be heard settling into the surrounding scrub oak and cedar. A sudden outburst of yapping can also be heard in the distant hills toward the mountains. A chorus of broken, quavering howls follows. "Coyotes," Joe says.

"It turned out," Isabel continues, "that the girl couldn't speak or understand the Tewa language of those pueblo Indians. But a young member of the tribe decided to take her for his wife and she remained behind when Coronado and his men returned to Mexico. Coronado agreed to this, so it couldn't be prevented. Señor Abeita, who had developed a deep affection for the girl, was much saddened. He hadn't himself understood his feelings until it was too late. He tried to arrange to come north again on other expeditions but was never able. He eventually married and settled in a valley south of Mexico City."

"And what became of the girl?"

"I don't know."

"So why did you tell me this story?"

"Because sixty years later it was his grandson who returned to New Mexico and established our family here. One of the reasons he came was because of the story, which his grandfather often repeated."

"Did he find out about the girl?"

"No. She was like the sun. She had gone over the edge of the earth, as far as he or anyone else knew. But the legend of her beauty and his grandfather's early love for her was like the sun's departing light. It drew him here."

"Oh. I see." Joseph looks at his wife. It is very dark now, and since the porch and house lights aren't on, he cannot make out the features or expression on her face. He looks out at the stars and at the obdurate silence and immensity of the desert surrounding and dwarfing the city.

Who's to Blame?

"I don't believe it," she said. "They fired you?"

"Yes."

"Well, why on earth would they do that?"

"They said I wasn't able to work fast enough. That I didn't show interest."

"Well, it wasn't much of a job. How could they expect you to show much interest?" Carolyn McFarlan was trying to be sympathetic. But she was worried and irritated. This wasn't the first job Tom had lost.

Carolyn went on to work that morning, as usual. She managed a book store. It didn't pay much, but it was their principal means of support, since Tom couldn't seem to hold a job for very long. He's frustrated, she thought. I can't blame him. A good education, and all he can find are menial jobs. But then, what did she have with a Masters Degree in Comparative Literature? She managed half a dozen employees who were earning near minimum wage. In her early thirties she seemed stuck, like her husband, without a clear future. I'm ageing without a purpose, she thought. She was putting on a little weight but was still considered cute.

Tom went out that day and registered for unemployment. In the afternoon he spent two and a half hours in the Buckhorn Tavern with his friend Don, also chronically unemployed.

That evening Carolyn was in a foul mood. She burnt the fried potatoes and seemed uninterested in the fact that the spinach was overcooked.

"When you're home, I'd appreciate it if you'd at least help out a little with the cooking," she said irritably as she placed the smoking frying pan and the still steaming cooking pot directly onto hot pads on the table in the dining nook of their small apartment. The kitchen behind her was full of smoke. The fire alarm in the hallway began to go off, and Tom went to unhook its battery without answering his wife.

They ate dinner in silence. Just as they were finishing, Tom said, "I'll type up a resume tomorrow."

"Good," Carolyn said, her mouth full of food.

That night Tom tried to make love to her. She submitted but was unresponsive. This was not new either. It was clear their marriage was coming apart.

Tom knew he should try harder, but he had lost enthusiasm for the job search, so it always took him longer. Unable to find work equal to his education, he had taken one menial job after another over the years, never able to bear the humiliation and tedium of any of them for long. Lately he had been spending too much time at the tavern with Don as well. In fact, often in the evening with both Don and his wife Patti. Carolyn rarely came along. She had to work, she would say.

Patti was very good looking. She and Don always quarreled, and the more Tom saw her, the shorter her skirts seemed to get, the more fetchingly unbuttoned her blouse. She and Tom laughed a lot together over silly things, often when Don was too drunk to join in the fun.

Carolyn became "bitchier" the longer Tom went without work. The more jobs Tom had lost or quit, the harder the next one was to find. The day came when Tom and Carolyn reached an unspoken agreement that Tom should sleep on the living room couch. After that they seemed almost unable to carry on any kind of civil conversation.

One night Tom had an argument with Don at the tavern. They got into a fight. Patti seemed more concerned about Tom's black eye and bloody mouth than about her own husband's injuries. This infuriated Don and he broke off his friendship with Tom.

It was at this point, or a short time thereafter, that Carolyn and Patti met at the public library. It was a small building, stuffy, loaded with book stacks placed close together, all on one floor in one extended area. They ran into each other near the fiction, and were standing close to the shelves of one of the book stacks in that corner of the room. They knew each other well enough but were not friends. Carolyn had always disapproved of Tom's hanging around with Patti's husband and she was suspicious of Patti's relationship with Tom.

The conversation began sweetly enough. It started with the usual surprised exchange of greetings, How are you doing? sorts of comments, and well wishes. But it grew ugly as they moved to the subject of their husbands. Patti seemed to be in possession of an amazing store of information about Tom. And she appeared to almost glow when she spoke of him.

"You keep your hands off Tom!" Carolyn finally blurted out.

"What are you talking about?" Patti looked surprised.

"I know that Tom's been seeing you at the tavern since he and Don broke off their friendship."

"Tom and I are still friends."

"Friends! A good wife doesn't have male friends that she meets in a tavern without her husband."

Patti looked maliciously at Carolyn, who had become red in the face. "A good wife," she said in a carefully measured voice, "doesn't force her husband to spend every night alone on the couch."

"How do you know...Who told you?" Carolyn could hardly speak. She burst into tears.

"For God's sake, Carolyn, calm down. Everyone's looking over here."

"I don't care. Let them look. Let them know how my husband's taken up with a...with a...well, with a whore who knows all his personal business." Carolyn was shouting.

Patti, trapped in a nightmare of embarrassment, struck out at the word "whore." She slapped Carolyn across the mouth.

Carolyn shrieked and raised her hand to strike back, tears pouring profusely from her eyes. But she withheld her blow, turned and walked quickly, stiffly out of the library, weeping volubly as she went.

All eyes were on Patti, including those of the librarian, who didn't quite seem to know what to do. Patti turned and began running her finger along a row of books on one of the shelves beside her, as if she were looking for a particular volume in that row. Damned if she was going to look defeated! After an interminable pause of several minutes, the library's patrons returned to their business. The librarian, who had hesitantly half arisen from her seat, had sat down again.

Patti found a book. It didn't much matter what it was. She went calmly over to the counter and checked it out. Then, in a quiet, self-possessed manner, she left the library. Outside in the fresh air on the front steps, she said to herself, "Whatever becomes of Tom will be as much his fault as mine. And Carolyn's too." She walked on down the steps and out into the sunlight, looking quite noticeable in her short skirt to a young man passing by on the sidewalk across the street.

Collateral Deaths

We were always racing down the roads in Vietnam, going too fast because we had the ridiculous idea that if you drove fast enough you'd be on the other side of the mine when it went off. I think in the end more people were killed in accidents than by road mines.

It wasn't just Americans who did this. I had a South Vietnamese Army friend—well, acquaintance—who was killed in just such a wreck. I have an idea what happened because I went into Da Nang with him once to get scrap lumber from the Naval shipyard and to steal a little more from a project some airmen were working on. The Marine guard at the Da Nang perimeter checkpoint, who was the only one present when we passed it on our way back to our units before sundown, told us the Air Force was planning on putting up a small building of some kind nearby, which was where we saw the pile of lumber. When I explained that my Vietnamese Army friend needed it for bunkers, he looked the other way while we loaded the extra lumber onto the truck.

My belief that my friend killed himself with his own driving is based on my memory of riding in with him that morning. He had driven his rickety truck so fast I thought it was going to turn over. And he did that because we had passed up the mine sweep team going our direction. This particular road was mined almost every night, and we went about a mile and a half as fast as we could down the middle of the road in a truck that had no shocks and was filled with choking dust. Why we drove down the middle, I don't know. But we sped along, metal peddle to the rusted out metal floor, until we reached the mine sweep team coming toward us. As we passed them, the Marines looked up through the blinding yellow dust cloud we were creating and saw me. The expression I remember observing on their faces through the swirling dirt was one of disbelief.

When Dong was killed, I was only told he'd turned the truck over. That was all. The rest is conjecture based on my experience of our trip together that morning.

Accidents took a lot of lives over there. Not every man is killed by the enemy in a war zone. People do stupid things or sometimes equipment doesn't work right. I myself had the left front wheel suddenly fly off my jeep and go rolling off into a rice paddy. I was doing somewhere between forty and fifty miles an hour but somehow kept the vehicle upright on the dirt road till it stopped. It was only my insane uncontrollable laughter while I was rolling around in the front seat afterwards that lost me the good humor and moral support of my passengers, a lieutenant and three men from another line company. I can't describe the look on their faces, but it was embarrassing to me.

At Phu Bai I knew of a gun crew that was killed when their one five five millimeter howitzer artillery piece blew up in their faces. And my platoon was shelled one night by the South Vietnamese Army. We didn't lose anybody but we were pretty unhappy. That's how I met Dong. He was the liaison for the South Vietnamese Artillery unit, one of whose batteries had fired those rounds. I happened to be with the lieutenant at battalion headquarters the next morning when he went in to make his report, and Dong was there explaining things, mostly promising it wouldn't happen again. Not that we had any reason to talk. Our night ambush patrols were considered more hazardous than the Viet Cong.

That brings up the worst accident I remember. The second squad was out on such a patrol and came in dripping wet early one morning in a dark, drizzling rain. As they filed into our muddy encampment in their ponchos and helmets, water running off them, faces hanging down and tired, one of the guys in my squad said, "Dave, what happened? Did you get anybody?"

They hadn't. We knew they hadn't because we hadn't heard anything since they left in the early morning hours.

It was just beginning to dawn. Dave looked up and smiled. His full rank and name were Private David Brombeck and he hadn't been in country long. We used to tease him about never having to shave. As he looked up, I heard someone shout to somebody else near where I was standing to break out the C rations for this patrol that was coming in.

Dave smiled and gave Lance Corporal Meyers the bird. "Yeah, we did it," he said, jerking his M-16 rifle up to point it at Meyers. "I got one like..." The rifle went off on automatic and Meyers, hit in the face, fell over into the mud.

Usually the company commander writes condolence letters to the family. I wondered if he'd told them Dave forgot to put his rifle on safety. He probably said something to the effect that "your son Lance Corporal Michael Meyers died bravely in the performance of his duty," which I suppose in its way is the truth.

Trying Times

She had a cultivated mind. But as an American she could not express herself as such, for it meant nothing. Oh, to be sure, she loved the opera and good music and shared this with others. But the operas and complex formal musical works she and her friends enjoyed had, for the most part, been written in other centuries and societies and were therefore considered safe. They could be enjoyed without an uncomfortable reflection upon one's own values and conduct. This held true of the great painters and sculptors as well. Their intellectual teeth had been carefully filed off by the solemn and ponderous institutional presence of the museums which contained them. There perhaps remained literature, but this excited only superficial discussion, since rarely read by most people. And the material value of science was too obvious to require, or indeed even permit, critical discussion. Finally philosophy, that proud speculative edifice in the air, was merely a form of intricate cloud chasing to the solid and busy citizenry of such as the present great republic.

Oh yes, there were history and political economy too. We shouldn't omit them. But after Hitler, Marx, Lenin and Stalin, this was overall a clearly dangerous topic, better left to experts and fanatics, like religion.

Martha Gorman was a plain little woman of strong sensibility. Her breasts were hopelessly small; her hair hung limp as a rag. Her wrists were too thin. But her eyes, dark and alive, were the great reservoir and mirror of the sensitive, spinsterishly conservative mind that lay behind them. Martha was a librarian in a small suburb of a big Eastern city. She was middle-aged and, unlike some of her colleagues in similar positions, especially out West, fully qualified in her field. She held a masters degree in library science. She had also never been married.

This latter fact didn't really matter. She lived alone in a small apartment and rather enjoyed not having to answer to another person's whims. Frankly, though she would never have told anyone, if the fires of physical passion burned too hotly within her now and then, she had ways of reducing them. Her one problem, as previously indicated, was that her wonderful mind was wasting away in a society gone to ruin in the midst of an unraveling of will and a riot of psychological pettiness and impoverished desire.

Martha spent hours in her apartment reading, thinking, but never committing anything to paper. At work, when not busy with the public or the book stacks or her three part-time employees, she did personal research and discovered many new things. Most importantly, she found that when immersed more than shoulder deep among her beloved books in the narrow aisles between the book stacks, a special odor emanated from their many pages. Slightly musty, it was redolent of the varied riches of former intellect and imagination.

Martha didn't care much for children. She considered that most of them were not well brought up. They were frequently loud, fussy, arrogant. But she almost always suppressed her irritation with a smile and soft expressions, except, of course, where a commanding demeanor was required. Spoiled children, she knew, were the necessary product of a society run by its merchant classes. Making money, or putting on a show of it, was time consuming and precluded any careful consideration of the finer nuances in effecting a moral refinement in one's offspring.

Sighing over such reflections on one stiflingly warm and close summer afternoon, when several young patrons were being a bit too rowdy in the children's section of the library, Martha Gorman got up from her seat behind the check-out counter, excused herself to two or three anxiously waiting customers (as they always were), and hurried to the scene of disturbance.

"Now hush!" she said pointedly but with some effort at sweetness. "You children must be more respectful of the rights of others." The children, two boys and a girl, immediately settled down. They were in a range of age between ten and twelve. Through the glass front of the library building, three bicycles could be seen lying together on the sidewalk. They were obviously theirs. The girl looked large-eyed at Miss Gorman, but the boys glanced furtively away.

Martha stood for a moment contemplating them. Those boys are trouble, she thought. She smiled at the girl and returned to the check-out counter. The first customer impatiently shoved a pile of books in front of her. He seemed to be in a hurry. His rush, no doubt, had to do with the minute or two he had lost, not with any destination that lay outside the building.

Miss Gorman had reached the last person in the short line when a commotion began once again in the children's section. One of the boys, perhaps in an attempt to tease the girl, had taken a book from her and would not return it. The girl, growing louder in her demands and exclamations and clearly insensitive to the boy's underlying affection for her, had suddenly burst into tears.

"This is intolerable!" Miss Gorman exclaimed. "Please excuse me for a moment." She left the counter and marched irritably toward the scene of conflict. The second boy, who had shown no interest in the fracas at first, now had the book. The frustrated little girl was beside herself. She turned to face the librarian as she bore down upon her.

"That's my book," the girl said. "They won't let me have it."

"That is not your book," the librarian answered shortly. "It belongs to the library."

"Well, he can't have it. I was going to borrow it."

"And borrow it you shall." Martha turned to the boy who had the book. "Give it me!" she said, holding out her arm and snapping her fingers. The boy obediently placed the book in her hand.

"Now if you children don't behave...If I hear another outburst...I... You will have to leave. Do you understand?"

"Yeah."

"Yes, ma'am."

"Yes ma'am."

Martha returned to the counter. The blue eyed young man who'd been waiting looked at Martha. Martha looked down at his one book. "Is this everything?" she asked.

"Yes."

Martha dated the card, slipped it into her file and handed the book to the young man. She was still angry. "No one cares about anything these days," she couldn't help saying.

"That's true," the young man responded, his facial expression sobering in harmony with the occasion. He turned and went out the front door. The book he was carrying was titled, Motorcycle Maintenance for Beginners.

Martha sighed. "Not even a thank you," she muttered to herself, looking after the man. She went back to her work.

The Letter

"I'm not opposed to mixed marriages," he said, "but I am opposed to uneven marriages in terms of education or class."

"Well, Lawrence, this young man is certainly getting an education. Sylvia says here that she met him at the university. She also says she's sure they are in love." Barbara Magruder spoke soothingly to her husband, trying to calm him. Their daughter's letter lay open on the white, marble topped kitchen counter. They were both standing in the red brick walled kitchen beside it. The morning sun, having just climbed above the neighbor's roof line, was sending its first direct rays through the windows. The nearest window was open a few inches and a fresh breeze came in over the sill, gently moving a copper pot and several other utensils hanging over an island in the center of the spacious, well lit room.

"What do we know about Koreans?"

"As much as he knows about us," Barbara went on. She felt as uneasy as her husband about this unknown factor which had entered their lives. Sylvia was their only daughter. "We're just going to have to trust her," she said.

"She's just a kid. And we've made her too idealistic, I think."

"She's twenty years old. She'll be fine!"

Lawrence went to work an hour late. An insurance executive, he was not unfamiliar with minorities, particularly Asians. There were a number of them working in underpaid clerical positions there at the home office. On the whole they were good workers. But, as he had often thought, they weren't like most other Americans. Their appearance and habits weren't the same. They looked different, they talked differently, and what was that stuff they brought in to work with them to eat for lunch? Not that he went into their lunch room, but he had passed by a few of them eating in the park across the street.

Most of the people he was referring to, when he thought of them at such times, were Southeast Asian boat people: Vietnamese and Laotians. But why shouldn't a Korean be like them too? He's from the same part of the world and probably not even an American citizen. Lawrence had never traveled in the Far East, and he couldn't imagine Sylvia eating balls of sticky rice lumped together and wrapped in vegetable leaves. And what was that awful, thick, brown sauce? "Nouc Mam," the Vietnamese called it. Fish sauce. A friend who'd served in the Vietnam War had told him it was prepared by letting fish decompose in a heavy salt brine. A sauce made from rotten fish. Unimaginable!

The executive lunch room, unlike those for the workers, was catered, located on the top floor of the twelve story office building where he worked. It was on the same floor as the executive suites: a quiet, tastefully decorated Elysium above the screech and bang of metal drawers and the snap, cough, crumple and tear of forty to fifty workers in a room, rushing, unstacking, sorting and piling mountains of paperwork. These rooms, these insurance contract initiation, addendum, change and cancellation factories, swarmed with noise and tensed motion, as though filled with angry bees, the short gray pile carpet becoming quickly covered each morning with staples flung in a continual shower from the forty or fifty desks.

The underwriters, elevated above these people on the two floors below the executive suites, fared a little better. They, at least, had cubicles, worked a little more methodically, deliberatively, carefully, used the phones now and then, and a few of the more serenely blessed even had glassed-in offices with closed doors. But these underwriters were mostly white, of European extraction.

Twelve o'clock. Lawrence sighed as he sat down in a comfortable booth. Tommy Popolato, the cook, came over and asked him what he would have. Tommy was a young man with hairy arms, a large hooked nose, dour eyes, and a certain indefinable manner.

"Can you do me up some fried egg sandwiches?"

"Sure, anything you want, sir. Drink?"

Lawrence thought about it. Tommy decided he hadn't heard him.

"From the wet bar, sir."

"No. Just a glass of iced tea, thank you."

The cook walked back across the noiseless red carpet.

"Lawrence, how are you doing?" Fred came in, walked over and slipped into Lawrence's booth. He pressed his arms against the soft leather cushions of the seat. "Damned nice," he said. "I fell asleep in here the other day. Popolato had to wake me."

The cook came up. Fred ordered his usual: a tossed salad with raw egg broken over the top. Fred was the company lawyer, a man of both Japanese and European American heritage. His mother, he loved to say in his usual joking way, had been one of the first spoils of war at the end of the Pacific conflict. Fred was underweight, a heavy drinker. He now ordered Scotch and water. He also always took special delight in devouring his salad in front of Lawrence or any other colleague he deemed sufficiently squeamish about his carefully orchestrated Asian culinary tastes.

The salad and sandwiches came to the table together. Popolato set them down carefully. The fried egg sandwiches smelled good. The raw eggs, with their yolks still unbroken, jiggled clear and jelly-like above the salad greens. The cook brought the beverages in a second round. Fred, whose Scotch and water was in a tall, sweating glass, downed half of his. "Thirsty," he said, sticking his fork into an egg and breaking it. The yolk ran over the salad greens.

Lawrence took a bite out of his fried egg sandwich, trying to ignore the revolting salad.

Fred leaned over as the cook walked away. "Did you know he was gay?" he asked confidentially.

"No. Who told you that?"

"Why he did. I was in here one afternoon and he just up and told me. He must have figured we had something in common, me being half Asian and him being gay."

Lawrence burst into laughter. He fairly rolled in the booth from it. "Ha ha ha—that's the craziest thing I—ha ha ha—ever heard!"

"It's true." Fred sat back and proceeded to eat in a dignified manner, being somewhat put off by Lawrence's overreaction.

Lawrence couldn't stop laughing. On the way home he found himself bursting into laughter again. Thank God he was in the car. Several motorists gave him wondering looks. He kept his windows rolled up, though it was warm under the afternoon sun in heavy traffic. He turned the air-conditioning on. He felt somehow relieved about his daughter, and when Barbara opened the front door, the first word out of his mouth was "Fred" and the rest was laughter.

Gifted

They were not wealthy. Their possessions were few. They lived in a small old house in the town of Belen, New Mexico. Their library of well worn, second hand books ran close to three thousand volumes and stuffed that old house like a swollen, road weary foot in a tiny, stiff, little shoe.

There was another peculiarity. This couple with one child, a girl who was eleven years of age, raised chickens, a motley collection of no particular breed, one dozen or so. Ostensibly the chickens were raised for eggs and occasional meat. But though the eggs supplemented the family diet, no chicken, young or old, yellow, brown, gray barred or red, plump or skinny, rooster or hen, ever graced the family board with its unwilling presence.

The girl was not like other girls, as her parents were not like other working class parents. For one thing, the girl, whose name was Priscilla, did not live up to the reputation promised by such a name. She was not pretty. She was, shall we say, not of a delicate carriage and taste. The fine art of combing one's hair on a regular basis had not yet occurred to her. Her shoes were scuffed and unpolished, her socks often dirty and tumbled down, her knees scratched, bruised, cut and scabbed over.

But the mind of this child was another matter. It shone like a star in the eternal dusty night of a small, Southwestern town. For though an indifferent student, Priscilla was judged by some of her teachers—those of greater patience and observation—to approach, in the nature of her mentality, something in the neighborhood of genius. There were things she seemed to know which they had not fathomed, until they heard them from her. Much of it was of a superfluous kind of information ranging over many fields, though to those who had seen the inside of her home, it was obviously gleaned from the numerous books that surrounded her.

But there was something else, a certain light which shone outward from some unfathomable inner recess. For this otherwise unprepossessing fifth grade child would make sudden, unexpected and penetrating observations, which were often surprising and of a disturbing nature. Whereupon, when questioned about her insight, Priscilla would assert with all the solemn innocence of youth, that she had learned everything she knew from observing the manner and habits of her chickens.

"My dear child," a kindly, older woman, who taught her geography and history, once remarked, "you could not possibly see into people the way you do, if you had learned all you know from chickens."

"But, Mrs. Sanchez, it's true. I've learned everything from them. They're just like people, if you get to know them as I have."

Mrs. Sanchez looked at the child standing before her in the empty school room. If only she could be taught to comb her hair, pretty herself up a little. Then the other children might not be so put off by her. They seem positively frightened of her at times, she mused. Children can be so cruel when they have something to fear. Priscilla must be so very lonely.

"Oh no ma'am," Priscilla said, chewing a strand of her shoulder length, sandy blond hair. "I'm not unhappy at all, or lonely either."

Mrs. Sanchez's eyes widened. "You see what I mean, child," she exclaimed. "Now how did you know what I was thinking?"

"I...I just felt it, ma'am."

Mrs. Sanchez frowned, shaking her head. Such a strange, gifted child, she thought. Surely her parents must understand. But why would they never answer the notes she sent home with their daughter? She resolved that very afternoon to go and see them at the first opportunity.

The following Saturday afternoon she arrived at the little brown house on Rosedale Circle. It was not often she took up her weekends to visit the homes of her students. But Priscilla was a special child. She longed to bring her into the orbit of the other children and to interest her more in her schoolwork. Not that Priscilla did so poorly with class work. It was just that she was somewhat indifferent, as though the fifth grade work were beneath the level of her interest.

Of course, Mrs. Sanchez was immediately taken back by the number of books crammed into the small, two bedroom, adobe style house. Here, she thought, is the true source of the child's brightness. Nevertheless, she consented to a tour of the chicken pen. There Priscilla pointed out the various temperamental quirks and personal habits of the inhabitants.

"There," she said. "That gray one. No, not the rooster. Yes, that one. She's only a year old. I'm sure she'll settle down. But she won't lay now in the nesting boxes."

"Really," Mrs. Sanchez said, feigning interest.

"Yes. We find her eggs all over the chicken yard."

"Why do you suppose that is?" Mrs. Sanchez asked, showing some genuine interest. Generally speaking, she was not fond of poultry. Their feathers were rather loose and got into things.

"It's because the other hens are larger and she's too nervous. It makes her shy, all that cackling and pushing and shoving." Priscilla looked up from the hen into Mrs. Sanchez's eyes. "Do you like public bathrooms?" she asked.

"Public bathrooms?" Mrs. Sanchez did not quite know how to answer the question.

"Yes. I mean with the stalls lined up side by side, so you know what's going on in the ones beside you."

"Well, I must admit I don't."

"That's her problem," Priscilla said.

In the house, Mrs. Sanchez found the girl's parents congenial. They appeared quite ordinary, except for their interest in collecting so many musty old books in such a small space. It seemed that Priscilla's mother had come from an upper middle class background where books had been a common feature in the home. Then her own habit of collecting them had blossomed into something of a passion over the years.

But were they aware of their daughter's extraordinary gifts?

Yes, in fact, they were. They had been aware of her solitary ways and ability to see unexpected things for quite some time. But they didn't have the slightest idea of what to make of their daughter.

Perhaps she could be encouraged to take a greater interest in school and even in her classmates.

No, they had tried that. She was truly her own person and would have to find her own way, which they were certain she would do in time.

"I'm not unhappy, Mrs. Sanchez," Priscilla added. "Really, I'm not." And the kindly schoolteacher had to resign herself to this fact: Some children were just different, maybe special. At any rate, it would all no doubt work itself out over time.

Keening

The sound of women keening. I've heard it before but not like that. It sounded like only a few voices, yet it was loud and could be heard above the rumble and creaking of the tank. There had just been a firefight in the village not more than an hour before. One of our patrols had encountered heavy Viet Cong resistance where they had least expected it, and they'd taken some casualties without being able to dislodge the VC. So they'd pulled back, surrounded the village and called for us on the radio.

When we got there, there was still an exchange of small arms fire going on, but it was light. The second and third squads had orders to enter the village from the south while firing on it from the west, then the first squad would approach from the northwest. A small river bounded the village on the east. That meant the Viet Cong would try to escape north, and that's what we wanted them to do.

An M-48 tank is not a comfortable way to travel. It's crowded inside, and everything you land on, when going into a hole or climbing out of one, is hard. It carries a ninety millimeter main gun and a thirty caliber machine gun at the tank commander's hatch in the turret. There are four crewmen. The driver is up front and below. That way, if he takes the tank over any mines, he's the first to know about it. That was my job. The gunner and the loader are in the main body of the tank, right behind and a little above the driver. They have just enough room to do their job.

As we approached the village through a rice paddy from the south, we could see movement on the village street just behind the two nearest huts. The tank commander relayed that information over his radio headset. We were slipping in the mud that was beneath the shallow water of the rice paddy. I felt the right track slip, and that caused us to veer suddenly to the right.

"Damn!" I said. We'd been stuck before and I didn't want that to happen now.

"Slow it down, Walt! Let it grip," the tank commander yelled.

We continued toward the village at a crawl. Someone opened up to the right of us and a red string of tracer bullets hit the thatch roof of one of the nearest huts and started it burning. At first you could just make out a little gray wisp of smoke, but then you could see the flames. In the background some figures were moving. There were four or five. One of them stopped and fired before all of them disappeared behind a hut three or four huts back. But there were more of them. A solid wall of fire opened up, most of it directed toward the Marines who had fired the burst of tracers from our right. All the while, as we approached, there had been keening, but now it stopped.

We moved slowly forward. The ninety millimeter gun swung around and lowered itself over my head. I heard my tank commander giving orders to the gunner but couldn't hear clearly enough to make out what they were. I knew anyway. That's why the gun and the tank were both pointed in the same direction.

The eeriest moment in a situation like this is when there's a lull, when all the shooting stops and there's just the radio chatter. Just the radio chatter and the creaking of the tank treads in the sloshy water, the diesel engine barely humming. Then the gun went off, the tank rocking backward while still moving forward, and you could see the round going. It was a heat round, high explosive, and the hut it hit, several hooches back where we'd seen the four or five VC, simply collapsed. It blew outward in a cloud of dust and fell in a heap. If there was anybody in or behind it, they were just corpses now.

"Hold it, Walt!"

I stopped the tank. The Marines to the west of the village opened up with heavy fire, and I could now see figures coming out of hooches and running down the village street toward the north. There were holes for cover and bunkers in those huts. The figures trying to get out were armed. The rest of the people remained in the holes.

The Marines to my right were moving forward, firing, running short distances in a leap frog fashion. There were still VC in some of the huts because they kept up heavy fire both to the south and west. We just sat there. The first squad had worked its way around from the northwest to the north of the village and to fire now would endanger them. Our job was done anyway. We had flushed out some of the VC.

Our infantry still took casualties. There was no small number of VC in the village. But their losses were greater, and I don't think any of them got away.

The infantry rounded up the people in the middle of the village street. They searched all the hooches, then burned them. Pajama clad bodies were everywhere, along the village street, on the road to the north and in the rice field beside it, with their weapons scattered around them.

Standing there in the middle of the burning village, surrounded by black smoke and flames, were silent staring faces, half of them kids covered with dirt and frightened, and three or four women keening. Probably the ones we'd heard before.

Tropic Heat

In the morning Jonathan had gotten up with his ten year old brother Tom, two years younger than himself, and they had run out into the Filipino sunshine to catch one of the rickety old sugarcane trucks that came rumbling along the tarmac road between Tarlac and Pampanga provinces on the way to Manila, passing through the nearby town of Angeles. They lived in the American housing area, known as Balabago, which lay just outside the main gate of Clark Air Force Base.

"We can catch it if we hurry," Jonathan shouted.

Tom, already trailing a half block behind his brother on the dirt road of the housing area, struggling in his black, Philippine made, car-tire-rubber shower clogs to keep up, answered, "Wait! I can't run in these things." But Jonathan had mastered those things in the three weeks the two boys and their mother had been in the Philippines, and he couldn't see why Tom shouldn't have done the same.

Melissa Hawthorne, a slender black woman of medium height, awoke wondering where her boys had gone. Then smiling, she thought with some real concern, I hope they are wearing their shoes. Melissa never let her children go outside barefoot, even in the hottest weather, and certainly not here in the tropics with so many things breeding in the soil and air.

Melissa went into the bathroom, relieved herself, pulled her nightgown over her head and got into the shower. Before turning on the water she looked at herself, cupping a long-fingered hand over the soft roundness of her belly. Her hand was warm, her touch gentle, caressing. Why doesn't he love me? she thought. She ran both hands over her arms and legs, now soaping herself with the water on. Her skin was smooth, shiny wet, the color tone of it dark, a kind of red mahogany like her china cabinet. A woman in her early thirties, she knew she was still attractive. At least she had never had any problem attracting men before she met Ted, and she really hadn't changed much in the thirteen years since, in her opinion. Well, other than fill out a little, which was certainly to her advantage.

When Melissa got out of the shower, she could hear a truck horn blaring out on the main road into Angeles. That's the sugarcane truck, she thought. They always throw the boys one or two of those fresh canes. It'll probably rot their teeth. She grimaced, smiling.

The front door opened and the screen banged shut. Technical Sergeant Hawthorne came in bringing with him a pocket of soft morning air. "Melissa." There was no answer. "Melissa. Honey, I'm home. We had some trouble with the intake on one of the F102s." There was still no answer. Sgt. Hawthorne went into the hallway. "Melissa?"

Melissa came out of the bedroom fully clothed in a simple, becoming house dress, but with a pink towel bound up over her damp hair. "Morning, Ted," she said flatly.

"Morning, hon, I was telling you..."

"Don't lie to me, Ted. I know where you've been." Melissa walked past him down the hall and into the kitchen. Ted followed her. He stood silently by the kitchenette table. Melissa was bent over getting a pan out of a cupboard. He looked at her slender hips. She filled it with water and went over and set it on the stove. Suddenly she straightened up, turning toward him.

She always looks so beautiful like that, he thought. And cold.

"I can't give you what she does," she said simply. "I wasn't brought up that way, to do those things with a man."

"It wouldn't hurt you to loosen up a little." Ted was ashamed of himself the minute he spoke. He loved his wife, and he knew he was losing her. But he couldn't seem to help it. In the six months he'd spent in the Philippines prior to the arrival of his family, he'd discovered a new dimension in life, as he described it, the appetite for which he just couldn't suppress.

Melissa came over to the table. "Ted, I want to go home," she said quietly. "Please, please send me and the children back to the States. We can talk about what to do when you return from your tour of duty. I'll wait until then before making up my mind. Maybe..."

"No!"

"Why?"

"The boys. The Air Force wouldn't understand. You just got here."

"Well, it's your fault!" Melissa turned away angrily. She went over to the stove, turned the heat down and got a box of oatmeal from an overhead cupboard. Ted sat down at the table, leaning his head on one hand, strumming the table with the other. "We'll work it out," he said, looking down at the table. "I know I can't go on doing this. It's not fair to anyone." He sat quietly for a moment. "I just can't seem to help myself," he said almost in a whisper.

Jonathan and Tom were walking contentedly back up the Balabago road. They each had a stalk of sugarcane several feet in length. Jonathan had peeled back the dark outer purple-brown skin of one end of his and was chewing the juicy, white pulp. Tom, holding his untouched, was looking up the road. "Hey! Here comes the bird man," he said.

"You want another one of those green parrots?" Jonathan asked between mouthfuls of syrup, spitting out the thoroughly chewed and dried pulp. "The last ones we got died." He wiped his mouth on his arm.

"That's because you forgot to feed them."

"You were supposed to feed them too."

The bird man came closer. The soles of his bare brown feet were calloused and covered with dust from the road. "You boys want Java bird?" he asked.

The two boys drew nearer to have a look. The bird man was carrying strings of bamboo cages hung on either end of a split bamboo pole. The pole was balanced on his left shoulder. Already, though it was not later than seven o'clock, the equatorial sun was high in the blue sky, a big yellow ball of fire beating down on them. There were beads of sweat on the bird man's forehead. He was middle-aged and the drops of perspiration were squeezed out of the leathery furrows of his forehead. He grinned, showing the number of gaps between his teeth. One large front incisor was gold capped, an ornament of which he was inordinately proud.

The boys stared at the beautiful gray and black rice birds. They were plump with flesh colored legs and feet and short, heavy, pink bills. They made a chink chink sort of sound as they hopped around in their cages. The day's humidity was already pressing upon the two boys, soaking their backs and armpits.

Tom looked at his brother.

"Mom wouldn't like it," Jonathan said, taking another chomp of his sugarcane and rolling his eyes at the intense, sweet flavor.

"You got any money?"

"Yeah, a little. Most of my allowance."

"I'll pay you back, okay?"

"Okay. But we've got to build them a bigger cage. And feed them right," Jonathan said, reaching into his pocket for the money. "Though Mom says it's parrot fever the other ones died of," he added reflectively.

The bird man undid the cages, detached a small one and fished his gnarled, stubby fingered hand into a larger one, reaching one at a time for two fat Java rice birds, which he put into the smaller cage. They bit him with their hard stubby beaks and he released them each time with a sudden flick of his hand, as if trying to toss them away from his fingers long enough to get his hand out of the cage.

Jonathan and Tom went home, laughing, talking, carrying the small, noisy cage between them, their chests swollen with excuses and excitement. Now and then Tom would stick a finger into the cage and yank it out with a happy, painful jerk.

Destiny

Patricio Valdes wanted to be an artist. As a boy he had followed the tinwork of his grandfather and had later learned the wood carving of bultos and retablos from his father. But as a teenager he had discovered through fine reproductions in books the mural work of the great Mexican painters: David Alfaro Siqueiros, Diego Rivera and Jose Clemente Orozco. This man Orozco, he had only one hand, he would tell himself, and yet he created those fine, dark works full of deep and troubled feeling. Siqueiros and Rivera also painted the Revolution with splendor and expressive power. But Orozco. It is he who has taken the Mexican soul in the unfolding of national rebirth and given it to the heart of every man.

Patricio, or Pat, as he was known to his friends in New Mexico, both Hispanic and Anglo, was seen as a quiet, somewhat self-absorbed young man who showed himself to be full of daring on certain occasions. For instance, he had once saved a friend from drowning in an irrigation canal when he himself was not a good swimmer. He had run ahead along one bank of the canal in front of his friend, who was struggling in the slow moving but strong current of murky brown water. Finding, as he ran, a large, dead branch of a cottonwood tree, and quickly breaking off some of its branches, he had thrust it into the water before the drowning boy, who was being overcome by the undertow. Then, when the boy didn't respond, he had climbed down the bank, risking the chance of falling in himself, leaned out, grabbed him by the shirt and pulled him to safety.

As a young man, Patricio spent two years at the National Academy and School of the Fine Arts in Mexico City studying painting. He learned much in the academy, but it was in the presence of the great frescos themselves that he grew in understanding. He felt what he could not have explained. And he copied over and over a number of the evocative, twisted figures of his favorite, Orozco, traveling often to such places as the University of Guadalajara to see his work.

Then he discovered, again through books, the coolly visceral work of the Peruvian Frenchman, Paul Gauguin, who had provided a beginning in Symbolist technique for the post-revolutionary Mexican painters. And he also found that group of early Twentieth Century European artists known as the School of Paris. His favorite among these was Georges Rouault, who frequently painted religious themes with the thick lines and translucent colors of a maker of stained glass windows, which Rouault had once been.

This brought Patricio back to his spiritual roots in New Mexico, where art, or craft, served the purpose of religion. For, in spite of all he had learned, he was uncomfortable in Mexico City. It was large and cosmopolitan in its rush of human destinies, while he was so only in spirit. Besides, his Spanish, when he had first arrived there, had contained a number of words that were of both English and Sixteenth Century Spanish origin, the latter characteristic being derived from his mother who was descended from a long line of Spanish settlers who had come nearly four hundred years ago to the northern part of the State. It made him sound foreign. Though he quickly overcame this minor handicap, he was made aware and remained sensible of the special character of his background.

Back in New Mexico, Patricio entered a period of confusion. If Mexico City had been too cosmopolitan, New Mexico now seemed unacceptably provincial. They do not produce universal art here, he said to himself with perhaps too much of the disdain of the young, newly fledged cosmopolitan. Perhaps Paris, Madrid or Barcelona was what he needed. But he had no money. Instead, now twenty years of age, broke, doubting himself and unwilling to practice his father's more modest vocation, he turned on momentary impulse and joined the Army, causing himself to be sent to Vietnam.

The war stunned him. It shocked him out of all remaining complacencies. For these Vietnamese, small of stature and Indian looking, were not unlike the Indians of both New Mexico and Mexico, but especially the Maya he had come to know in the South of Mexico on several recreational trips to the Yucatan. They were not so far removed from a strain of blood which ran through his own veins as well. And they were being butchered, old men, women and children alike, by their own people and by Americans. He returned to the United States, he felt within himself, as a much older man.

Ten years passed. After being released from the Army, Patricio intermittently attended classes at the University of New Mexico without matriculating. He drifted into odd jobs. He continued the habit of drinking he'd picked up in the military. He could produce no original work of consequence. He was certain the thread of painting within himself had been damaged, even cut. He married a beautiful young girl of good family, whom he truly loved, but he was an indifferent provider. The marriage resolved itself into quarrels, bitterness and separation, having produced one child. Then a miracle happened.

Alone, desperate, convinced he had completely lost his way, Patricio began to paint as he never had before. His conceptions were clear, simple, powerful. He showed a few to his estranged wife. Though untutored in such things, she saw immediately that a transformation had taken place. Others saw his work. They, many of them, suddenly knew what he could no longer believe about himself. Patricio, falling ever more deeply into a trough of confusion, hardly able to swim in the turgid water of an increasing emotion, beyond any apparent formulation of thought, was creating in swift, powerful strokes a new language of the eye and heart. What it said no one could put a name to, but everyone knew, and that was its strength.

Patricio began showing his work in small galleries in Albuquerque, then, shortly after, in Santa Fe and New York. His reputation began to spread quickly over the next few years and collectors as far away as Europe and the Far East bought his work. He achieved international renown. Never divorced, his marriage survived the dark years and his daughter grew to a stable and lovely young womanhood, though he did not live to see it. There were no other children.

Patricio was never a regional artist. That is for certain. He died at age thirty-eight of sudden heart failure in 1984. There were retrospectives in New York and Paris in 1987 and 1990. He belongs now to the world.

A Ferment of Years

In the crash of '87 he lost everything. If he hadn't pulled out of the stock market then, he would have been all right. Stocks went back up. Or if he hadn't been tempted in the first place into stock market speculation with all his retirement savings. Or at least if he had not put a second mortgage on his Long Island home to feed the ravenous junk bond machine, as he has since been inclined to refer to it... All, all of it gone in a nervous puff of smoke!

Georgios Vernadakis was a son of immigrants. His boyhood in the Astoria section of Queens, New York near the East River had been pleasant enough. His father had opened a fruit stand before he was born and expanded into ownership of a bakery as well, by the time Georgios was in his teens. The strong goat cheese and fresh smell of the big, golden, round loaves of bread his father sold had been a recurring stimulus to what would become the memory of his childhood. And, as he was an only child, the bakery store and fruit and vegetable business together had earned enough to get him an electrical engineering degree at a good school.

George served a stint as a junior officer aboard a Navy minesweeper near the end of World War II but did not get into any action. Discharged from active service in San Francisco, he had remained on the West Coast for two years to gather experience with a new company there, then went back to New York, where he found similar work in electrical research with a small firm.

All this is well enough. It is sufficient detail concerning the ordinary life of an ordinary man. What might be added is that George married, produced, reared and educated two children, and looked in regularly on his parents during the remainder of their lives. He was a good husband, father and son. His wife, and close friend for forty years, passed away the year before the crash.

Well, in the Spring of 1988 George sold his house on Long Island, realizing very little cash from the sale, though he had owned the house for nearly thirty years. He moved to Seattle, a city he'd visited several times while on shore leave in the Navy, and rented a small house on the nearby Kitsap Peninsula close to the town of Bremerton, where he began the experiments for which he will be remembered and is presently growing in renown.

From childhood George had always expressed an interest in botany. He went about collecting plants where he could find them, gathering seeds and germinating them in small pots set on the east facing window sill of his bedroom on the relatively sunny corner of Twenty-first Avenue and Hazen Street. This interest remained with him all his life. But another interest, electricity, had seemed the better choice for a career. Or so his father had advised and he had dutifully assented.

Now that he was retired, widowed (his children busy with their own lives), and conveniently too poor to have any other worldly aspirations, George was ready to combine these two interests. For he was convinced that electrical fields could be used to enhance, even significantly accelerate, rates of growth in organic matter. He called this process rapid oxidation, because he believed electron energy levels could be controlled with electromagnetic forces in such a way as to influence the speed of chemical change without disruption of the metabolic process. He was excited for he had held a germ of this idea in his heart from early childhood. The problem was finding a means of applying the energy field to living plant tissue, varying frequency levels, measuring results, and discovering an appropriate catalyst for change. He set to work.

A stocky man with a thick bush of white hair, usually uncombed, and a broad, hairy chest, he could be seen puttering about his house in apparent Neanderthal heaviness on warm summer afternoons, and especially evenings, beneath the bare bulb of an unshaded light, dressed only in a thin pair of boxer shorts. A pungent odor seeped from this dwelling where he lived alone. And this odor was a mixture of the sweet scent of potting soil and green herbage and a light but acrid emanation of body smells from the all too frequent habit of forgoing a nightly bath or washing of soiled clothes that were lying about the house. Late at night too, neighbors, or those among them curious enough to stay up for the occasion, would see George in the bare lighted rooms, still in the underwear he'd slept in, sometimes, they suspected, for weeks, tending to his pots, which covered every window sill.

The neighbors thought him odd. Those who had visited him, mostly children, for he was also believed to be quite harmless, reported that several tables, in what normally would have been considered the living room, were covered with more plants in pots, some growing only in water, and bits of tissue in petri dishes, all hooked up by electrical wires or transformers or subjected to inexplicable apparatus which the children could not even begin to describe.

George, a trained scientist, was a meticulous experimenter. He kept the minutiae of his observations in clear, well organized notes, written in calligraphylike print and stored in neat folders set in a kitchen cupboard. These formed the substance of several articles he published in science journals. For George was becoming known to a diverse community of thinking men and women far removed from his little house in the wet green woods.

One morning, having driven to the northern extremity of the Kitsap Peninsula, so as to be able to think in the open air, and looking out through the dark, evergreen woods into the gray, early morning mist of Puget Sound, he saw several, large, ominous shapes half emergent from the twilight of fog and sifted sun. They were the huge, gray hulls of warships of the U.S. Navy.

Perhaps it was the several of them together, or the effect of the fog, partially obscuring all but their menacing, big gunned, iron massiveness, and his knowledge of the tremendous firepower they were capable of delivering. Whatever the cause, the result was a shudder that raced down the spine of Georgios Vernadakis. He got into his car, drove home, gathered his notes and began writing. For, inexplicably, at that moment a final problem was resolved.

What he wrote was not an article, but a book. It was the summation of what he had learned and thought over a period of five years. Gone were the tentative explanations of what had appeared to be tantalizing but inconclusive results. Here in plain exposition was the means to alleviate famine throughout the world.

George is still at home on the Kitsap Peninsula. His leisure is increased and his habits more orderly. Due to the close proximity of dark, evergreen forest, which virtually surrounds him and his little house, and to the predominance throughout many months of the year of overcast skies, moss grows up to his very door sill. He has a small porch, the damp timbers of which are slowly rotting, and now finds time to spend his afternoons sitting on it. He observes the nervous chattering of gray chickaree squirrels with their bright orange underbellies, perched high in the hemlock and fir trees surrounding him. He responds to the intense querulousness of the indigo-blue Steller's jays, which are hopping from branch to branch, peering this way and that at an ornery world with black, beady eyes. And he is sympathetic—well, understanding—of the pileated woodpeckers, knocking themselves brainless in their hammering search for grubs and insects beneath the bark of stumps, fallen logs and weathered old trees.

Meanwhile, here and there throughout the United States and elsewhere, in universities and private laboratories alike, many minds are at work on the experimental results and carefully wrought theoretical conclusions that have been recorded in a little book.

G. Lowell Tollefson

In a Wounded Country

When the military authorities released him from the hospital, then shortly thereafter discharged him from the Army, he thought his troubles were over. With his war disabilities he was no longer considered fit for service, but he was certainly fit for life! An annoying buzz in his head was the only problem.

Lester Bernard went home and married the girl he'd always loved, a beautiful, shapely young woman who'd become a source of inspiration, hope and fantasy to him in the wet, hot jungle. He was sure pleasant thoughts of her had kept him alive during the worst moments after he'd been hit in the chest, arms and head by an exploding mortar. Carol was waiting for him. That was the thing that kept him going.

Lester took a day job and enrolled in night classes at the University of Idaho. He was interested in game management and wildlife biology. Having thought a lot about the cool, pristine forest wilderness of central Idaho while he was in Vietnam, he knew that would be the place for him always, far away from all the craziness of people.

But Carol soon became pregnant. They should have been more careful. At any rate, these things happen. The continuous buzzing in Lester's head made concentrated study almost impossible anyway. So Lester left the university and moved to Seattle, Washington, where he could find better paying work to support his wife and coming child. He took a job at Boeing Aircraft, and the company's insurance policy covered Carol's pregnancy.

Electronic bench assembly work was immensely boring. The buzzing increased in intensity. Lester began to drink more than usual. Little Charlotte was born in mid-December. She had Lester's expression, his turn of mouth, curious and daring, Carol would sometimes say.

In late January Lester was caught unexpectedly in the massive Boeing lay-offs following Congress' failure to support domestic production of the supersonic transport plane. The unemployment lines were long and snaked all over the cold, crowded, echoing room where Lester picked up his unemployment compensation check every other week. The weather was an endless, cold, blowing spray that never managed to fall on top of anyone's umbrella but always blew under it.

Little Charlotte got pneumonia and had to be treated with antibiotics by the "country doctor," a free medical service offered by the County. One made visits to this doctor by climbing a long, winding, back staircase to a small, third story room in a little, moss dampened, wooden building in a gray, dreary looking neighborhood of unadorned, concrete block apartment buildings.

There were several one hundred eighty degree turns in the narrow stairwell. Lester and Carol carried Charlotte eagerly up through them behind the lumbering, gasping efforts of a young man several hundred pounds overweight. He huffed and puffed, heavy kneed, stopping to gulp for new breath at each landing. It took him twenty minutes to ascend the stairs. His bulk blocked the way, and no one could go around him. It was twenty extra minutes of worry for the frightened parents.

Seattle was in a slump because of the Boeing lay-offs. To make matters worse, the shipyards were now firing people too. A sign went up on Interstate Five: "Will the last person out of Seattle please turn out the lights." Rush hour traffic on the stretch of freeway nearest the University of Washington campus was frequently in a snarl due to the presence of anti-war students lying on the roadway, blocking traffic. At the same time, vigilante off-duty police in street clothes ran about the campus with baseball bats and wooden clubs, looking for stragglers among the protestors.

Continued drink, no job prospects, and increasing tension between Carol and himself had only made Lester's head worse. The buzzing sound had become more articulate. There were actual voices, music.

"I can even make out the songs sometimes," Lester told Carol.

"Maybe it's the drink. You could cut down on the drinking. You know we can't afford..."

"It isn't the drink. That's the only thing that helps."

"It's gotten worse since you started drinking heavily like this."

"I'm telling you it's all I've got to relieve the stress. You don't know what it's like to hear voices and music all the time. I actually hear people talking, Carol. Like an announcer or something. I think it's a radio station."

Carol looked at her husband in silence. She didn't believe him. Hardship was dulling her senses. She wasn't sure of anything anymore. "I don't know," she said, turning away.

"Damn it, Carol, don't you walk out of here on me! I'm hurting badly. Can't you see that?" They were in the living room of their one bedroom, North Seattle apartment.

"What about me? What about Charlotte? Don't we matter? All I hear about is your problems. We could've lost Charlotte. And all you can do is complain about imaginary voices and get drunk. I think you just don't want to look for work."

"Don't want to look for work! I've been looking all over." Lester jumped up out of his armchair in anger and accidentally knocked the lamp over. "Imaginary voices?" He picked the lamp up and set it on its table. "I'd like to see you hearing this all day and night without stopping. I'd like... Oh, the hell with you, Carol!"

She had left the room.

Lester went to a Veterans Administration hospital. They x-rayed his head. The doctor then explained to Lester that when he was wounded in Vietnam the surgeons had failed to remove a piece of shrapnel embedded in his brain. It had not appeared to produce any visible impairment at the time and removal was dangerous, if not impossible, with the present technology. Apparently, the small piece of shrapnel was behaving like an aerial or tuner, picking up certain frequencies. But how it transmitted these tiny electromagnetic impulses to the brain as sound no one could as yet explain.

"I want it out, doctor. I can't stand it anymore."

The surgical procedure, once begun, took several hours to complete. A team of surgeons assisted. The operation appeared to be a success, but afterwards, in the intensive care unit, Lester's heart simply stopped working.

Seattle eventually recovered from the bust. The war ended, and the nation settled down to go on to greater heights of prosperity and greed. Carol, deeply shaken with guilt, nevertheless eventually remarried. Charlotte came of age, a beautiful, intelligent young woman, sensitive and slender like her father. She also had her father's eyes.

The Seduction

Patricia Gonzales sat down in the living room of her boyfriend's second floor brownstone apartment. She was five feet, six inches tall, slender but full figured and sandy blond with a clear complexion, carefully plucked brows, gray eyes, a pert, small, upturned nose and an equally small mouth. She wore mauve lipstick, which accentuated sensuous, full lips. Her hair was thick, unevenly cut to just below the ears and swept loosely back. It resembled new mown hay, recently wind turned and gilded under a layer of autumn frost. She wore tiny pearl earrings and smelled of spring flowers.

Derek Berrington was in the kitchen, where he kept his liquor in a cabinet above the sink. Derek was tall and dark, rather handsome, small boned, looking a good deal more like a Spaniard, which he wasn't, than his girlfriend did. Patricia's mother was Irish.

"Who did you say brought you?" he asked loudly from the kitchen so his girlfriend could hear.

"I didn't. I took a cab." Patricia leaned back on the sofa, putting her head on the firm cushions behind her. She ran her hands out beside her, feeling the rich brown and green tweed texture of the upholstery. Her finger tips communicated with her spine. "I rode the subway to Fifty-ninth Street and Fifth Avenue and then caught the taxi," she said, staring up at the ceiling, where a large fan slowly turned.

"Well, I hope you didn't run over any bicycle messengers," Derek said, laughing as he walked into the living room with a tall glass in each hand. "Not that there wouldn't be plenty of others to replace him." Patricia grimaced. He set one drink down on the glass coffee table top in front of her then sat down beside her, leaving a space of half a cushion between them. Patricia sat up, straightening her skirt, and picked up her drink.

"It's cold."

"Yes. I used plenty of ice."

Patricia smiled. "Do you always try to heat your women with liquor and freeze them with ice at the same time?" she asked.

"Sometimes." Derek put a hand on Patricia's skirt covered leg and, feeling her muscles tense, removed it. She was wearing a full cotton plaid skirt that come to below her knees. "Whatever works," he added.

Patricia blushed.

"Listen," Derek said. "Why don't we have dinner here and then go out? The concert isn't until eight."

"I thought that was the plan," Patricia said, setting her drink down.

"Well, it was, but I wasn't sure..."

"I'm looking forward to it."

"Okay." Derek got up. "I'll shove something in the oven. Roast suckling pig. He died with the sow's teat still in his mouth," he said, disappearing into the kitchen.

"That's awful!"

"Well, I made a casserole out of him anyway. You won't recognize him. And he tastes an awful lot like turkey."

In the kitchen, Derek put the already prepared clear glass casserole dish into the oven. It was baked brown along the edges. He turned the oven to three hundred and fifty degrees. Since he had previously cooked the dish in the late afternoon before Patricia arrived, it was only a matter of reheating it. He shut the oven door.

He couldn't get the thought of Patricia's body off his mind. He had had his hands on it before. He had had his hands inside her dress, for that matter, but they had never made love. The scent of her perfume filled his brain like an intoxicating vapor. Would she ever let him go all the way? She had resisted him twice, letting him undress her, fondle and caress her, but always stopping him, even to the point of crying and locking her legs together, when he began to undo his own trousers. He couldn't understand her divided mind. After all, she was a grown woman.

"Derek."

"Yes." He answered from the kitchen.

"That wooden clock on the mantle. Did you buy it here?"

"No. Mom and Dad gave it to me for Christmas last year. I think it was a subtle hint to organize my life better. I guess they figured that if I saw the clock every time I walked into the living room I would put some effort into arranging my day."

"You could have put it in the bedroom. I mean, if you didn't want to see it."

"It's too big."

"You do all right anyway."

"They think I come home from work and just lay around listening to music or watching TV."

"Do you?"

"Sometimes." Derek came into the living room. He saw Patricia had finished her drink and went to refill her glass.

After the second glass Patricia was flushed. She thought her tongue seemed thick sometimes when she spoke. She was sure she sounded drunk. They were eating their meal at the coffee table. Patricia's hair was a little mussed by her own hand and her skirt was a little above the right knee. At one point, while they were eating and talking, she noticed Derek looking at her knee (he was sitting to her right), and she smiled. She didn't cover it. "Did you know my great grandfather was a vaquero?" she said.

"A cowboy?"

"Well, sort of. He bred fighting bulls in Spain. My father describes him as having been a very p-passionate man." Patricia spoke slowly to make her words clear. She set down her third drink, half empty. She was determined now to overcome her inhibitions. So, forcing herself to finish saying what she would not normally have said, she added, "He fathered nine children. Nine sh-hildren," she repeated, leaning back on the cushion behind her, still holding her fork. She closed her eyes.

Derek looked at Patricia but didn't answer. He was also feeling the alcohol but not as much. She's mine this time, he thought simply. She's ready and willing. But he got up and went to the closet for his sport jacket and Patricia's light coat. "We'd better get moving or we're going to be late," he said. "We can clean up this stuff when we get back."

Patricia looked at Derek and sat up. Her eyes were moist. She did not get up. The fingers of her left hand, which was still placed primly in her lap, trembled slightly. "Let's not go," she said. "I'd rather stay here." Derek closed the closet door and walked over to the sofa.

G. Lowell Tollefson

The Restaurant

Probably the most significant fact about the Dos Hermanas, or Two Sisters, Restaurant is that no one who works there knows anything about two sisters who have had any connection with the place. There is a town near Seville, Spain, by that name, but the restaurant owners have never heard of it. The restaurant serves Mexican food, but neither the owners nor any of their employees are Mexican or of Mexican descent.

This restaurant, which has its busiest season during the warm, relatively dry tourist months of the summer, is located in the town of Port Angeles on the northern tip of the Olympic Peninsula in western Washington State. A typical day begins at ten in the morning when the morning cook and prep cook come in together. They, along with one waitress, serve lunch. It is not a busy time. The busy time begins at five in the evening. This is when American tourists coming back across the Strait of Juan de Fuca from Victoria, Canada, begin unloading at the nearby ferry dock.

To get an inside view of this fundamental American institution, the semifast food emporium of one sort or another of ethnic fare, let us enter the back door with Arnold, the afternoon prep cook. Arnold is of medium height, a little paunchy in the middle. He is still in his twenties but already balding. He enters the kitchen directly from this rear entrance and is greeted by one of two cooks on duty. This one happens to be the male half of the establishment's proprietorship, the female half being destined to arrive a few minutes later to head up the evening's team of waitresses at their busiest time.

"You're late," says the owner. He is a big, broad faced, freckled man with curly red hair and a bushy mustache. He is twenty-eight. Almost everyone involved with this restaurant is in his or her twenties or early thirties. There are, in fact, only two exceptions: the dishwasher, not yet arrived, who is a seventeen year old high school dropout, and an indeterminate percentage of the five or six waitresses, who may be older. The owner-cook flips a pan of fajitas eight inches into the air. Flames from the stove curl into the black, cast iron frying pan underneath the flying fajitas, blossom upward over the green, orange, red and brown cuts of meat and vegetables as they return to the pan, and then go out. The cook is obviously impressed with his own agility and does not turn to look at Arnold, whom he is addressing. He is now sliding the pan rapidly back and forth over the gas stove top, giving its contents a good shuffle and causing new flames to dance merrily over them. On one side of him, a younger man lifts a strainer of chimichangas, or deep fried burritos, streaming oil, out of a tank of boiling, dark brown grease and replaces it with another strainer full of raw nacho chips. "It's quarter after six," the owner says. "You were supposed to be here two hours ago. It's a good thing Mary"—the morning prep cook—"decided to stick around awhile."

"Sorry man, I had an emergency."

Clarence, the owner-cook, grabs a plate from above his head, rattling a stack of them, pours the contents of the frying pan onto it, steps over to the steam tray behind him, and ladles some beans onto the plate next to the smoking fajitas. He dabs a little pale green guacamole sauce topped with sour cream into the remaining space on the plate, then spreads shredded cheddar and jack cheeses over the beans for both flavor and yellow and white color. He adds a lemon garnish, a bit of parsley, sends the plate clattering onto the stainless steel counter through the serving window, and hits the top of a metal bell with his fist.

As luck would have it, the waitress who picks up the plate is the other owner, just arrived. "About time you got here," she says, looking through the serving window at Arnold, who is still standing in the middle of the crowded kitchen floor, an expression of guilt on his face. There are beads of sweat on the balding portions of his head. The kitchen is humid, heavy with an odor of grease, beans and cheese.

(The secret for making refried beans in this place is to simply mash the newly boiled ones to give them an appropriate used look. These properly mashed, newly boiled beans, of course, may last several days, since they are prepared in large quantities. So they are generally stored white hot in big, yellow, plastic buckets that originally contained cold pickles or other refrigerated condiments. However, no trace of plastic flavoring has ever been detected in a vintage supply of three day old beans. Not by any customer, at least.)

"You could've called," Clarence says, reaching under the stainless steel counter into a refrigerated cabinet for a container of pre-rolled, pale white enchiladas. This is the substance of the order requested on the ticket just retrieved by Clarence from a row clipped above the service window. He puts several of these enchiladas on a clean plate, covers them with a thick, dark brown chili sauce—his own indefinable invention, to which he attributes the entire success of the restaurant, ignoring its convenient location within a block of the ferry dock—and sprinkles cheese over the lot. The cheese container is nearly empty. "Need more of this," he says, shoving the clear plastic, rectangular box into Arnold's hands.

"I didn't think of it," Arnold says, referring to the phone call he should have made. He disappears into the big walk-in cooler behind the kitchen to retrieve two twenty pound blocks of cheese, one cheddar, the other jack.

There is another cook in the room, this one a hired employee, though not without that share of arrogance appropriate to positions of leadership. He is trying to fish tamales out of a hot steamer and manages to drop one on the floor. "Damn! Mike, get that, will you?" The young dishwasher he is addressing has just stepped inside the back door. He is late too, but that is normal. This second cook, a short wiry man, is cushioned under each of his shoes by a layer of cheese, which is stuck to their soles. In fact, the floor is covered with lettuce, cheese, red and white onion skins.

"Sure, boss," says the kid. He grabs a mop out of its bucket in a corner of the kitchen by the back door, takes it over to the big metal sink basin, which is full of dirty dishes, gray water, ugly soap bubbles, etcetera, and plunges it in.

"God!" says the morning prep cook, a woman with a kitchen conscience. "I could throw up!"

"Never mind," says the second cook in an intense, falsetto voice, still addressing the dishwasher. "Get me some more chicken for enchiladas."

The prep cook, mumbling to herself, goes back to work chopping onions on the wooden counter that takes up the center of the room. Upstairs, heavy wooden chairs can be heard scraping the floor, or kitchen ceiling, in the restaurant loft. There is laughter, the clatter of dishes, the tink of glasses, clink of silverware, and a confused rumble of voices. People are having fun. Mexican songs, sung in Spanish by an American woman with a good voice and fine legs, are up on the stereo system. The walls, both upstairs and downstairs, are hung with paintings of Mexican bandits, or revolutionaries. The upstairs banister is draped with a serape, and a terra cotta lazy Indian is asleep under his sombrero near the bottom of the stairs.

Sunday Afternoon

"Dickens is a realist," Rebecca said, putting down her copy of Martin Chuzzlewit. She ran a hand through her hair, lifting her head and pulling the long, chestnut strands of it up off her young neck and dropping them over the green and blue plaid arm of the six foot living room couch, where she lay full length, propping her head on a matching pillow. "I've known more than one Pecksniff."

"So have I," Dick said. He was leaning back in an overstuffed armchair, which also matched the couch and which was placed at a ninety degree angle to it. The armchair faced a television set which was not on. In the afternoon half-light of the partially darkened room it could be seen that the nineteen inch glass screen of the set was quite dusty. A Sunday newspaper lay piled in a disheveled heap on the floor beside the chair, the poor quality coloring of a front page photo glaring in a narrow beam of light. "But where have you seen anyone as innocent as Tom Pinch, as pure as Mary, or... Well, I might allow for a Mr. Chevy Slyme. I think I've known one or two of them."

Rebecca laughed. "You're such a cynic, Dick. Ow!" She sat up. A big, yellow tom cat was sitting on the floor beside the arm of the couch where she had been lying. It was well-fed, tiger striped. It looked up at her with wide, wondering, green eyes. Their pupils were a little enlarged. "He clawed me!" Rebecca exclaimed. "He was playing with my hair and he clawed me. The little beast!"

"You wanted a cat."

"I did? Wait a minute, Dick. You brought this thing home. Shoo! Go away." She waved an arm at the cat.

The cat leapt out of the way of her hand, went off nonchalantly a few paces and lay down under the footrest of Dick's chair, facing Rebecca, its forepaws placed primly out in front of it, its ears pulled back, as if to say: Strange behavior. The cat's precarious position under the collapsible footrest seemed to indicate its greater faith in Rebecca's husband. It began to purr.

"Oh, go bother someone else," Rebecca continued, feeling guilty, waving her arm at it. She lay down again, her large bundle of hair placed carefully under her head this time.

"That someone else being me, I suppose," Dick said without altering his sprawled position on the fully leveled chair.

"Who else?" Rebecca answered matter-of-factly, lying flat on her back, looking up at the ceiling. "When did you last change his box anyway?"

"Since when is it my job?"

"Since you brought him home."

Dick got up, raising the back of his chair, lowering the footrest and scattering the cat. He opened the living room door. The cat went out. "It's hot in here," he said. There was no breeze. But there were birds outdoors somewhere. Finches, no doubt. Their muffled chirps sounded like the squeaking of mice.

"You're letting all the flies in." There was no screen door.

Dick sat down. "There's room for us all."

Rebecca leaned toward him, putting her hands together in a supplicating posture. She said in a small, mock sweet voice, "Please, Dick dearest, O honeyed knight, gallant and noble..."

"All right." Dick got up and shut the door with a bang.

"You didn't have to shut it so hard."

"You wanted it closed."

Wearily: "Yes, I wanted it closed." Rebecca closed her eyes. It certainly was hot in the room. She was two months pregnant. A fly landed on her nose. She brushed it off irritably, without opening her eyes. "I feel a little queasy," she said.

"It's all those pickles and ice cream you've been eating." Dick was once again sprawled comfortably in the chair. The cat was nowhere in sight in the front yard, but they wouldn't have noticed.

"Very funny! It's probably the heat."

"Probably."

The afternoon sun slipped quietly over the western mountains of central New Mexico, as they both dozed where they were, in a small subdivision high on a mesa south of Albuquerque, in the half-light of a semi-darkened room in which the curtains had been only partially opened.

Routine Business

On the morning of Tet at the end of January 1968, the North Vietnamese Army marched into the city of Hue in military formation and took it over. They assassinated most of the South Vietnamese officials who had anything to do with the United States. We found civilian bodies piled into mass graves all over the place. There were no American or South Vietnamese combat troops in the city at the time of the takeover, but there were plenty of CIA agents. They wore civilian clothes and were pretty conspicuous. Many of them escaped out of Hue through the underground sewers. They were brought to First Marine Division forward headquarters at Phu Bai combat base for debriefing by the General, and it took four weeks for American Marines and South Vietnamese troops to retake the city.

Just before Tet, Khe Sanh had started up and the siege ran on until the middle of April. All these activities produced a lot of captured weapons. But the losses didn't stop the North Vietnamese. Even now as we were carrying the weapons south to Da Nang in a military convoy, there was a bloody fight going on in a nearby mountain valley not far south of Phu Bai. A company of Marines, while in the middle of thick, high canopy jungle, had stumbled unawares into a North Vietnamese regimental base camp. When we left Phu Bai, they had been pinned down for three days with the bodies of their own putrefying dead piled beside them. I had heard a firsthand description of the stench and flies over the radio. You could hear weapons firing and feel the fear. Reinforcements were having to work their way in to them on foot because the jungle canopy was too thick to reach them by air, even to take out the dead and wounded.

It was hot and dusty as always on the slow, winding road that led south through the Hai Van pass on the sixty mile trip to Da Nang. The surrounding hills were covered with short dense brush jungle that appeared to be light green, almost tan in the shimmering heat. We passed some Army engineers working on a part of the road.

"They're up there," one of them said, pointing to the hills. The hills were sunny and quiet. I was riding shotgun in the hard, right front seat of a shock absorber deprived two and a half ton truck loaded with captured weapons, many of them new and still packed in the original cosmoline jelly. We were near the rear of the long column of vehicles, mostly trucks and a few radio equipped jeeps.

We had only gone a few miles past the engineers when there was an explosion and a black puff of smoke ahead of us. Because the front of the convoy had gone around a curve, we couldn't see what was happening. We were forced to stop. Small arms fire started, and we leapt out of the truck and took cover along the side of the road.

More small arms fire, then nothing. Someone signaled and we climbed back into the truck. As we continued on around the bend, Private First Class Thornton, a thin blond Marine about eighteen or nineteen, who was driving, said, "Must've been a mine."

"Or an RPG."

"Think a rocket propelled grenade would have made that smoke?"

"If it hit the diesel tank."

When we got around the bend, there were two disabled trucks and one of them was burning. There weren't any deep, wide craters in the road to suggest a mine. Several other trucks were pulled over and a couple Marines were standing beside the road. We slowed. A lieutenant came over to the driver's side window. Not far behind him stood a Marine with a radio, speaking into his handset.

"Keep it moving," the lieutenant ordered.

"Did we get any, sir?" Thornton shouted.

"We're looking." He pointed toward the hills. I couldn't see anybody or hear any shooting.

"What about us?" Thornton added.

The lieutenant pointed to the side of the road a little ahead of us and a good distance from the burning truck. I could see a number of Marines, some standing, some kneeling or squatting. I realized there was a corpsman with them and there were bodies. Whether dead or wounded I couldn't tell at first. It turned out to be several wounded and two dead.

PFC Thornton was in an excited mood most of the rest of the way to Da Nang. He talked continually for twenty minutes about his desire to see combat, which he hadn't done. Then he fell silent, concentrating on the road.

"They never quit," I said after awhile.

"Wish I could've been with the platoon that went in after them."

"I haven't heard anything."

"Yeah."

Going back to Phu Bai was different. We left the weapons and vehicles at First Marine Division Headquarters in Da Nang and returned on a C-130 transport plane. They marched us in through the open rear rampway and jammed us in there, in the dark cavity of the plane's fuselage.

"All right, move it up! Belly button to asshole, Marines! Let's go!"

We were jammed so tight we couldn't move. It got hotter and hotter. Sweat poured. It was dark. Finally the engines started. They had long since shut up the rear end of the aircraft. When the plane took off, we fell over, all in one mass because we couldn't move. The rifle or canteen sticking in my ribs was uncomfortable, and if it had meant anything, I would have been embarrassed about my sweat running down onto the guy underneath me.

The Heritage

David Monford stood and looked out over the land he'd inherited from his grandfather. It was several thousand acres of dry range, located south of the little town of Mountainair in central New Mexico. Already late afternoon, the weather was hot, the sky an almost cloudless, searing white-blue, the earth parched to silveriness and burned a khaki brown. But there was a light breeze. So David stood beside his car on the side of the road, facing a rocky, forested spur of the Manzano mountain range, while an occasional motorist sped past him.

"Why?" David asked aloud. "Why me, Grandfather? I'm no farmer."

He knew that because of his mother he had always been a favorite of his grandfather, Juan Mondragon. For David was an only child, and his mother was the youngest of five. She was such a late arrival she hardly knew her brothers and sisters as siblings. Then her mother died at age fifty of cancer, the same disease that was to claim her when David was in his teens. So Juan had raised her alone from the age of twelve, his other children being already grown. And David had many cousins, all of dual Hispanic parentage, except himself. I can't even speak the language, he thought.

He got back into his car, drove a short distance down the State highway, and turned off onto a dirt road. He did not want to take his new Ford Escort over this road because of the rocks, gullies and possible washouts. So he went very slowly. A harrier hawk glided low to his left, circling over rabbitbrush and cactus. It tilted in flight now and then, turning and going back over the same area.

Plenty of cottontail and cottontop out there, David thought. He remembered hunting rabbit and scaled quail on his grandfather's ranch as a boy, using his grandfather's old 410 gauge shotgun. You had to be patient and observant, able to get close, and a good shot.

The property extended to the base of the mountains, where the dominant prairie shortgrass and cactus gave way to woody growth: juniper, piñon pine and scrub oak. A little further in the distance, on State forest land, were tall stands of ponderosa interspersed with hemlock and gambel's oak, and these in turn gave way at successively higher elevations to fir, spruce and golden aspen. There were apple orchards too, now gone wild in the lower valleys. Their fruit was firm and sweet. These old orchards, some planted long ago by Spanish settlers, were the source of the mountains' name.

As slow as he was going, white dust still rose high behind David as he bumped over rocks, ruts and holes. He turned off onto a gravel driveway, now little more than an overgrown path. In front of him was the house. He got out of the car.

It was a small, frame house, once painted yellow with a green trim. The porch was in need of repair. The front screen door was off one of its hinges. David pushed the main door open and went inside, where it was cool and dark. He could see in the dim light that there was no furniture, not even appliances. Aunts, uncles and cousins had seen to those. The house smelled musty, and the rough, wood plank floors were covered with sand that felt gritty under his shoes. There was evidence of mice or some other kind of rodent. David went back out into the blinding sunlight and descended the porch steps.

What am I going to do with this property? he thought. There haven't been any cattle run on it in years. If the house is like this, what are the sheds, corrals and barns like? I wouldn't know where to begin anyway.

As David stood near the porch, he thought of his father's advice. "Sell it," he'd said. But then his father, an Easterner from the Mid-Atlantic States (where he himself had been taken in his early teens after his mother had died), cared nothing for the tradition, the old stories of Spanish settlement his mother had told him when a boy.

As David stood there, a young coyote stepped out from behind a dense, low growing juniper. It stopped abruptly, as if surprised to see him, its forelegs straight and tensed, its hindquarters bent, ready to spring away.

David remained motionless, watching. Must've been onto a cottontail, he thought. I'm probably the first human he's ever seen up close.

As David did not move, the coyote seemed to relax a little, cocking its head. Then David shifted his weight, and the coyote darted away amongst the sunlit brush, its tawny coat disappearing into the gray and sandy colored landscape.

David got into his car and backed it along the driveway slowly, grimacing as he scraped its paint on the branches of an intruding apache plume. The bush was beyond its flowering stage, now covered with cotton tufts that would soon float into the surrounding desert. Out on the dirt road he looked for the hawk he'd seen, without finding it, and wondered where the coyote had gone. This land is so stark compared to the lush, green, forested, water fed hills of Maryland, he thought. Everything in nature holds its own separate place here.

On Highway 14 David headed north toward Tijeras Canyon, then west to Albuquerque, from which he'd just come. He decided he would continue on across country to California, as he had planned. It had been a year since his grandfather had passed away and left him the land. So far he'd been unable to reach a decision about what to do with it.

Flight of the Condor

The line was long. The day was hot. Tom was at the end of the line, and no one else seemed to be coming into the store. So Thomas Jefferson H. Smith waited. He was not named after the famous American statesman, but after an early nineteenth century Englishman, Thomas Jefferson Hogg. This was a source of embarrassment. Life was always getting in another dig at him. In fact, at this time, as was so often the case, he was unemployed.

"Hey, let's get a move on up there!" An impatient young man ahead of Tom wanted to pick up his Friday evening six pack of beer. This small store on the outskirts of Dallas, Texas, sold cigarettes, beer, wine and hard liquor. That was it. The store was the last stop along Skillman Road before going out into the legally dry suburbs. Big, fairly expensive homes on carefully manicured lots, but no booze. Hence the long line.

"Okay, okay. Can't you see I'm working alone?" The young woman behind the counter was the only one there. The man helping her had gone into the storage area in the back for something.

Things could have been worse. Earlier the line had snaked for fifty feet outside the front door of the store. Now at least they all fit inside, even if it was a little snug among the rows and rows of glistening wine, whisky, vodka and gin bottles.

"Well, hurry it up," the young man insisted in a lower, more subdued tone.

Soon he was at the counter, for the young woman was working very fast, dashing back and forth between the counter and register with money and change. The cash register was on the back wall behind the brown, wooden counter. The young man leaned on the counter. The young woman, a redhead whose curls were pasted to her forehead with sweat, was too rushed and irritable to notice that he was actually handsome. He looked at her with his dark, expressive eyes, mentally seeing her without her clothes on as she went to the register with his twenty dollar bill.

"Damn!" the young woman said. She could feel his eyes on her back. She banged the register drawer shut and went to the door leading into the back room. "Mike, I need some change out here!"

A thin, sallow, wispy blond haired man, wearing wire framed glasses and in his thirties, appeared with several wads of money. She took them out of his bony fingers with their carefully filed, undamaged nails (he was an assistant manager). Then she went over and opened the register drawer to put them into their appropriate compartments. She removed some of the change and brought it to the young man. He left the store. The line went down.

Now it was Tom's turn. He was the only customer left in the store. Someone had bumped into and broken a big jug of inexpensive red wine. It was pooled on the beige, linoleum tiled, concrete floor and people had walked in it, including Tom. No one had been available to clean it up. The assistant manager who had brought the change was still fooling around somewhere in the back, whatever he was doing. He no doubt figured the young woman could handle things alone. It was probably cooler in the back. The front end of the store now reeked of sweet alcohol.

"What'll it be?" the young woman asked at the counter. There was a pause, and in that infinitesimally tiny moment all kinds of things ran through Tom's mind. What'll it be? she had asked. He was, after all, lonely and, unfortunately, neither good looking nor of a winsome disposition. So, "One pack of Marlboros," is what he said.

The woman looked at him in disbelief. He had waited all that time for one pack of smokes? But she said nothing and took his money. He was kind of thin. Must really need them, she thought. She was also a little irritated because he had handed her a twenty and she knew the drawer was low again. She didn't know he couldn't really afford anything more than the cigarettes. She leaned over the cash drawer, surveying the barren field of coins and small bills. Tom noticed the bra straps that passed over her shoulders under her light cotton blouse. It was very pretty. How lonely he was!

Suddenly the young woman turned away from the register and went into the back. She left the drawer wide open. Must be tired, Tom thought. He observed that the drawer would be within arm's reach if he leaned over the counter a little, the aisle between the register and counter being quite narrow. He saw that, while most of the compartments were empty or nearly empty, the stack of twenties was deep.

Tom had never stolen anything before. Yet he was the only one in sight. This place must make a damn good profit, he thought. They could afford to lose a little. And he badly needed it. Tom leaned over the counter, but he hesitated to reach for the money. God would understand, he reasoned.

The young woman walked back into the room. Tom pulled himself away quickly. The woman glanced at him and went to the register. She loaded it and pulled out his change, dawdling over the twenties as she did so. Tom waited on the other side of the counter behind her bra straps and her freckled elbows. Satisfied that all was as it should be, she turned to the counter. "Here's your change," she remarked. She threw a pack of cigarettes in front of him as well.

The look she had given Tom was a strange one. On his way home he couldn't decide whether it meant, why didn't you go for it? or, I understand what it feels like to be on the bottom, or, boy, are you ever honest or chicken or something! All of these things were written in her face at once. At least, that's what he imagined.

On the other hand, it could've been that she was needing to scratch herself somewhere inconvenient and was just impatiently waiting for him to leave. Or maybe she wanted to mop the sweat off her forehead with her forearm but was reluctant to express herself in such an unfeminine manner in his presence. Tom didn't know. One thing was certain though. Someone needed to clean that wine mess up off the floor. Maybe she was anxious to do that. The sticky liquid was beginning to draw flies. Big Texas flies, the size of condors or eagles.

All in a Day's Work

On January 31, 1968, the North Vietnamese Army marched into Hue city in regular formation. There was no one to resist. They rounded up twelve hundred South Vietnamese government workers. American CIA operatives escaped through the sewer tunnels.

Months later, an American patrol came upon a suspicious mound near Hue and dug into it. They found hundreds of decapitated bodies. Several more mass graves with similar contents were discovered.

At 1st Marine Division forward headquarters in Phu Bai, a major was addressing a corporal. Beside them was a table covered with aerial photographs.

"You see," said the major proudly, "I determine each morning's fire mission on the basis of these photographs and intelligence reports of varying reliability."

"To interdict enemy movements," the corporal said. "But what about the villages?"

The corporal left the command bunker and walked toward several rows of hooches. He knew what those artillery rounds would do.

Cruelty

He was a nervous child, introspective, sometimes cruel. Siblings there were none. He had no father. Only a mother provided sustenance to his clandestinely inflorescent soul.

Tommy Lee Marcowitz was eleven years old. "Mother," he announced one bright, sunny morning, "I shall become a scientist. I will study the souls of things."

"Scientists don't have much to do with souls," his mother said with a condescending smile of happy appreciation.

"Then I shall change that," was his high pitched response. He turned, ramrod straight, upon his heels and went perfunctorily out-of-doors with a bang.

In the back yard, sunlight fell everywhere like a bright shroud in dense yellow splashes. It lay in a fiery consuming readiness at the bottom of the red painted wagon that had been his since the age of seven. It hit the concrete back door steps with a pop and a glare and skipped out onto the lawn where it sank long fingers into the coolness of the earth. Clouds hung in it like parachutes, soft, billowy and white. The pale blue sky, a translucent jellyfish, positioned the glaring ball of it, as though it were a hot yellow mouth, directly over Tommy's head. He felt it, like a hand, warm and tight upon his shoulders.

In the garage, which was still cool in the early morning, and which was detached from the small white frame farmhouse his mother had rented for them just outside Baltimore where she worked, he found his refuge. Not that he needed it. But it felt good to be in the dim light, next to the car, amidst the oily, musty odors near the wall, where Thelma the cat and her four kittens were housed in a carton box.

"Hello Thelma."

The big yellow cat opened her big yellow eyes, yawned, stretched her paws and began to purr. One of the kittens, a black and white one, was feeding. The other three were wrestling, tumbling and trying to crawl up the steep, smooth sides of the box. Tommy reached down and took one out. He held it in his hand like a sausage. The mother mewed.

Outside, Tommy looked at the yellow kitten, which was tiger striped like its mother. In the bright sunlight the kitten seemed to squint.

"Good," he said, satisfied he'd made a careful analysis, and pulled a small note pad and pencil out of his pants pocket. "Its eyes are not used to the daylight." He wrote that down, laying the kitten in the grass.

Perhaps it was the coolness of the lawn, which was well watered, green and high, in need of clipping. Upon touching it, the kitten sprang immediately into action. It leapt upward, arching its back, and bounded about in a circle. Then it began to walk through the grass in an elegant, high-necked manner somewhat like a cheetah. Presently it sprang, an action which was followed by several small pounces. Then it came up with a grasshopper, which got away and flew off somehow in spite of a furious battering of paws. The kitten, turned about, glancing over its own back, flailing the air with its forepaws while standing on its hind legs, looked as if it were shadow boxing an unseen opponent. The grasshopper circled away clumsily, veering, making a crackling sound and showing bright orange underwings.

"Good." Tommy wrote in his notebook the simple observation: It knows what to do. It can hunt.

He picked the cat up and proceeded to the front of the house. A long, raised porch stretched the entire width of the simple edifice. In the middle of it was the front door. The porch was made of wood, but the floor of it was painted gray, as though it were made of concrete. The porch was raised perhaps two feet off the ground, fronted by a broad wooden staircase with balustrades on either side. These too were painted gray. The staircase was centered on the front door of the house.

The open space beneath the porch was fully enclosed. It was a musty, dark place, paved with loose dirt and littered with boots, pails, a few pop cans.

Tommy opened a small gate to the right of the steps and, placing up the kitten inside, shut it fast. He then peered into the dusky, pungent odored light through close wooden slats. The kitten, sniffing about in the semidark, was already investigating a rubber rainboot. "Good," Tommy said, getting up and walking away. "It's not upset about being away from its mother...yet." The kitten was four weeks old.

It was three in the afternoon before Tommy's mother finally took him shopping with her. He'd been waiting all day. The kitten had been mewing for some time, and he had kept careful notes concerning its behavior.

"What's that awful mewing?" his mother asked when they had gotten into the car.

"Oh, just one of the kittens."

"Must've wandered off from its mother. Hmmm." She hadn't looked into the box, which the mother cat had long since left in search of the missing kitten. This meant, of course, that the three in the box were also putting up a fuss. "Strange, I thought I heard it earlier in the house."

Tommy and his mother were gone two hours. Upon their return, Tommy felt lazily content with a belly full of cold chocolate ice cream. Though it was hot outside and in the car as well, he had been satisfied by the cool, soft, creamy flavor of his treat. They pulled into the garage.

"Sweetheart, what on earth could be the matter with that kitten? It's still carrying on," his mother said.

Tommy got out of the car, went over and looked into the carton box. The big yellow cat was not there. The three kittens were now asleep.

"How are they doing?" his mother asked from the other side of the car. She was gathering two grocery bags from the floor in front of the back seat.

"Fine."

"Well, one of them isn't doing so well. You better find him."

"Okay."

Kneeling before the front porch, Tommy pulled out his notebook and observed: The mother cat is not anywhere around. She must've given up and gone hunting. This one is okay. It knows something now that the others don't know. I think it'll grow up to be a wise cat with this kind of early education. I'll make further notes of its progress.

He closed the notebook. A strange thrill had excited him as he wrote. It was something almost sexual in the way it had passed through him. He opened the little gate.

The Prize Tomato

Fred Falsopp had retired from one thing or another. No one was sure of what it was. He was known for his gardening: the beautiful banks of blue larkspur, yellow-centered white and lavender asters, and vermilion roses out in front of his home, fronting the street. There was a large, leafy green vegetable garden in the back as well.

One morning Fred's wife stepped out the back kitchen door into the August sunshine and called to him. "Honey!" Like her husband both in age and build, she was a portly woman in her mid-sixties. At this particular moment she was flushed with excitement. "Fred, they're coming in today."

Fred was tending his tomato plants, which he had neatly staked at the sunniest end of his garden. All superfluous branches had been carefully and systematically nipped in the bud, so that the plants were no longer crawling vines, as God had casually intended them to be, but were compact, upright bushes—bushes set with heavy, bright red, perfectly formed fruit.

"Oh, Fred, I'm so excited!" His wife came up to him. Her nose twitched sensitively at the pungent odor of the tomato plants, for Fred had just watered them. "We haven't seen little Bernice since she was a toddler. Eight years it's been. She's eleven now. Ha-a-a-chew! Can you imagine that?" She wiped her nose.

"Yes, I can imagine it, Alice." Fred's voice was patient, almost weary. Alice was not a gardener, and she was so excitable. He was squatted next to a particularly fine tomato. Like an only child, it was the sole occupant of its vine and surpassed all others in size and unblemished beauty. He did not turn to face his wife but reached under a leaf, pulled out a bug, and crushed it between his fat fingers.

"All you care about is those tomatoes."

"They give me pleasure, Alice."

Alice stood there looking petulant. "I suppose you're going to enter that one in the county fair."

"Might as well. You won't let me enter you." Fred was facing his plants, hiding a grin and the crinkles around his eyes.

"Oh, Fred, you're impossible! Anyway, I came out here to tell you they're coming in this afternoon. We should be at the airport before three." Alice turned and hobbled up the kitchen steps, grumbling about prize tomatoes, the allergies they produced, the invention of steps, and about impertinent husbands as well. She entered an old frame farmhouse, though it was located on a large lot along a town street. Inside the kitchen she smiled and began to sing softly to herself as she went about her chores.

In a little while Fred came in. In his hands was the big tomato.

"You picked it!" Alice said with surprise. "But the fair isn't until..."

"Doesn't matter," Fred commented gruffly, brushing past her. "Here, let me wash this fellow up." He elbowed into the sink, turning on the tap. "It's for our Bernice," he said simply.

"What's she going to do with it? Honestly, Fred, I really wonder about you sometimes." Alice was smiling, standing behind her husband with her hands propped on her wide hips, watching him. She could not decide if the big man or the big tomato seemed more ridiculous to her now. And she wondered if her daughter's new husband, the third one so far, would be any better than the last. People get together like cats nowadays, she reflected. And when they grow old, they're all strangers.

Ambush Patrol

We knew of movement in the valley and that the Viet Cong were using the village to resupply themselves with rice. So we left one night from our little clearing on a hilltop in the jungle and set up near the village. The village lay along the bank of a river and we had the river to our backs along with a copse of brush jungle. There was a trail coming out of the village that passed between us and the surrounding rice fields.

The night was overcast. It was the long cold drizzly rainy season that comes after the monsoons. But it wasn't raining. Just damp and cold for Vietnam.

"Mark." The Marine next to me whispered, motioning toward someone further up the line. I could see Sgt. Curruthers, my squad leader and the leader of this patrol. But in the dark I could barely make him out and had to strain. I was awake but had been in the same position for so long I was in a kind of stupor. I could make out that he was holding something. Quietly I unhooked a grenade from my shoulder strap. I nudged the guy on the other side of me. He carefully slipped his rifle selector from safety to automatic and nudged the next man.

In the village there had been dogs barking. But they'd been barking all night. Every time someone got up to take a leak, I suppose. I heard what sounded like a faint mumble of voices. I was thinking that I was probably imagining it when suddenly they were there.

Two men on the trail and further back, others. My heart started going like a heavy hammer. Not fast, just hard, and I started worrying that I would have to breathe loud enough to be heard.

The two men had stopped for a moment, looking back. Then they proceeded toward us. They were both carrying Chinese carbines. Carefully I pulled the pin from my grenade and carefully dropped the pin to the ground. My left hand was sweaty. The spoon of the hand grenade lay beneath my thumb.

The two men stopped again, looking back along the trail. The others were coming into sight out of the dark, a fairly large group of them trudging along with heavy burlap bags full of rice slung over their shoulders. The Viet Cong guards were wearing clogs but some of the porters were barefoot. They were villagers.

We would have to take them all. You couldn't discriminate. Two more guards came into sight behind the group of six or eight porters. The porters were bunched up and were acting confused or unwilling. One of the forward guards, close enough for us to make out the irritated expression on his face, said in a low, sharp voice, "Di di mao!" Hurry up.

I saw the sudden swing of Sgt. Curruthers arm. I threw my grenade. The two explosions were almost simultaneous. Then everyone else along the line opened up.

The grenades had landed among the porters. I saw the two guards in front go down under automatic fire and heard the screams and groans of the porters. I was firing my M-16 rifle now and we all kept shooting as the bodies fell and were twisting and turning, trying to scramble or drag themselves off the path. Behind them the other two guards fired once and bolted. Chinese SKS carbines don't fire on automatic. One of the guards fell on the trail and the other got off into a rice paddy. The field was dry after harvest with no standing water, so he didn't make any noise. But you could see his silhouette against the low horizon of the fields. Several of us stood up and cut him down.

Immediately Sgt. Curruthers got up and we all moved off quickly to another nearby tree line. From there we could see across the small field we'd crossed to where we had been before and where the porters' bodies were still scattered on the trail. We waited a good twenty minutes, never taking our rifle selectors off the firing position. Normally we would have had them off safety from the time we left the hill, but there had been an accident a few weeks before and Sgt. Curruthers had ordered us to keep them on safety till we needed them.

A small pebble hit my arm. I saw Sgt. Curruthers get up and we all got up. We walked quietly toward our handiwork, close enough to get a good look, then turned west away from the river toward the platoon encampment in the clearing on the hill.

The Mystery of Light

He had proposed, in a philosophy of science colloquium at a non-prestigious western university, that, for a general field theory to be developed in physics, there must be a shift in the perspective of science. The response from his colleagues was silence, a few remarks such as, "ahem, very good," "an ingenious approach," etc., then indifference. Other more easily understood theses which were presented at the colloquium were discussed at length that afternoon. But not his. So the unremarkable Dr. Lloyd Harkins returned to his small college in the Midwest, where he continued teaching without notice or challenge.

Within a year he had published a slender book titled, The Role of Probability and Reason in the Formulation of Theoretical Frameworks. It was more revolutionary in content than in its title. But some few who took note of it said in jest that the title was longer than the book. It was soon forgotten. Dr. Harkins went on teaching, retired as professor emeritus, and took up final residence in a retired persons condominium. He had never married and never issued a second book. Within a few years of the book's publication, he had even stopped making contributions to the professional journals.

Lloyd, as he was known to his fellow retirees, rarely took his meals anywhere but in the basement of his condominium. The condominium was a self-contained community. In that same basement were several small shops, including a book store, which sold his favorite westerns, a tobacco seller, and a barber. On the first floor were the offices of the few medical professionals who provided services to this retired community.

"Hello Lloyd," a woman said to him one evening as he entered an elevator in the basement, returning from his customary supper. This woman had long had an eye on him, and he considered her attractive, but the habits of a bachelor so long nurtured in solitary living are not easily dismissed.

"Miss Brenda." He nodded, trying not to catch her eyes in a lingering look. He did not know why she was referred to as Miss Brenda. He believed her to have once been married.

"I have good news for you." She was unusually cheerful.

"Oh?"

"There's a young man to see you. Something about a book you wrote a long time ago. He says it's become very important now."

Lloyd looked at Brenda. He had not mentioned the book to anyone in years. The sincere kindness in her eyes indicated her good will.

"Thank you," he said warmly.

She smiled.

Having missed the first floor, Floyd rode up and then back down in the elevator. He got off and went straight into the visitor's lounge.

A neat, carefully dressed man in his thirties rose to greet him. They shook hands and sat down in comfortable armchairs.

"Dr. Harkins, I'm from the De Broglie Physical Research Institute in Maryland."

"Yes, some years ago I was impressed with the research being done there in particle physics. But I'm afraid I haven't been current in the field for some time."

"Oh, yes sir. You don't realize just how current you are. Recent research has led us to some startling conclusions. Falling back on previous assumptions, we have found them untenable in light of the new discoveries. Your book..." The younger man paused.

Lloyd looked at his visitor with curiosity, but did not speak. Something awoke in him.

"I'm sorry. I forgot to introduce myself. I'm Harvey Shanks. I'm a theoretical physicist myself."

"Yes," Lloyd said simply. Is someone reading my book now? he thought. Are physicists reading it?

Harvey Shanks continued, "Your willingness to take a different tack, sir, has led several of us to believe there may be hope for a unified field theory after all: one rational structure that will encompass all the observable forces in the universe. A simple edifice cleanly built. I mentioned the research problem—the difficulty in accounting for certain recently discovered phenomena—how some of our theoretical assumptions would no longer support our observations. Then several months ago we came across your book with its marvelously simple suggestion for a shift in perspective."

"George Berkeley was my inspiration," Lloyd interrupted, his voice gravely with mounting emotion. He checked himself. After so many years, a rush of excitement seemed—undignified. But he could hardly contain his excitement.

"Yes. Berkeley." The young Dr. Shanks hesitated, flushed, looking at the older man whom he held somewhat in awe. He went on, picking up the thread of his thought. "I only wish I could've thought of it myself. What you say is that if the laws of nature and the laws of thought are—symmetrical... I believe that is your term." He looked at the elder man with the thinning white hair, sunken, gaunt features, but alert gray eyes growing ever more piercingly sharp as his interest in the subject rose. He felt a little daunted by those eyes.

"Go on." Lloyd said, grinning broadly. He closed his mouth and tightened it down to a smile.

"You understand my meaning. I'm merely restating your thesis. Empirical science has come a long way since Galileo first gave a close, careful scrutiny to the workings of nature. But as you pointed out, any theoretical framework is a creation of mind superimposed upon the existing structure of what we perceive. What we perceive is sensory input organized within a subjectively held space-time continuum."

"That's right," Lloyd Harkins added. "There can be no insurmountable conflict between two different operations of the same mind, such as thinking and perceiving." It was his turn to flush. He turned a crimson red. This was the sort of discussion he had longed for throughout a good part of his adult life.

"Wave mechanics and particle physics are on a new footing," Harvey Shanks continued, moving toward his point. "All force can be understood as expressing the relationship of sensory data. Such data are arranged within the four coordinates of the space-time continuum. But this requires the abandonment of any unity of physical attributes assignable to matter, even at the subatomic level. Each sensory datum should be understood to stand independent of every other, merely combining with the others in some momentarily existing proportion in an ever-changing distribution throughout the continuum.

"So in this view, light and other forms of energy are the shorthand by which the accretions we call matter, at any one point in time, are related to those of another point in time. Light and other forms of energy explain motion and change. They make them possible for us to conceive.

"But, by this definition, motion and change are an illusion created by our limited apprehension of time. If we saw everything in universal time, there would be no motion and change, no differentiated forms of matter. What isn't differentiated can't be perceived at all. So there would be nothing—everything and nothing at once." Dr. Shanks stood up. "Dr. Harkins, we would like to hear you speak about this at a special colloquium at the Institute. Can I tell my colleagues you will come?"

"Yes," Lloyd Harkins answered mildly, while remaining seated.

Harvey Shanks was on his feet because at that moment he felt the need to be.

G. Lowell Tollefson

A Curious Disposition

In the American housing area of Balabago in the Philippines, the boy had built the chicken coop himself. Now, many months later, having crawled inside the only compartment of it he could fit into, he found it cramped. He sat on the ground amidst dust, feathers and chicken droppings with his knees drawn up almost to his chin and his head bent over nearly to his knees. Outside, the noon tropical sun pressed mercilessly upon the tin roof. Waves of moisture laden heat wrapped around and closed heavily through the chicken wire sides of the coop. A cock crowed from a nearby masonry fence, though it was midday.

A muffled sound of clucking and peeping came from the cool, crowded growth of water loving plants aligned along another yard wall extending at ninety degrees from the one the rooster had chosen. There a spray of dirt made its appearance now and then through green leaves as one hen, then another, took a dust bath. Tiny spindle-legged brown and yellow mottled chicks darted in and out of the dense foliage, snipping off blades of grass and searching for small insects and even smaller pebbles.

The boy, aged twelve, reached one arm into an adjacent compartment of the chicken coop. The door through which he groped was small, not more than a foot above the ground. So he couldn't see what he was doing, but had to feel his way. This compartment was also behind him, since he sat with his back to it, looking out into the yard through the chicken wire.

He groped carefully for the nest, felt the clutch of warm eggs. There were feathers between some of the eggs, a few of the feathers stuck to them with dung. Even from where he was he could smell the eggs, their narrow warm promise of life. The hen wasn't there. She was off foraging somewhere, perhaps in a neighbor's yard, getting him into trouble.

The neighbors didn't like his odd assortment of barnyard fowl. This included about thirty chickens, half a dozen ducks, a pair of pigeons. The pigeon loft was a small box fastened on top of the chicken coop. There was also a bitch dog, forever in heat and always followed by a litter, an assortment of cats in various states of wildness, guinea pigs, frogs, tadpoles, small green parrots, rice birds, a monkey and one crane, which the boy had recently acquired by some means or other of trade from a local construction worker who had presumably caught it in a nearby rice paddy.

The crane, stretched out on the ground and looking perpetually awkward and uncomfortable, was tied by one leg to a stake in the back yard. The bird was large and rather ugly, long limbed, long necked and long beaked with a dull brown plumage. And unbeknownst to the boy, the neighbors were presently making certain righteous noises to one another about the cruelty of the boy's possessing such an animal. Perhaps this was because the crane was a wild bird, constitutionally free, and thus in violation of its constitutional rights.

The boy slipped his fingers around a single egg. This was a dexterous act of great delicacy and immeasurable poise, because his arm was extended behind him, his body twisted a little to one side. His hand was getting numb from the pressure of the top of the tiny entranceway, which severely pressed upon and limited movement of his arm. Sweat ran down his forehead into his eyebrows and eyes. He licked the salt from his upper lip.

"Got it!" he announced. A chicken clucked rapidly somewhere, the nervous clucking terminating in a strained screech, as if someone had stretched its throat. There was apparently a skirmish out in the yard. A chicken, perhaps a hen or young cockerel, had violated the social rules of engagement and had been summarily returned to its proper square on the chessboard.

Carefully, slowly, even painfully, the boy withdrew his arm from the compartment behind him. It came out miraculously all of a piece with one egg, very warm. He held the egg up for inspection and sniffed it. It smells meaty, he thought. Perhaps that was because of the weight of it, the solidity, the pulsing heat in his hand. There was a faint peeping sound.

"A talking egg," the boy observed.

He set it down in the dirt beside him and took into consideration what might be inside. He'd never looked into an egg before, though he'd known a number of them to hatch. They always seemed to carry out their metamorphoses in the middle of the night, unseen by him. In the morning a hen would appear followed by chicks, where there had been only eggs the day before.

The boy picked the egg up again. It left a small oval depression in the loose soil. A rooster crowed from another fence wall.

The fences were made of cinder block. They contained in their open spaces—since the blocks were not placed directly over one another, but set ajar—innumerable gecko lizards, round leathery white gecko eggs, insect chrysalises, interesting spider cases and such. Domestic goats and water buffalo grazed in a field beyond this wall, for there were no houses within a hundred yards in that direction.

The boy often took his ducks out there to throw them into the air and watch them fly home. They swooped down low over this field and looked as if they would smash into the cinder block wall, but always cleared it. There were lots of big, colorful, orange and yellow winged grasshoppers and many birds in the field.

A second rooster crowed, young and awkward of voice, issuing to the first rooster an adolescent challenge for possession of the yard's pleasant crop of hens.

The boy moved the egg gently and heard the chick peep. He then noticed a hairline crack in the tan colored shell. At one end of the crack was a tiny hole.

"It's hatching," the boy whispered. He spoke in hushed reverence, as if it were a secret, and, indeed, his heart raced at the mere suggestion of such a momentous and holy event.

He did not reflect further but began pushing the event toward a conclusion by peeling away bits of shell. Tiny little specks around the hole were removed at first, then larger pieces. What emerged, almost hot to the touch, and perhaps a little surprised, was a very wet, balled-up little chick. It lay helpless in the palm of his hand, staring upward at him with what appeared to be one huge dark eye. In its soaked condition, its neck also looked long and disproportionate. The egg tooth was visible at the end of its beak. It was more like a prehistoric lizard than a bird.

The boy held it close to get a better look. Peep, peep. The sudden expression of life—or was it personality?—startled him. In his cramped position he was in an awkward way. Thus he dropped the little bird, reflexively catching it between his knees. Lifting it again, he saw its beak working. Open and shut. But there was no sound. Something hung out of its little body.

The boy set it down on the ground. He stared at it. The beak kept working.

It's suffering, he thought in horror. And I caused it!

Clearly he must do something. He picked it up and began to turn its head, twisting its neck into a coil. It took a long time.

War is Hell

Mark and I went on R&R at the same time. But I had only two months left to do in Vietnam and he had six or seven. We flew back from Hawaii in an airliner. Very nice. But all the way back he kept his face buried in a pillow set on a tray pulled down from the rear of the seat in front of him. He missed his wife and seemed to have the idea he would never see her again.

I managed to pick up a couple bottles of rum in Guam and one of them broke in my suitcase. Stunk like a distillery. We drank the other one the night we arrived in Vietnam. The roads were already closed so it was too late to get out to our unit. Mark got so blubbering drunk he slept in the middle of the floor of the hooch we were staying in for the night. And we both reeked from the rum, which we'd spilled down the front of our utility shirts. Some of the clerks in the hooch with us there at First Marine Division Headquarters thought Mark was strange. Not for the drinking but for the absolute abandon and sullen mood with which he did it. But I understood. After all, Darlene, his wife, whom I'd met, was a good looking woman. It's hard to go dry for six months after spending a week getting all wet again. Besides, the clerks thought I was strange too.

We were welcomed back to the battalion command post the next evening with a night of perimeter guard. The following day we would go out to our separate line companies.

Mark was a big blond Swedish looking guy. He was a little livelier that night. Vietnam kind of grows on you.

It was during my watch and his break that the Viet Cong hit us with one of their probing actions. It didn't amount to much. Just small arms fire from across the river. But it got Mark up groggy and irritated. I think he was still half soused. And it kept us both awake.

The sergeant of the guard came by. He approached us in the dark without a flashlight, so as not to be picked off by the snipers. We guided him in with our voices, because we were on a knoll at the end of a finger of land extending out with steep mud banks from the main hill. The wire was down on part of it too, which was not supposed to be the case.

"Eighty-one mortar crew is going to get some illumination up," he said.

"Good. Can't see anything but the muzzle flashes."

"Nothing to worry about. It's just a probe and their angle of fire is too high to do much. Where you guys from?"

"Mike company," I said.

"Lima company," Mark said.

"I used to be with Kilo. Too short now. I've got less than thirty days left in country."

Mark looked away toward the river and the muzzle flashes. The VC seemed to be shooting mostly at the main part of the perimeter. Mark and I were lying on top of the bunker, and Sgt. Hamner was crouching behind it because of the occasional whine of a bullet overhead. The bullets sounded like mosquitoes, and none of them were hitting anything. Then there was a dull thunk and a pop. The round white ball of a flare opened up above us and swung from its parachute. A little bit of movement could be seen in the village across the river. The air smelled damp and green, or even brown like the sluggish river water below us. Heavier fire was now being directed from our side, along the main perimeter, toward the Viet Cong. I squeezed off three rounds toward the movement I'd seen, but there was no return fire and I didn't see anything else.

"We had some LBGBs in the water a little earlier," the sergeant said.

"How many?"

"Six."

"What the hell's an LBGB?" Mark asked.

"Little bitty gook boat." Sgt. Hamner wasn't smiling, but I could see in the flat white glare of the flare light that the corners of his eyes were crinkled.

"Oh. So what happened to the sampans?"

"Nothing."

"Nothing?"

"Yeah. We thought they were going to cross the river toward our side, so we held fire to get a better look. But they didn't cross. The bridge guards who spotted them were disappointed."

"War's hell!"

"See you guys." The sergeant went off toward the next bunker.

There were a number of flares up now, and the shooting had stopped. The place was lit up like day and we had to contend with the metal canisters from the flares. They made a loud whistle coming down and put a pretty good dent into whatever they hit.

Mark started laughing, rolling over onto his back. "Ha ha ha."

"What's the matter?"

"Ha ha ha ha."

"Damn it, Mark, what's so funny?"

"Ha ha. Can't you see it? Ha ha ha. Tomorrow's headline in the Stars and Stripes: Marine killed by falling flare canister. Ha ha ha ha. Ha ha ha ha ha."

I remembered after we went back out to our separate companies, that Mark had told me he'd frozen once under fire. Frozen stiff and couldn't move. It had bothered him a lot, he said, until he realized it would ever happen again.

And it didn't. The Marine Corps presented his wife and new born son with the Silver Star he earned.

Gray Lady

1

It was certainly true she had failed him. He was thinking of Denise, his live-in girlfriend of the past two years, who had only left him this morning. She was a strange sort. Fancy free. And he was possessive. He might've been willing to marry her. But what did that matter now?

Tom Martin placed three dollars on the bar. It was enough to cover the tip as well as the last beer.

"Be seeing you, Tom."

Tom turned around and nodded to the bartender, who was picking up his glass and the money. With one swipe of a rag, the bartender restored the varnished wooden surface of the bar to its dark luster. He was young, stocky, handsome, square jawed, short and had close-cropped blond hair. He looks like a pit bull, Tom reflected. This was not an unkind thought but an observation of fact. Terry—that was the bartender's name—was probably a very effective bouncer. He looked it anyway, and it was always good to take note of such things.

Tom, already halfway across the barroom, threaded his way through the remainder of it in the dark, carefully avoiding closely packed, small tables surrounded by laughing, talkative people, most of whom he didn't know. He went out into the night air. It was winter in Seattle, which due to its weather and drab office buildings was known as the Gray Lady. At present, he was met by a cold drizzling rain. Rain made of the tiniest stinging drops that always came at you with the wind at an angle, rendering an umbrella useless.

Tom pulled his heavy raincoat up around his ears and over his chin and began to trudge steeply uphill toward the rundown residential area known as Capitol Hill. He walked quickly, his chin tucked into his chest, the rain pouring off his bare head and running in rivulets down his forehead onto his raincoat. He could hardly see while crossing several intersections, but there wasn't much traffic at night, especially away from the downtown area.

At home in his small, third floor apartment in his less than savory neighborhood, he reflected on his present misfortune. He was sitting in the living room beside a yellow, water-stained wall that had once been a brighter shade of white. His coat had been left hanging on a chair in the kitchen dining area, where it was making a pool of water on the floor. He had dried his hair with a dishtowel, and that particular article was now wadded up on the counter next to the sink.

Denise, he reflected, was a strange girl. They never really had gotten along. He was sitting in dim light, one small lamp, garnished with a forty watt bulb, turned on at the opposite end of the couch.

Why was he so depressed? Denise was a very thin, plain faced, fiery orange haired girl, who didn't have much in the way of a figure. He wanted to believe she wouldn't be of much interest to any other man. But she had a way with them. She had a way with him.

The doorbell rang. Who could that be this late? he wondered. He got up groggily to answer it.

It was Denise. She was standing there soaking wet, her hair hanging limp to her shoulders. "I forgot something," she said matter-of-factly. She paused.

Tom didn't say anything.

"Aren't you going to let me in?"

Tom stepped out of the way of the door. "You have your own key," he said.

"I know." Denise passed through the door. "But I thought I should ask, since I left you this morning."

"Just like that?"

Denise looked at him quizzically. Tom shut the door, and Denise hung her coat in the kitchen opposite his.

"I mean you leave for no good reason this morning, and now you're back."

"I left," Denise said wearily, "because you refuse to trust me." She looked at him with her blue eyes, eyes that always conveyed a deceptively childlike simplicity.

"Well, you're always flirting. Making eyes at people when we're out."

"I'm not supposed to look?"

"Oh, come on, Denise. A good looking guy walks into the bar and your voice starts to rise. Hell, he and everyone else knows you're interested! It's embarrassing."

"I've never been unfaithful to you."

"I know."

"I don't think you do. I think because I wasn't a virgin you assume...."

"I don't think anything, Denise. I guess I just don't know you."

"That's for sure."

"Well, you don't know me either."

"I'm starting to."

"What's that supposed to mean?"

They were still standing next to the kitchen chair where Denise had hung her coat and Tom had followed her. A moment of silence ensued.

"Where are all your things?" Tom asked. "You packed up all your clothes and took them with you this morning." He was hoping she would say her suitcases were out on the landing or down in the foyer inside the front door of the building. He really did want her to come back.

"I said I forgot something," Denise answered ironically, a hint of mischief in her eyes.

"What? Your toothbrush?"

"Yes."

"Oh, come on now."

Denise went into the bathroom and came out holding up a toothbrush.

Tom's heart sank. "You came back just for that?"

Denise smiled and went over to the kitchen chair her coat was hanging on, picked up this very wet outer garment, ignoring the pool of water it too had made on the floor, and put it on. "Yes," she said, the same ironic look in her eyes.

"Well, good-by," Tom said. He didn't go to the door. He figured she'd let herself out.

"Aren't you going to ask me to stay?" Denise asked.

"But you didn't come to stay. You didn't bring your clothes."

"So?"

2

Tom and Denise went out to the bar Tom had just come home from. They sat at a small table for two, drinking beer. Denise always said she didn't like the strong taste of hops, but she could put away beer to the point of drinking most men under the table. She had grown up in the dry, hop growing country south of Payette in southwestern Idaho.

Terry, the bartender, came over to the table with two beers in open brown bottles on a tray. He was very squarely built, and his crew-cut blond hair added to that effect—the effect of his looking like a trim, but heavily fortified, military armored personnel carrier in motion. "Howdy," he said smiling broadly at Denise. "Thought you'd be ready for a second one."

"Sure," Denise answered. "Put her there." She tapped the center of the table with her index finger. Something in the gesture seemed coy and alluring to Tom. But he resolved to remain calm.

Terry took up the two empty bottles, then, picking up the old wet paper napkins that were under them, replaced each one with a clean white napkin. He set a fresh beer bottle on each napkin.

Tom pulled out his wallet. Terry held up his free hand, the one not holding the tray and empty bottles. "Pay when you leave," he said. He was talking to Tom, but he was looking at Denise, a rather sweet expression on his face. Denise returned the look in kind.

"See what I mean," Tom said as Terry walked away.

"See what?"

"You and Terry flirting."

"I wasn't flirting," Denise said, sounding genuinely surprised. The look on her face would've proven her innocence to most people.

"Oh, what's the use?" Tom said. He poured some beer into his glass and noisily sucked off the head of foam as it rose above the glass.

A four member band, which normally came in after nine in the evening to play, had been setting up behind them. Suddenly it launched into a song. This band played and sang soft rock.

The bar was more of a lounge than a tavern, or maybe it was something in between. It had an old upright piano which the band didn't use, and it was located below street level down a narrow set of concrete steps. There was a left wing, second hand bookstore above it, opening directly off the sidewalk. Several blocks away, going steeply downhill towards Elliott Bay, was the open-air market, located beside the water. The market would be closing soon. Denise and Tom decided to go there to pick up some fresh vegetables, then take a walk south along the waterfront. They finished their beer, put money on the table and left the bar. Terry didn't even see them go. That was all right with Tom.

The market was noisy as hell. People were hawking everything. It stank of fish and boomed and shook with the coarse crowded shoving of people. The rain had stopped, and they were under a roof anyway. But the wet breeze, blowing in from the open street side, pressed against their wet raincoats and made them shiver. They hurriedly bought some tomatoes, green peppers, cheese, and two pounds of fresh salmon they couldn't afford, and walked back out into the night.

They wandered out onto a pier, the glassed-in, covered portion of which was closed and locked. So they stood beside a wooden rail and looked down at the murky water. The water was slopping at the piles underneath them, smelling of salt, seaweed and, well, oil and rust. The water, black with the night, seemed to move with the thickness of oil as it sloshed against those big, slimy, round, log piles. Out on Puget Sound the hoot of a tug could be heard. It was pulling some kind of flat metal barge. Beyond it stood the huge gray outlines of two naval warships. They couldn't be seen now, but Tom had noticed them earlier in the day, lurking in the distant fog like ominous ghosts.

"Do you want to walk over to Sally's and get your stuff?" he asked, leaning over looking at the piles. Denise was staring up at the cloud cover overhead, noticing how the light coming from the tall buildings massed behind her was reflected off it. Far to her left a spotlight from SeaTac airport hit the low ceiling of clouds and bounced off, slipping along its undersurface as though it were contained in a jar.

"No."

"What do you mean no," he asked. "You don't have anything to wear."

Denise looked at Tom as he was rising from bending over the rail. "I'll go tomorrow," she said.

On the way back to their apartment they were accosted by a street person asking for money. It was not immediately clear whether this person was a man or a woman. He or she had long, unkempt hair but no beard, and was completely enveloped in a brown, oversized overcoat. Tom pulled a handful of change out of his pocket and gave it to the person. They were still near the waterfront, one block up from it on First Avenue.

The tug hooted again, heavy voiced. A light mist began to fall. Cars passing on wet city streets made a swishing sound as they went by. Their headlights carved white tunnels into the mist ahead of them under the isolated, glaring street lights. When one of these cars turned a corner, its beams of light would swing like the boom of a sailing vessel and go, as it were, independently onward, leading the car away along the new street.

Continuing to labor uphill beyond the downtown area, Tom and Denise began to climb into the relative darkness of the Capital Hill neighborhood. Street lights became rare, cars even rarer, and the dull yellow windows, of those four, five, and six story buildings that had either the grace or humility to be occupied, offered little illumination. Somehow it was always colder up here, the wind nastier.

Inside the apartment Tom and Denise fell asleep fully clothed on their bed, their coats making fresh pools of water in the kitchen. Little nut-brown cockroaches, in spite of Denise's effort to keep things clean, ranged freely over the kitchen cabinets and walls. All the lights were out except the one in the bathroom, which illuminated part of the bedroom, and which had been left on as a convenience and a warning to roaches to stay out of that part of the apartment.

3

In the morning Tom got up first, then Denise. Since he was in the bathroom first, he took his time toileting, showering and shaving. When he came out, Denise shoved past him mumbling something about his slowness. Before he could answer, she shut the door and raced to the toilet.

Tom and Denise lived on the edge of an abyss when it came to finances. They seemed to like it there. They had met while they were students at the University of Washington, at which Denise was still attending classes, while Tom cast about with his liberal arts degree from low paying job to job. It was while they were still both students that they had learned all their bad habits. One of the worst of these was that they now considered themselves to be intellectual giants. But they were learning. The Gray Lady was a good teacher.

Meanwhile, in their present semi-knowledgeable absence of experience in things practical, they decided to enjoy this Saturday morning, since the sky was temporarily blue. As they walked downhill toward the open-air market, a gray lid of cloud began to move toward them from the west. By the time they were seated in the small coffee and pastry shop which was located on the second floor directly above the still closed, open-air market, the cloud had passed over them and was getting a good fix on the general lay of Elliott Bay and Puget Sound. While they were eating their croissants and drinking their narrow, ironstone cups of espresso of a consistency somewhere between solid and liquid, it continued onward and hooked up with the Cascade Mountains to their east. Now everything was shut in under a blanket of semidarkness, from the Olympic Mountains on their west to the mountains on the other side. The sun was a dull and ineffectual heat spot behind all that gray.

Outside the cafe window looking down on Puget Sound, seagulls were flying at just their level. The gulls in this part of the world bore a remarkable resemblance to rats and stray dogs in other places. For they ate anything. Right now, the little devils, giving off their ornery, piercing, wild cries, were simply sailing back and forth past the window like so much paper refuse borne aloft on a strong wind. It was clear the birds expected one of them to open the window and hand out food. It was their moral duty. But Tom and Denise, being in the amoral early years of adulthood, chose to ignore them. After all, they had each owned dogs and knew the beggary of both species rather well.

"Want to go up there now?" Tom asked, sipping the last of his coffee. It wasn't hot. The ironstone cup it was contained in reminded him of a miniature toilet. Such was the shape of it. At the bottom of it, regardless of the angle at which he tipped the cup, a brown chocolate sludge refused to budge. He set the cup down.

"I suppose," Denise said, looking out the window at the gulls without really seeing them. "What do you think those big old ships are doing?" She was referring to the huge, navy battleship and its single destroyer escort. Though well out into the middle of the sound, they loomed eerily in the uncertain light, and the battleship seemed as big as a mountain or an iceberg. The water was gray like the cloud cover overhead. A mist left over from the morning fog connected them. The ships, of course, were also gray.

"I don't know," Tom said informationally.

"They give me the creeps," Denise said, pulling in her thin shoulders and shuddering.

On the way up to Sally's apartment, which was not far from the downtown area, Tom decided to try a bold new tactic with Denise. "Want to get married?" he asked. He wasn't at all sure this was what he wanted to do. After all, they had everything they needed now.

Denise looked at him in surprise. "What for?" she said and looked back at the street.

Tom shrugged his shoulders, and they walked on.

Sally had Denise's suitcases setting beside the wall just inside her door. Tom and Denise came in and sat down in the small living room. Sally was a good looking, if rather large-boned, young woman: tall, dark haired and shapely. But she didn't have much use for Tom. Tom had never seen her with any man.

"Come back for your stuff, huh," Sally said, going into the kitchen.

"Yeah," Denise answered from the living room couch.

Sally came in and set a cup of instant coffee in front of each of them. She had on a purple, silk housecoat that was not fastened very securely at the waist, so Tom could see well into the top of it as she bent over.

"No thanks," Tom said, referring to the coffee.

Sally ignored him and sat down in an armchair across from them. "You two make me laugh," she said after an interval of silence.

"What do you mean?" Denise asked, drinking her coffee. Tom was always amazed at how much of the stuff she could put into that nervous little frame and not be shaken apart by it. Too much coffee made him a wreck.

"Well, the way you two are always quarreling," Sally said.

"Maybe it's the weather," Denise said. "It's so nasty and cold out there. Keeps us on edge."

"Yeah," Tom agreed.

Sally burst into laughter. "More than likely you guys make the weather," she said. "It suits your temper."

Some friend, Tom thought.

Denise didn't think anything of it. She and Sally were like sisters.

When Tom and Denise went back outdoors with the suitcases, it was raining. So they decided to call a cab. Another extravagance the pocketbook couldn't afford.

When they got home, they decided to leave the suitcases for unpacking later and go down to the Seattle Center for the afternoon. There probably wasn't much going on there, but it would give them an excuse to ride the monorail, which was at least mildly entertaining. And the Center itself would at least be a different shade of gray.

Hue City 1968

It had taken three hours to clear all the North Vietnamese soldiers from the lower end of the street and another hour to bring the truck up past several security checkpoints along the other narrow streets leading into it. The military two and a half ton truck had come without a load so as to be able to quickly take out the dead, which were stacked like logs beside a building. A part of the building's front wall had been blown away, the shattered masonry littering the street. The bodies by the damaged wall were partially covered with dark green plastic ponchos, which looked gray in the rain, the water running in rivulets off the ponchos and dripping from the dead men's boots. The uncovered legs and boots had become soaked until they were black. Dark clouds hung over the city with its narrow streets, and the rain came down in a cold thin spray.

The men who had come with the truck were part of a graves registration detail which was also gathering the bodies of Marines on several other streets. As the three men from this detail and the driver dismounted from the truck and began moving the dead, a sniper opened up from a rooftop across the street. The men took cover behind a low wall in front of a building adjacent to the one facing the bodies. They returned fire, chipping bits of stucco off the façade of the building across the street and splitting tiles on its roof. Though they could not see the sniper, a heavy concentration of automatic weapons silenced him.

When there was no further response from the rooftop, the Americans continued retrieving the bodies of their countrymen in the drizzling rain, putting them into the truck and fastening the tailgate with a clang of metal and rattle of chains after the last of them had been loaded. There were seven of them. The driver started the truck's engine, filling the damp air with the heavy fumes of its diesel fuel, as two of the men climbed into the back of the truck and one got into the cab on the side opposite him. The truck began to move slowly down the wet street against the rain and away from the sound of small arms fire and several explosions which could be heard coming from further up the street, where the platoon was advancing.

Aunt Julia

Julia Morgan had been known by the sobriquet "Aunt Julia" since about the age of thirty-three. It wasn't only her many nieces and nephews who referred to her thus, but most everyone she knew. No one could've said why.

Perhaps it was her appearance or possibly her manner. Physically she was tall and large but not notably overweight. Solid. Yes, solid is the word. Presence. Where reason fails, imagination may supply an image. She also wore thick-lensed glasses in a large, pointed frame swept upward at the corners. These hung heavily upon a nose that could not adequately support them. They were perpetually sliding down. She, in response, was forever putting them up, particularly when punctuating a verbal point with a terrible thrust into the middle piece of the frame with her index finger.

People naturally stood back when she spoke. It was a matter of providing room for the greatness of her manner, the volume of her expression, the immensity of her words. This habit of stepping back, or rocking upon one's heels in an attitude of arrested flight, whenever she was aroused to vigorous elocution upon an issue, generally any issue, was shared by her first husband, John. John was not a small man, but he seemed to feel diminished in her presence, and often found himself retiring with a drink to the solitude of his front porch for long periods in the evening.

When these two were in their fifties, he died, suddenly struck down, carried away, it would seem, by some obscure, debilitating illness which aggressively weakened him with shivers and fevers, until one day it shook him still. There he lay, finally at peace. His passing was like that of a tree toppled by winds. Yet on his deathbed his last generous act was to offer the suggestion in a quiet voice that he might be going over to "the other side" to prepare her a place. Though it was generally thought he had gone to find some rest.

After what might be described as a decent interval of quiet mourning, Julia set out on an extended tour to visit all her family and friends. These were scattered throughout North America like pepper in a salad. They were in both Canada and the United States. Julia's visits were sometimes prolonged. The journey lasted several years. In the end, all were of one accord in agreeing that their dearly beloved Aunt Julia was truly herself once again. It may have been suspected she had never been otherwise.

It is several years since then, and Julia is still widowed, living quietly in the northwestern section of Lancaster, Pennsylvania. Well, quietly by her standards. It is summer, and she is presently in her back yard, which she has converted into a vine, rose and occasional weed entangled garden. A neighbor has been fastened adroitly to the low fence adjoining their two properties by an uninterrupted flow of words coming from Aunt Julia. Contained therein are stock market quotes, something about the weather, the current malaise in both religion and politics, and, of course, a few comments on the subject of lawns and gardening. The neighbor, a young man in his twenties who was a moment before simply trying to mow his tiny lawn as quickly as possible after work and before dinner, is now trying desperately to extricate himself from those invisible verbal entanglements holding him to the fence like one of Julia's vines. A grasshopper, gripped in the sharp, unremitting beak of a shrike and hammered mercilessly against a hard tree limb till it falls into pieces, would certainly know something of his predicament.

"Really, Aunt Julia, I must go. I told my wife we would....and....dinner....yes....well, that could be ....I agree with you there....yes....well, I've got to go....I know....some people are like that....well, yes, I hadn't thought of that...." and so on.

"And do you know, Don,"—that is the young man's name—"that those very ones up in the State House now are the rascals who gave in to the milk lobby and made such laws? Imagine. It's a veritable subsidy.

Price fixing is what it is, and at the expense of ordinary people too. People like you and me. Just plain folks who...."

Saved by the bell! Don's wife is calling from the back door. She knows full well she is rescuing her husband, but smiles sweetly at her neighbor. "Hello, Aunt Julia." She waves to her. "How are you this evening? It certainly is pleasant out. Yes, nice breeze." She waves again and shuts the door quickly. It isn't verbally safe out there.

Don, armed with a firm excuse, makes his hiatus, trailing his apologies behind him. "Whew!" he says, getting in the back door of his house and facing his wife. Neither of them dares to look out the window. "I bet she's still talking," Don says.

"Serves the fence right," his wife responds. "I can't get a thing to grow on our side of it."

Several months have passed. It is fall. The weather is cool, crisp and sweetly melancholy. Leaves are turning, and nearby Buchanan Park, along with the surrounding farm country, is alive with reds and golds. Pennsylvania reds and golds which have a mellow quality, inducing thoughtfulness. Crisp underfoot leaf litter is sifting onto roads. It is left ribboned along curbsides by subtle breezes. There is an indefinable cleansing in the air. Most importantly, Julia has found a man. The neighborhood has gained a reprieve.

The gentleman who is paying her visits, which are carefully and joyfully observed by all the neighbors ensconced in their hidden retreats, peering over windowsills, peeking from behind curtains and shades, glancing through half-closed blinds—this gentleman is indeed a marvel. For he is well-dressed, almost natty in appearance, though a little corpulent about the midsection. He has a large head with big ears. His hair is cut short in a butch. There is hair in his ears, for that matter, a bump on his nose. But overall he is handsome, all the neighbors willingly agree. They wish it to be so.

Aunt Julia now has a purpose. She is an object of most pleasant attention. For this man comes regularly—several times a week. He takes her out places. They were once seen in a restaurant. He was listening patiently, a pleasant smile on his face.

"Just what Aunt Julia needs!" one and all agree. In truth, it is what they have been hoping for.

The gentleman's name is nothing less ordinary than Smith. Perhaps he is descended from a long line of metal or woodworkers. Such lineages become lost in the mists of time. The immediate neighborhood is atwitter with meaningless speculations like this. It is all they have to go on at present. At any rate, it has formed a worthy topic for more than one family gathering at the dinner table. Grave pronouncements have been made. Weighty speculations from heads of households have been considered. There have been smiles.

Meanwhile, what is not known by the public is probably of greater moment. One of these facts is Mr. Smith's first name, which is Orrey. There is also Orrey's employment. He is a bookkeeper at a Pennsylvania State liquor store. Now herein lies the deep kernel of meaning: bookkeepers do not make much, and Orrey is facing the bleak prospect of soon being put out to pasture in the vacuously dry meadow of social security checks and Medicare payments, for he is in his sixties and diabetic. His present apartment is small and cramped. The interior paint is becoming drab and the general quality of lighting is poor. Orrey has few valuable possessions.

On the other hand, Dearest Little Pigeon—for she has been so named by the gallant and affectionate Mr. Smith, who has a way with words—is rather comfortably situated. She owns her house, collects her husband's social security and has money in the bank and elsewhere, rating at interest. John was an industrious man.

Orrey knows Julia is "well off." Julia knows that Orrey continually showers her with courtesies and compliments. Most importantly, he listens to her. Listens interminably without complaint. It would seem he has no opinion of his own but the one of considering it important to hear hers.

On this very evening—it is somewhere in the middle of the week—Orrey arrives at Julia's door with a bouquet of flowers in hand. The flowers are pink carnations and express the limit of Orrey's budget.

All eyes are upon him. The month is not February, so it is not Valentine's Day. It is not an anniversary or Julia's birthday. The neighbors know what this means. A single pulse has synchronized the hearts in every observing household.

Orrey puts a large finger on the little doorbell. Presently the door opens. There is an exchange of words, which none of the anxious neighbors can hear. Julia is presented with the bundle of flowers wrapped in green and white tissue paper. Her eyes light up. A collective sigh passes like a tiny wind up and down the street.

The door opens further. Orrey lumbers in, doffing his hat, and the door is closed.

Silence.

"Pigeon....I....I...." Orrey is standing just inside the outer room, head bowed, hat in hand. He fumbles with the hat. He is a large man and is quite at a loss for words.

"Yes, Orrey."

"I wanted to give you those."

"Oh. Oh, well thank you, Orrey. It is sweet of you. Come on in." Apparently disappointed at first, for she was expecting something more, Julia takes the flowers into the kitchen. She gets a transparent green vase down out of an overhead cupboard, cuts the stems short, fills the vase with water from the sink, and plunks the flowers in. She gets a small bottle out of another cupboard and drops an aspirin into the vase.

All this while, Julia has been talking. For it is, as always, her wont to fill the air with chatter when the emptiness begins putting on too much weight. Orrey follows her to the kitchen, then turns around and paces back into the living room. He must screw up his courage.

Here comes Julia. She puts the vase on the coffee table. Orrey is standing in the middle of the room. She turns around to face him. "Aren't they lovely," she says.

"Yes they are." Orrey clears his throat. "Pigeon, darling....honey, Julia....damn!"

"You don't have to cuss." There is horror in Julia's voice but a crinkle in her eyes.

"Yes, ahem, well. Marry me, will you, damn it!" Orrey lets out a bellowing laugh and steps toward Julia, arms open. It is the best he can do.

Julia, stunned, or at least appearing to be, falls into his arms. They hug, then kiss with tears in their eyes. Finally, Julia will always have someone to talk to. She begins right away. There is laughter and joy.

Perhaps twenty minutes pass. They are still talking animatedly. Or rather, Julia is. But Orrey does get a word in edgewise: They will be married in a few days, and he will move in with her. He can transfer all his belongings in an afternoon, he informs her. That's settled then.

The doorbell rings. Talking, laughing and planning, they open the door together. There is no one outside. But a bottle of red wine is sitting on a porch step.

The Boss

"Don." The voice came over the intercom, young, inexperienced, irritatingly youthful.

"Yes."

"Bring a box of form 3051D up to my office, will you."

There was a pause, a moment of hesitation. Then, "A case?"

"Yes, a case."

Another pause. "Okay, boss. Whatever you say."

The voice over the intercom had sounded tinny and weak. It always sounded weak. It had echoed in the basement among countless shelves stacked high with office supplies: forms, pens, printer ribbons, etc. These items all together constituted the extensive plumbing of corporate life. Without them an executive will would not flush.

Donald Radnor, a short, stocky, bristly man, who somewhat resembled a sea urchin come ashore on stubby legs, was wearing a kidney belt in support of his bad back. Therefore, regardless of any actual presence of discomfort, he grumbled as he searched the shelves. Then, having identified the form, he went to a stack of boxes arranged against a wall and chose one. It weighed sixty pounds. Yet it was not large enough to justify use of a dolly, especially since he would not have been able to tilt the dolly up in such a way as to hold the box in place. So he carried it to the elevator.

The elevator let him out on the first floor. This was the home of lower middle management at corporate headquarters. Above these unfortunate souls were middle middle managers, and above them certain specialists, such as lawyers and accountants. On the very top floor of the building were the plush office suites of the several men—and one woman—who controlled the destinies of hundreds in the building and thousands across the land.

Don stepped off the elevator groaning. When on this floor he had a tendency to make the most of the pain which was now truly beginning to occur in the small of his back. He was middle-aged and his belly was large. Had it not been for the kidney belt, one or two buttons might have been open near the bottom of his shirt. Trudging down a hallway defined by two arbitrary rows of soft, flannel, gray, room dividers, he came to the cubby of Mathew Johnson and stopped at its entrance. He cleared his throat.

The young man inside the cubicle did not look up. He was busy with paperwork or with some sort of form. Perhaps it was a business letter he was writing. He was holding a pen, occasionally making marks on the paper with it. Also, he was leaning his chin on the palm of his other arm, which was propped upon its elbow near the edge of his desk. There was a studied air of concentration about him.

"Sir." Don did not care to reduce himself to servility in applying such a term of respect to a mere boy, but the box was heavy. "Sir, you wanted the forms?"

Mathew looked up, his thin face with its bony nose and narrow chin like an alligator's, his blond hair and pale blue eyes suggesting a youthful manhood not yet fully attained. He might've been all of twenty-two or twenty-three, might not yet have made serious use of a razor, for that matter. For, in spite of the longish rather than rounded nature of his features, his was a baby face. "Put it over there," he said, pointing to the corner of his cubicle.

On the way to the elevator, Don fumed. He could've at least said something civil, he thought.

Mathew, concentrating on his letter, for it was a letter to one of the sales representatives who supplied him with office paraphernalia—Mathew also was feeling a bit unpleasant. His stomach muscles were tensed. His lower jaw bone protruded on either side of his neck. His face was beginning to flush, his neck reddened. "Damn!" he said and wadded the letter up and threw it into his trash can.

The problem had arisen approximately a month before. That was when Mathew had assumed his present duties, fresh out of college: some ivy league, Eastern, pink-finger school Don could never keep straight in his head. Mathew was the son of the woman on the top floor. He was being introduced to the corporate structure—from the ground up, you might say. The fact that he was privileged and had supplanted a much better man, in Don's opinion, was bad enough. But the fact that his parent, and mentor within the company, was a woman was even worse.

It was true that the man Mathew had replaced had been given a promotion, but that didn't matter to Don. To him Mathew was the son of what should have been a housekeeper, home provider, baby-care giver.

On the other hand, it didn't help that Mathew did have something of an attitude. He saw no reason why he, a man of intellectual attainment and good manners, should not receive the fullest cooperation from his rather earthy and little educated employee, who was, after all, rightfully confined—except when summoned—to the bowels of the building.

In truth Mathew was a little afraid of Don. Though short, Don was a big man. Quite hairy. He had the abrasive temper of asphalt, whereas Mathew felt himself to be of the tenderness of new rubber. Well, and Don had come in for overtime one Saturday smelling of alcohol. True, he had put in an extraordinarily good day's work. But Mathew had been offended, feeling he should have said something morally corrective or at least moderately authoritative, yet not having had the courage to do so. It was this sort of thing that upset him.

Down in the basement, Don referred to his new boss as "the bubblegummer." It made the several employees who worked under him laugh as they went about filling orders and putting incoming forms and articles in their respective places on the shelves.

The basement was lit by white neon lights. Ugly glaring things. However, the shelves were high enough to block them. Thus it was semidark and rather dingy. Directly adjacent to this large room in the cellar was the printing and copy room. Many of the office forms in the corporation's daily use came from there. Other printing needs were jobbed out, especially those in need of high color resolution, for the equipment was old. In fact, the cleaning fluids used to remove ink from those old offset plates in the copy room made life manifestly unpleasant at times in the stockroom. It stank.

Ventilation was poor. There were no windows. And once, exhaust fumes had somehow gotten into the ventilation system from the loading dock on the first floor. In short, this basement was truly the bowels, or hold, of the corporate ship. It was the place where countless faceless and low-paid oarsmen came in unending succession to work, grinding out a monotonous existence in daily rowing.

Several weeks passed. Don was growing ever more insubordinate. Surly was the term Mathew would've used. He was already considering who Don's replacement might be, as chosen from among his subordinates. The problem was Mathew hadn't the least idea of how to fire him. Or what for, really. Yet, surely he must handle his position with decision and firmness. At any rate, if worse came to worse, he hadn't the least doubt he would find support for his actions on the top floor.

The problem was he hadn't yet an inkling of that carefully guarded, corporate secret known to experienced managers, which was the studied habit of maintaining a strategic blandness in all affairs of an emotional nature. It was how businesses survived, how they functioned on a day to day basis without messy explosions or without becoming hopelessly mired in the egoistic quicksands of the human continuum. In other words, what he didn't know was that he must avoid confrontation at all costs. If he needed to get rid of Don, it could certainly be arranged. But he, the direct supervisor, must not be the one to actually fire him. A gray and indefinable intermediary was required, someone of faceless antecedents and demeanor, toward whom it would be useless for Don to vent his anger.

Alas, Mathew was but a mere youth. He could only envision a direct standoff, and that was frankly terrifying. The big ugly brute might pounce upon him and elongate his neck in a farewell shake. He—that is, Mathew—might die. It wasn't that he, given the usual overconfident urgings of his youth with regard to mortality, was afraid of death. He could conceivably handle that. But, lord, what an embarrassment! What a scene! Besides, a man like Don probably didn't wash his hands after using the restroom. He, Mathew, could contract some sort of filthy sickness and suffer a lingering illness, wasting away before the horrified and bewildered eyes of both his mother and his girlfriend.

His dad was deceased. That's how his mother took over a controlling interest in the company. She was a thin, nervous woman. So was his girlfriend. Rich people can't afford to be fat. They're too busy fighting the unending battles of high finance. He lived with his girlfriend. Or she lived with him. Someday they would probably marry.

Don had met this girlfriend. She had come downstairs in a haughty manner demanding something for Mathew. Don had immediately observed how short her skirt was, how bony her knees. What a hag, he thought. Though he did find her somewhat attractive. It was her arrogant manner that offended him. Who did she think she was? Dracula's wife? No, she was only Dracula's girlfriend, Don informed himself with a smile.

So it went. Mathew worried. Don stewed. Mathew contracted strategies for dealing summarily with his recalcitrant employee, always falling short of concocting means for actually firing him.

Don devised devious ways to irk Mathew. He would delay orders, misaddress them, send the wrong forms upstairs. Once he delivered fifteen sixty pound boxes of form 3052C, which Mathew didn't need. He had had them set in Mathew's office while Mathew was at lunch. It was a Saturday. They were working a half day overtime in the basement. So Don dismissed the other stockroom employees immediately after lunch, leaving a few minutes later himself.

Needless to say, when Mathew returned he worked up quite a head of steam, enough to power the Seattle to Sitka ferry along its route and back again. Nevertheless, there was nothing he could do till Monday.

Monday came. Mathew got to his office late, about a quarter after nine, and immediately summoned his adversary.

Don stopped at the door of Mathew's cubicle, looming in the midst of it, in spite of his short stature, like an Alaskan Kodiak bear. Mathew stood up. He was visibly shaking with rage and perhaps a little fear. His features were by turns pale then red. Don sported the slightest hint of a sick grin upon his face.

"I want those out of here," Mathew said, pointing to the stack of boxes. He had hardly been able to move back and forth between them and his desk all Saturday afternoon.

"Why?" Don asked, his face smooth as pudding. "You asked that they be brought up."

"I did no such thing," Mathew shouted. He withdrew the pointing finger which, in his preoccupation, he had left hanging in the air. There was a sudden hush in all the surrounding cubicles. Mathew was aware he was being embarrassingly loud. But he didn't care. "If you don't get those out of here now, you're fired!" he said in a voice almost as loud as that of the previous remark.

Don shifted his eyes over to the boxes. No other part of his body had moved, not even his face.

The pistons inside Mathew's chest were pumping faster and faster. Blood rushed to his eyes. They began to bulge. His lips trembled and were outlined in a thin, eerie circle of white.

Suddenly Don stepped into the cubicle and picked up a box. He knew when far enough was enough. On his way out, he stopped at the door of the cubicle. "I'll be back for the others," he said blandly.

In truth, he sent two of his subordinates up with dollies to retrieve the rest.

Mathew settled for the morning into near exhaustion. He slumped down in his chair breathing deep and slow. For all the world, he looked like a little boy who could not quite reach the surface of his desk.

However, by late afternoon he had recovered. When he left at five o'clock, he was feeling quite cheerful and whistled a recent movie tune on the way out the front door of the corporate building. He had, after all, assumed his first mission of uncompromising command and had steered his ship through a heavy storm. He'd gotten his sea legs.

The Brawl

It was all smoke and mirrors—literally. A place called The Parakeet. Located in the town of Jacksonville, North Carolina just outside the Marine base at Camp Lejeune, there were mirrors on all the walls, a long bar and a bandstand in the corner near one end of the bar. Few women. There weren't many in the town. But plenty of Marines in various stages of intoxication.

It is November tenth, the Marine Corps birthday. It is also Nineteen sixty-eight, the height of the Vietnam conflict. Three men are sitting in a booth along the wall opposite the bar. The wall is lined with such booths, and small, independent, round tables fill the space between them and the bar. The room is packed, heavy with smoke and noise, even when the band isn't playing. Someone is singing the Marine Corps hymn. Several other voices join in.

One of the men sitting in the booth, talking, smoking and carefully drinking a beer, pulls up a shirt sleeve, showing a long scar on his lower arm.

"Flesh wound," he says to his two young admirers on the other side of the table inside the booth. He is himself in his early twenties.

"I'll drink to that," one of them says. He picks up a pitcher of beer from the middle of the table, which already has a few wet spots from spilled beer. Several crumpled, wet, paper napkins are scattered on the bare table top. Refilling his heavy glass mug, he spills a little more. He has short, cropped, red hair, almost a bright orange, is all of nineteen and obviously fresh out of boot camp. Sitting next to him is a young man of similar age and sophistication.

"Hey, take it easy. I paid for that." The other young man takes the pitcher and pours some beer for himself, loudly sucking the foaming white head off his glass mug. But he also manages to spill some.

"You guys are drunk."

"Yeah. Show me that scar again. You get it killing anybody?"

"More than I want to think."

"How many did you get?"

"I don't know."

The one young man looks over at the other with red hair.

Someone shouts from a table in the back of the room, "Happy birthday, Marines!" He mounts his chair and then climbs up onto the top of his table, from which he plans to better broadcast his message. But, balanced only on a center pedestal, the table falls over under his weight, sending him sprawling onto the table next to him. Two men from the other table get up and throw the sprawling man onto the floor. They straighten their own table, laughing, and one of them goes to the bar to refill their overturned pitcher, which is retrieved unbroken from a pool of beer on the floor.

The two young men in the booth turn back from watching this event to look at the war veteran. "I'm going there soon," one of them says. "Shipping out in January."

"You'll be dead in a week," the redhead says, drinking off his full mug of beer.

"Screw you, bastard! You're going too. We'll see who gets it first."

The drunken man has now gotten up off the floor. He staggers to the center of the room and stands there looking around. The Marines at adjacent tables ignore him.

"Hey, grunts," he shouts. "I'm Recon. Nobody's better than Force Reconnaissance." He staggers but manages to remain on his feet. He's a small man with powerful arms and shoulders and a haircut the length of the redhead's.

"Sit down," someone next to him says. This man, a tall, slender, dark haired Marine infantryman with the Marine Corps bull dog mascot tattooed on his upper right arm, gets up. "You're too damn drunk to even stand up."

"I can handle you and twenty others like you." They scuffle and surprisingly the recon man pins the taller one to the table where he'd been sitting. Others get up. Someone attempts to pull the recon man off the taller man. Someone else hits the third man with a chair from behind.

"Shit!" The veteran in the booth gets up, drops his cigarette onto the floor and wades into the fight. Soon everyone is in it, the band has scuttled behind the bar and the young redheaded Marine is throwing wild punches which hit nothing but air. The heavy impact of a beer mug on the back of his head knocks him almost senseless to the floor. He lies there weak and half-conscious on his folded arms. Someone proceeds to kick him in the face. He turns his face downward and covers it with his arms.

It is perhaps twenty minutes later. The young redhead regains consciousness and stands up. His gray flannel jacket is soaked in blood. MPs are inside the bar and police are at the door, where they remain, apparently preferring to let the military police restore order. Tables and chairs are overturned everywhere, but none of the mirrors on the walls is broken. The redhead sees his friend, the veteran, standing in a line with several others, including the recon man and the tall Marine. They are being watched by two MPs. Another MP is getting information from the bar owner. The redhead, still somewhat dazed, starts picking up chairs and standing them on their legs.

"That guy needs to see a corpsman," the MP talking to the owner says, turning around and addressing the other two MPs who are guarding the row of Marines. Another MP comes in from the entrance and takes the young man outside.

"So you think you're tough, huh?"

The redhead is lying on a cold, bare, steel table in an antiseptically bare, chilly room. He has taken off his jacket, shirt and T-shirt and is positioned on his stomach. The man speaking to him, a Navy corpsman, has a needle in his hand.

"What about novocain?" the other corpsman in the room asks.

"He doesn't need it. He's a tough Marine. Aren't you, buddy?" The first corpsman begins sewing the two inch gash in the young Marine's head. The redheaded Marine grips the front steel legs of the table until his knuckles turn white through his freckles. The room is silent, the other corpsman, not wanting to watch, having left the two men alone.